BRIDGET WALSH was born in London to Irish immigrant parents. She studied English literature and was an English teacher for twenty-three years, before leaving the profession to pursue her writing. Bridget lives in Norwich with her husband, Micky, and her two dogs. *The Innocents* is the second novel in the Variety Palace Mystery series.

Praise for *The Tumbling Girl*

'A narrative that neatly weds historical detail and quiet wit'
Sunday Times

'Walsh does a splendid job depicting Minnie's flea-bitten yet appealing theatrical world and Albert's monied yet treacherous milieu'
Wall Street Journal

'Walsh's diligent research pays off in spades here, and her rich and nuanced portrayal of the period will leave readers feeling like they're on the soggy streets of London. Imogen Robertson readers will be eager for a sequel to this un-put-downable mystery'
Publishers Weekly (starred review)

'A sparkling novel and a complete delight to read. The characters and world are wild, vivid and enchanting. A wry, warm and proper rib-tickling slice of dirty Victorian gothic . . . I can't wait to see what Minnie and Albert are up to next'
Julia Crouch, author of *The Daughters*

'Beautifully evocative, deftly plotted and with engaging characters, it was a page-turner from beginning to end'
Sheila O'Flanagan, author of *What Eden Did Next*

'Brilliant . . . Beautifully written . . . keeps you guessing till the end'
A. J. West, author of *The Spirit Engineer*

'Minnie Ward is a woman you want to follow through all the wicked twists and turns of Victorian London. It had me on the edge of my seat until the final page'
SJ Bennett, author of *Murder Most Royal*

'A brilliantly written page-turner. A bravura performance tumbling us into a compelling mystery in a vivid, richly imagined world. You can smell the greasepaint and hear the roar of the crowd on every page'
Imogen Robertson, author of *The Paris Winter*

'*The Tumbling Girl* is gripping, dark and thrilling and takes the reader on a rollercoaster journey from music hall to gentleman's club and back again; all in the company of two engaging protagonists' W. C. Ryan, author of *A House of Ghosts*

'I absolutely loved *The Tumbling Girl*. Bridget Walsh is a fresh and fabulous new voice in historical crime fiction' Elizabeth Chadwick, author of *The Summer Queen*

'One of the most engaging double acts I've read in ages. Delightful, dark and depraved' Trevor Wood, author of *The Man on the Street*

'Rich in period detail, Walsh's thrilling debut melds authentic, believable characters with a perfectly executed plot set against the backdrop of a finely drawn Victorian London' Mark Wightman, author of *Waking the Tiger*

'Smart, funny and expertly plotted, *The Tumbling Girl* cartwheels off the page . . . A cracking start to a charismatic and distinctive series' Emma Styles, author of *No Country for Girls*

'A racy and thrilling ride that doesn't let up till the last sentence. Superbly done' Femi Kayode, author of *Lightseekers*

'An accomplished crime murder mystery, with an addictively gritty plot and truly remarkable cast of characters . . . deliciously dark and compelling' Essie Fox, author of *The Somnambulist*

'Walsh resurrects the culture and crimes of Victoriana without cliché or condescension, but with warmth, wit, remarkable texture and rare authority' Tom Benn, author of *Oxblood*

ALSO AVAILABLE IN THE
VARIETY PALACE MYSTERIES

The Tumbling Girl

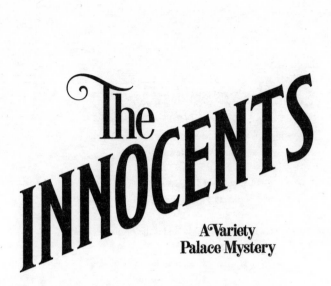

The INNOCENTS

A Variety
Palace Mystery

BRIDGET WALSH

GALLIC

Gallic Books
London

A Gallic Book

Copyright © Bridget Walsh, 2024

Bridget Walsh has asserted her moral right to be identified
as the author of the work.

First published in Great Britain in 2024 by
Gallic Books, 12 Eccleston Street, London SW1W 9LT

A CIP record for this book is available from the British Library

Typeset in Fournier by
Palimpsest Book Production Ltd, Falkirk, Stirlingshire

ISBN 978-1-913547-52-3
Printed in the UK by CPI (CRO 4YY)

2 4 6 8 10 9 7 5 3 1

For Micky

Love is like a tree: it grows by itself, roots itself deeply in our being and continues to flourish over a heart in ruin. The inexplicable fact is that the blinder it is, the more tenacious it is. It is never stronger than when it is completely unreasonable

VICTOR HUGO

TRAFALGAR THEATRE, LONDON

12 DECEMBER 1863

'Cram them in,' Taylor had said. 'Every one of them kids is money in our pockets.' But Freddy Graham was worried. There were so many, for a start-off. By his reckoning, at least a couple of thousand, squashed in together, sharing seats, little ones on older ones' laps. And precious few adults to take care of them. The youngest weren't much more than babes in arms, the oldest maybe ten or twelve. The worst age, in Freddy's opinion. Too young to be responsible, but old enough to make serious trouble. There were a handful of the bigger lads now, up in the gallery, leaning over the rails and spitting on the kids down below. Little bastards.

He was only the stage manager. It weren't his job to worry about front of house. He certainly wasn't paid enough. And maybe he needn't have bothered. The show was going well, after all, although most of it didn't make much sense to him. It was the first time they'd staged a pantomime, and he wouldn't be too concerned if it was the last. That scene where the King had fallen on the baby and squashed it, and then the Nurse had inserted a bellows in its arse and brought it back to life. Load of old nonsense in his opinion. The kids lapped it up, mind.

To give them their due, Williams and his crew all knew what they were about. They'd performed this show a hundred times, at least. And they were good. The children loved the ghost illusions, the talking waxworks. Although, to Freddy's mind, the pantomime story seemed like a poor excuse to sling together a load of acts that didn't really belong on one billing. Give him a nice melodrama any day. You knew where you were with a melodrama. Pantomime was just nonsense. Why have a conjurer at a baby's christening? From his position in the wings, Freddy could see all the wires and ropes, the secret pockets, the suspicious-looking boxes that were just a little too large, or just a little too deep. But from a distance, down in the stalls, up in the galleries, it must have really looked like magic.

He hadn't been too pleased when they'd released those pigeons, mind. He weren't fond of birds at the best of times, and in an enclosed space they scared the hell out of him. And guess who'd be the one clearing up after them?

He looked at his watch. Nearly five o'clock. Only a few more minutes to go. He peeked out at the audience from the wings. They were growing restless. They'd been promised presents at the end of the show. Freddy had his reservations about that. The best part of two thousand kids in the theatre, half of them up in the galleries. There was no system, no way of making sure everyone got a present. But Taylor had shrugged. Said it weren't his business. Well, whose business is it, Freddy had thought, if it ain't front of house? Taylor had barked at him that Williams and his troupe had made a promise, and it was up to them to figure out how that happened.

'And now, ladies and gentlemen, boys and girls,' Williams said, his commanding voice reaching across the packed auditorium, 'Sleeping Beauty has been restored to life. Evil has been vanquished. Good has been rewarded. We have come to the close of our magical entertainment.'

Excited cries erupted across the theatre. Poor little buggers. From the looks of most of them, there were precious few treats in their lives. And this would only be some bit of old tat: sweets, most likely. Maybe a whistle or a cheap doll that would fall apart before the child got home.

Williams smiled, throwing his arms wide in a munificent gesture. 'I believe you know what time it is. It's *present* time!'

Shrieks exploded from all around the auditorium. The older kids started stamping their feet. Christ, Freddy thought, they'll start chucking up in a minute, they're that excited. As if on cue, a little girl two rows from the stage leaned to one side and vomited in the aisle.

Freddy swore under his breath, turned away and nipped down the short flight of steps to the cupboard where he kept all his supplies. His hand reached instinctively for the bucket and mop, but found only empty air. Some bugger had been in there, taking his stuff, not putting it back. Swearing again, louder this time, he headed down the corridor and found the bucket nestled under a rail of costumes, the mop upended next to it. There were a few inches of dirty water in the bucket; enough to clear up the sick. Freddy was mentally rehearsing his complaint to Taylor when he heard a noise.

Something wasn't right. A great disgruntled roar from somewhere out front.

Freddy made his way back into the auditorium. Williams was randomly scattering small items into the audience, the other performers lending a hand. Children leapt across each other, hurling themselves in front of the sweets, grasping for them. The bigger kids, the boys mainly, were getting most of the bounty, grabbing and pushing smaller kids out of the way.

Freddy frowned, glanced around him. Williams and his crew were only throwing stuff into the stalls. How were they gonna get anything up into the gods? Freddy looked upwards and realised what the noise was. The children crammed in the galleries had noticed they were missing out and were heading for the staircase leading down to the stalls.

Even from a distance, Freddy could see they had a feral look about them. This could mean trouble, particularly from those bigger lads who were leading the way. He dropped his bucket and mop, gestured frantically to the ushers nearest the stage, but they were paying no attention, too busy trying to control the mayhem down in the stalls. Freddy looked behind him. Where was Taylor when you needed him? Or anyone?

The kids in the stalls were shrieking with delight, flinging themselves in all directions to grab the bits of nonsense. Freddy caught Williams's eye, made a gesture for him to stop, but the actor just shrugged and carried on.

Another sound started to emerge underneath the screams of delight. More shouting, but different this time. Urgent. Desperate. It was coming from the stairwell. And then he realised, with a sickening lurch, that the door into the stalls was still bolted. A long bolt at the bottom that slid into a hole in the floor. Once bolted, a gap of exactly twenty-two inches was left. They'd measured it carefully, room enough to ensure only one person could get through at a time. The usher could check their tickets before letting the next one in.

Twenty-two inches. And maybe a thousand children trying to force their way through.

Freddy stumbled forward, tripped over and staggered down the aisle, only just managing to right himself. Some older kids laughed and jeered. Any other time he'd have given them a clip round the ear, but he needed to get to that bolt.

He ran, his breath coming in gasps, his lungs burning. No one else even seemed to have noticed. Two ushers were lounging on seats at the rear of the stalls, chatting. He shouted at them, gestured towards the door, but they laughed, mockingly cupped a hand behind an ear to show they couldn't hear him, or didn't want to, and turned away. They never bloody took him seriously. He shouted again, but his voice was lost in the shrieks and squeals and screams. How had no one else noticed the screams?

4

By the time he got there, a child had become wedged in the doorway, then another, and another. One on top of the other until they reached almost to the top of the doorframe. He bent down to the bolt and grasped the handle. Tried to wriggle and wrench it free. It was always a bit sticky; usually he had the knack but his hands were sweating and he couldn't shift it. He tried again, pulling desperately at the top of the bolt. It wouldn't budge. And then it dawned on him. It had bent from the weight pressed against the door. There was no way of pulling it free. The weight of one child, even half a dozen children, couldn't have bent the bolt. So how many were there behind the door?

Freddy reached up and tried to pull one of the children out from the top of the pile. But they were so tightly wedged in. He was afraid to drag at them, pull harder, for fear of breaking their little arms or legs. Were some of them already dead? He'd lived long enough to know what death looked like, the blank eyes, the lips parted as if to speak. But they couldn't be, surely? Fleetingly, pointlessly, he remembered the scene with the Nurse and the bellows.

Freddy couldn't see past the wall of bodies in front of him, couldn't tell for sure what was happening to the other children in the stairwell. But he could hear them. Children crying for help. For their mothers. And, above his head, the sound of hundreds of little feet clattering down the stairs. They were still coming. Three flights of stairs there were. Seven feet wide. He couldn't think why he was remembering all these numbers now. The stairs turned onto landings, so that all those who were thundering downstairs couldn't see what lay ahead. Until it was too late to turn back.

He felt a change in the auditorium behind him. Williams and the other performers had noticed something was amiss and had stopped dispensing gifts. Then Taylor appeared from somewhere, and the ushers were behind Freddy, clawing desperately at the children.

'Take them from the top,' Freddy shouted. 'You've got more of a chance of getting them out. Pull them from the top.'

But no one was listening. There was just a frenzy of arms, hands, trying frantically to pull someone, anyone to freedom. Grasping for any child they could reach.

Freddy moved away from the crowd of helpers, grabbed Taylor and gestured towards the west staircase. They usually kept it locked. Easier to control the crowd, Taylor said, if they only came through one doorway. Easier to stop anyone slipping in who hadn't paid. Freddy fumbled in his pocket for his keys, found the one he needed, and unlocked the door. He raced up the stairs, Taylor wheezing behind him, then across the walkway linking the two staircases. Children were still pouring out of the gallery, heading towards disaster. Christ, would they never stop coming! Freddy ran past them, pushing them out of the way. He blocked their entrance to the east staircase and pointed them back towards Taylor.

Then he carried on across the walkway to the other staircase and looked down.

Freddy wasn't a churchgoing man. He'd given all of that up years ago when a pastor assured him he was heading straight for hell. So he wondered if maybe he was already dead, because what greeted him was surely worse than any vision of hell he'd heard about at Sunday school. A sea of arms, legs, heads. Fingers grasping the air but no longer moving. Tiny mouths held open, emitting one last silent scream. Lips parted for a final desperate intake of breath that came too late. He stood for a moment, overwhelmed, not knowing where to start. They were dead. All dead.

Then he heard his own name. 'Mr Graham? Please, Mr Graham.'

The voice was familiar. He followed the sound and glimpsed a twist of red hair peeping out from a pile of bodies.

6

His neighbour's child. Six years old. She'd broken her ankle a fortnight ago, jumping off a wall, and had been walking with a crutch ever since. How had she survived? And what was her name? For the life of him, he couldn't remember it.

Freddy lunged towards her. 'I'm here,' he said. 'I'm coming. Hold on.'

He stumbled forward, felt something soft beneath him. He looked down. An arm, the child no more than four or five. He couldn't see if it was a boy or a girl. He moved forward more tentatively, trying to avoid stepping on anyone. Then realised the pointlessness, and ploughed on, telling himself not to dwell on what lay beneath his feet, but only what lay ahead of him. A living child calling his name. There were bodies piled high around her, and he lifted them, pushed them aside, not allowing himself to think about what he was doing. How each of these bodies was somebody's daughter. Somebody's son.

He reached her. She was tucked into a corner of the landing. Her crutch had somehow got wedged in front of her and acted as a barrier. It had given her just enough space to breathe. He reached behind the crutch and lifted her out, cradling her head in his hand, her hair soft and fine as thistledown, her little heart thumping in her chest.

Holding her tightly, murmuring words of comfort all the while, he staggered back along the walkway, down the west staircase and carried her outside. He sat her down carefully on the pavement. There were other children, standing or sitting, moving aimlessly or not at all. It was raining, but no one seemed to have noticed. They huddled together instinctively, staring blankly into the distance, or reaching blindly for a hand to hold. Toys lay discarded on the ground. An older girl who seemed to know his neighbour's child pulled her close. Freddy still couldn't remember the little girl's name.

He turned back. He had to rescue whoever he could. And some

of them – lots of them, surely – were still alive. If they were making noise, they were alive.

Later, when they had finally freed all the bodies and laid them out in lines on the pavement, Freddy walked up and down the rows and counted them. He had to do it twice, because he figured he must have got it wrong the first time. But he hadn't.

One hundred and eighty-three of them. One hundred and eighty-three kids who weren't going home.

He walked back into the empty theatre. The air was thick with the sharp tang of piss; so many of the poor mites had wet themselves in fear or desperation. All down the stairwell were little caps and bonnets, torn from heads and trampled underfoot. Buttons with lengths of thread attached. The sole of a little boy's boot torn from the uppers. A red hair ribbon ripped from a girl's head. A hank of blonde hair with blood at the roots.

ONE

She wasn't their usual bookkeeper; he had six months left to serve if he kept his nose clean. This new woman – Mrs Dorothy Lawrence – was younger than Minnie had expected, somewhere in her twenties, maybe thirties, with a pleasant, open face, and rather beautiful hair which she wore elaborately dressed. Minnie peered more closely; if any of it was false hair, it must be the expensive stuff, 'cos it looked like it was all her own. She wore what seemed a simple, almost severe dark-navy dress. But Minnie could see it was cut perfectly to highlight her impressive figure. There wasn't a straight line about her. She was all curves and magnificent hair. She belonged on the wall of a fancy art gallery.

Mrs Lawrence hadn't shown any surprise that a woman could manage a music hall, which made a nice change. Now they'd spent twenty minutes in total silence as she'd looked over the books, wincing on occasion and peering at Minnie over her glasses before resuming her perusal.

'Before you took up the reins, the Variety Palace was thriving under Mr –' she said, glancing down at the papers, 'Mr Edward Tansford. Why is he no longer in control? He is still the co-owner, I take it?'

'Mr Tansford was deeply affected by the tragic events of last year. He's finding it difficult to return to work.'

'Well, I would suggest he overcomes any emotional compunction and gets himself back to the Variety Palace quick smart.'

Emotional compunction, Minnie thought. Unbidden, an image flashed into her mind. Blood. A life leaching away before her eyes. Tansie's cry. She bit her tongue. Right now, she needed this woman's help. Once they were back on their feet she'd tell her what she could do with her emotional compunction.

Mrs Lawrence looked again at the papers. 'You appear to have been haemorrhaging performers over the last few months. Any reason?'

'They're a superstitious lot, theatrical types. Some of them started to say the Palace was cursed. What with the murders and all.'

The other woman blinked slowly, then measured her words as if each of them was worth a shilling. 'Murders? In the plural? How many are we talking about, Miss Ward?'

'Three. Well, more actually, but three people who worked at the Palace were murdered.'

'I see. Numbers like that might render the most confirmed sceptic a trifle superstitious. And these murders, they were solved?'

'Oh, yes. We caught the killers.'

'*We?*'

'Me and a private detective. Albert Easterbrook.'

Mrs Lawrence frowned. Then sighed. 'But *you* are not a private detective, Miss Ward?'

'No. I'm a writer. For the Palace and a few other places, but mainly the Palace. And now I'm managing it. In Tansie's – Mr Tansford's absence. It's complicated, I'll give you that. But all you really need to worry about is the profit and loss.' She nodded at the tattered notebook and bundle of papers on the desk.

Mrs Lawrence extended an elegant finger and tentatively

touched the bundle, as if afraid of infection by association. 'Judging by this, it would be correct to assume that bookkeeping isn't one of your many talents.'

'No,' Minnie said, forcing herself to remain calm as her lips stretched to a thin smile. 'In between writing enough to keep the wolf from the door, taking on a management role I ain't suited to, and helping to solve the murder of my best friend, I ain't had time for much else. I thought bookkeeping was what I'm paying you for.'

The other woman gave her a hard stare, and then started to explain – at great length – exactly where the problem lay.

'Impending doom.' The words hadn't actually been used, to be fair, but that was how it felt to Minnie. Mrs Lawrence had definitely said 'deficit', 'closure' and 'trouble'. The bottom line was they needed to pull in more punters, or the Variety Palace could be out of business before Easter.

She scurried through the back streets to the Strand, lowering her head against the chilly November winds, and ticking off everything she'd done that morning, alongside her painful hour with the bookkeeper: pacified the butcher who was waiting for his payment; hurried along the carpenters who'd been hired to produce a dozen hinged scenery flats, and so far had produced only two; nipped into the Gaiety and unsuccessfully tried to persuade Gertie Steadman, the juggling fire-eater, to do a turn at the Palace. Longingly, she thought of the days when all she'd had to do was knock out a few songs and sketches.

Pulling the stage door of the Palace behind her, she narrowly avoided colliding with Betty Gilbert in the cramped corridor. It was only twenty minutes to the matinee and, as usual, chaos reigned. Betty, dressed in form-fitting bloomers and corset for her turn as an acrobat, shouted in passing, 'Bernard's looking for you, Min.'

Minnie sighed. If Bernard Reynolds was looking for her this close to curtain-up it couldn't be good. Usually consigned to 'thinking parts', a few weeks ago Bernard had suggested a sketch where he dressed in an animal 'skin' and performed a song-and-dance routine. She must have had a sudden rush of blood to the head, because she'd agreed. Nothing had gone smoothly since.

She hurried down the flagstone corridor to her office, although she still thought of it as Tansie's. Maybe she could hide there for the next twenty minutes.

No such luck. Lounging in the upholstered chair she'd installed for a little bit of comfort, with his feet firmly positioned on the desk, was Tansie. He'd regained the weight he'd lost after Cora's death, and was slowly starting to assume some of his old flamboyance. Today's choice of suit was a dark-green velvet which Minnie had to admit was rather smart.

'Comfy enough?' she barked at him. 'Sure you wouldn't like a little cushion? A blanket? Little tot of something while I'm up?'

He glanced up from the newspaper he was reading, refusing to rise to the bait. 'Kippy's looking for you,' he said. 'His favourite hammer's gone missing. And there was something about the trapdoor not working again.'

'And you couldn't have seen to it, I suppose? Given it was your bleedin' idea in the first place?'

Against her better judgement, Minnie had agreed to Tansie and Bernard's ambitious plans for a star trap. It covered an opening in the stage, beneath which Bernard stood on a platform, ready for his entrance in what was ambitiously – and fraudulently – billed a magical menagerie. Kippy, the stage manager, released a counterweight, and Bernard was propelled upwards for a spectacular entrance, appearing to fly through the air. Rehearsals had not gone well.

Someone coughed gently behind Minnie. She turned to see

Bobby, one of the stagehands, a lad of seven or eight, with a steaming mug of tea in one hand and a large pork pie in the other. He smiled at Minnie, then slid past her to place the tea and pie in front of Tansie, who nodded his thanks before breaking off the crust and feeding it to a small black-and-white monkey who sat on the desk in a miniature deckchair.

'Oh, and Bernard's on the warpath,' Tansie said. 'He's been asking after you all morning. Been anywhere nice?'

Minnie took a deep breath and recounted her morning to Tansie in language that would have made a navvy blush, before requesting that he shift himself or she'd be inserting the pork pie and the mug of tea up a certain part of his anatomy where even his own mother wouldn't venture.

Tansie smiled broadly, revealing the flash of a gold tooth.

'What?' Minnie said.

'It's the first bit of fire you've shown in months, Min. Nice to have you back.'

He sprang up from behind the desk and the three of them made their way to the stage, the monkey seated on Tansie's shoulder eating the remains of the pie crust and shedding crumbs behind him like a furry Hansel.

From the wings, they peeped out into the auditorium, which was filling slowly. This was the bit Minnie loved, those few minutes before a performance started. It reminded her of her own first visit to a music hall, sneaking out of the house against her mother's instructions and hiding behind some woman's skirts so she could get in without paying. Even though she'd known she'd be clobbered when she got home, it had all been worth it when the curtain went up and she was transported into another world, where everything seemed possible.

'You could squeeze a lot more in,' Tansie said. 'Few more tables and chairs. Little ones on their mothers' laps. We could charge the bloaters extra for wear 'n' tear.'

Minnie glanced down at Tansie's stomach. 'We don't charge *you* extra.'

Tansie shrugged. 'What was it that accountant said? "Financial peril", weren't it?'

'Which reminds me. You know what you'd be really good at, Tanse? Running this place. Like you're supposed to.'

Tansie shook his head. 'Too soon, Min.'

'I understand, Tanse. Really I do. I was there, remember? But it strikes me you ain't finding it too soon to go poking your nose in at every opportunity. So, no offence or nothing, but is there any chance you could sling your hook? You're either here or you ain't. You can't be both.'

He looked affronted. 'I'm only trying to help, Min.'

'Well, you ain't. All you do is come up with hare-brained ideas that cost money and don't work. I've got enough to deal with, Tanse.'

'Like what? Besides running this place? You doing much for Albert?'

'*With* Albert. I worked *with* him, not for him. Remember?'

'No need to get the spike,' Tansie said. 'I only asked.'

Minnie sighed. It was herself she was angry with, not Tansie. Her relationship with Albert Easterbrook was complicated, and not something she wanted to spend much time thinking about.

'To answer your question, Tanse, I'm too busy here to be developing a sideline as a detective.'

Tansie looked down at his shoes, a beautiful pair of highly polished oxblood brogues. He drew invisible patterns across the flagstones of the backstage corridor with one foot. 'You can't hide forever, Min,' he said quietly. 'You need to move on.'

'Like you have, you mean? Your best mate is a monkey, Tanse. Even you must know that ain't normal.'

He shrugged. 'At least I don't spend every minute of my life inside this place.'

14

A few months ago, Minnie had moved into two rooms tucked away behind the upper gallery. It saved a lot on rent, but it wasn't the healthiest arrangement. Some days she never left the Palace. Once upon a time that would have bothered her.

A bell rang. The show was about to start. Quiet descended backstage, punctuated by the opening salvos of Paul Prentice, the unfunniest funny man in London, who hadn't taken any of Minnie's hints that maybe his music hall career was over.

Minnie slipped out of the wings and back to her office. Frances Moore, one of the dressmakers used by the Palace, was waiting for her. An unassuming-looking woman, tall, with features so fine and dainty it looked as if her face had been drawn with a very sharp pencil. The kind of woman you might pass in the street and pay no mind to. But look more closely and you'd see she had a delicate beauty about her. She was one of the best dressmakers within five miles of the Strand and insisted on being called Frances, never Fran.

Frances gestured towards a package wrapped in brown paper and tied with string on Minnie's desk. 'Done,' she said. Minnie knew before she even opened the parcel that the work was going to be exquisite. And she was right. Two tiny ballgowns with billowing tulle skirts covered in sparkles that would catch the light with every movement on stage. The Fairy Sisters were going to be delighted. Unexpectedly, Minnie felt tears prick her eyes. She must be going soft in her old age.

'They're beautiful, Frances. You could charge us twice what you do, you know.'

'Don't go letting Tansie hear you saying that. Besides, I like working for the Palace. Where else could I get free tickets and all the beef sandwiches I can eat?'

Minnie ran her eye over Frances's slender frame. 'I'm surprised you can manage even one of those sandwiches. And all I'm saying is, you could charge a lot more for your work.'

Frances shrugged. 'I do charge more. To those that can afford it. Word has it that the Palace might be in a little – trouble?'

Minnie sighed. You couldn't keep anything a secret on the Strand. 'Things have slowed down a bit. It'll pick up again.'

''Course it will. In the meantime, you let me know when you need anything more.'

Five minutes after Frances had taken her money and left, Minnie was hanging the two tiny dresses on the rail in the backstage corridor when she heard her name and turned to see Bernard bearing down on her. Behind him was Kippy, the two men clearly vying to see who could reach her first. Bernard was hampered by a pair of hooves on his feet but he still won.

'I need to talk to you, Minnie,' he said. 'In private?'

'I don't know what Bernard's latest gripe is,' Kippy said, 'but we need to discuss that bleedin' star trap. It still ain't right.'

When first installed, the platform had propelled Bernard upwards, but the trapdoor on the stage had failed to open. Bernard had been game, you had to give him that, but there were only so many blows to the head a man could take. Kippy had worked tirelessly to improve the mechanism until the trapdoor opened but Georgie Carter, who was playing the part of a zookeeper, kept forgetting where to stand and had fallen through the trapdoor with such astonishing regularity Minnie wondered if it wasn't Georgie who'd taken the blows to the head. Endless rehearsals, and a series of chalked crosses on the stage, had finally impressed on him where not to stand. Foolishly, Minnie had thought the problem was solved.

'It's the propulsion on the platform,' Kippy said. 'There's too much force, and I ain't sure I know how to fix it. Bernard almost landed in the flies this morning during rehearsals.'

Laughter erupted from the audience. 'Paul's going down well,' Bernard remarked, 'given he learned most of his jokes from Moses.'

'So maybe we abandon the star trap altogether?' Minnie suggested.

'My sentiments exactly,' Kippy muttered. 'We're a music hall, not bleedin' Drury Lane.'

'As if I need reminding,' Bernard sniffed. 'But I am not prepared to abandon the mechanism simply because we are suffering a few teething problems. Would Irving stumble at the first hurdle? Would Kemble? No. The star trap stays.'

'So is that why you wanted to see me?' Minnie said hopefully.

'No. It's a private matter. Your office?'

Paul had completed his act, and emerged backstage looking decidedly pleased with himself. Out in the auditorium Harry Gordon, Tansie's stand-in as master of ceremonies, was regaling the audience with promises Minnie was pretty certain the next act couldn't fulfil. Carlotta, a sheen of sweat visible on her upper lip, slid nervously past Minnie and waited for her cue from Harry.

'Can it wait, Bernard?' Minnie said. 'We could have a chat after the show, if you want.'

'Promise me you'll make the time, Minnie. It's important.'

She sighed. Everything was a matter of the greatest urgency with Bernard. Then it turned out to be a complaint about running order, or a mess in one of the dressing rooms, or whether he should make his entrance on the second or third bar of music.

'I'll make the time,' she said. 'Promise.'

'I've been thinking, Min,' Tansie said, sidling up behind her and making her jump.

'I thought I could smell burning.'

'There's a mate of mine. Handy Mick. Reckons he could install a water tank and pump beneath the stage for a fraction of what you'd normally pay. We could have all sorts of fancy effects. Rivers, fountains, waterfalls.'

'Is this the same Handy Mick who flooded the Star last month?'

'It weren't his fault that porcupine got loose.'

'You don't think there's a danger, if we start mucking about with rivers, fountains and waterfalls, that we'll just end up drowning someone? Given that we don't seem able to get a bleedin' trapdoor to work properly?'

'You gotta dream big, Min, if you want to achieve greatness.'

'Well, I'd just like to achieve a single performance where no one ends up with concussion.'

As if on cue, a deafening crash from the stage made them all jump. The monkey grabbed hold of Tansie's hair, resulting in a stream of whispered curses from Tansie. Minnie would happily have dispensed with plate spinners but Tansie was adamant the punters expected to see one. Carlotta was so inept she must be keeping the potters of Stoke-on-Trent in luxury biscuits. Luckily, the audience seemed to think it was deliberate and were whooping with delight. Minnie looked at her pocket watch. Only another hour and a half to go.

Two hours later, the Palace was blissfully quiet. The show had gone surprisingly well, the audience had departed, and most of the performers had nipped out for a quick bite before the later show. Minnie settled herself back in her comfy chair and removed a small card from her purse. 'Ward and Easterbrook,' it said. 'Consulting Detectives.' She ran her finger across the surface, remembering Albert's joke about not being able to stretch to vellum. She'd been carrying the card around since the day he'd given it to her, removing it from her purse every now and then to gaze at the words and think about how different things might have been.

She had promised to help him. But every time he appeared, needing her help with a missing pet, a cheating husband, a stolen item of jewellery, she had told him she was too busy at the Palace. Which was true, but still. Lately, he hadn't been coming around so much. It was probably for the best. Every time she saw him she felt herself slipping back into a world she had spent the last nine months escaping from.

But she missed him. Particularly at times like this, when she was so tired she felt like she was melting at the edges. Or when she felt completely alone, even though she was surrounded by people. What she wouldn't give to have him close by. To lean into him. She had done that once. He had smelt of clean sheets, and she had wanted to stay there.

She held the card gently between her finger and thumb for a moment, then opened a desk drawer and dropped it in among the pencils, old song sheets and other detritus.

A gentle knock at the door roused her. Bernard stood in the doorway, his costume swopped for a brown serge suit, although he had not been entirely successful in removing the last traces of his stage make-up. The whiff that wafted across the room told Minnie he had reapplied his goose-grease pomade to the remaining strands of hair he meticulously combed over his pate.

'A moment of your time, dearest one?'

Minnie nodded and gestured towards a chair.

'It concerns my brother, Peter. He's on the missing list. We meet every Wednesday for an early supper between the matinee and evening performances. He didn't appear last week.'

'So something came up. That German fella – Otto something, weren't it? – is he back in town?'

Bernard shook his head firmly. 'Our Wednesday meetings are sacrosanct. No matter what the distractions, Peter is always there.'

'You been to his digs? His place of work?'

'His landlady hasn't seen him in nearly a week. He's been working at the Fortune, but they're dark at the moment. Refurbishment. I tracked down one or two of his chums, and they haven't seen hide nor hair of him since Tuesday, when the Fortune closed.' He paused, playing with a gold signet ring on his little finger, the entwined initials of his parents engraved on the surface. He seemed uncertain of how to go on; Bernard was never normally lost for words. 'This isn't like him, Minnie. Not at all like him.'

'I'm really sorry, Bernard, but I ain't doing any more detective work.'

'Of course, of course. I was just wondering if you could speak to Albert about it. Perhaps he could exert some influence with that police officer friend of his? I've reported Peter as missing, but the officer I spoke to seemed somewhat indifferent. I thought – perhaps – with your connections, you might be able to pull some strings.'

'Why not have a word with Albert yourself?' Minnie asked.

He shook his head. 'I barely know him, dear heart. It wouldn't take up much of your time, surely?'

'I'll ask. But I can't promise he'll do anything with it. He's very busy these days, you know.'

'Thank you,' Bernard said. She waited for the Shakespearean quotation or the anecdote from his glittering acting career. But there was nothing. He simply gave her a gentle smile and left.

She sat for a few moments, questioning why she felt so reluctant to speak to Albert. It was purely business, after all. Simply asking a favour for a friend. She could be in and out of there in no time. Hardening her resolve, she rose, grabbed her bonnet and coat from the back of the door and made her way out into the chilly November evening.

TWO

Albert Easterbrook removed his hat and loosened his tie. He was glad to be home. The church had been bitterly cold, the graveyard even colder, an easterly wind whipping at the mourners' ankles and making everyone huddle inside coats and scarves. But it had gone well, if such a thing could ever be said of a funeral. Now the real mourning would begin, when he would need to come to terms with his loss and all it meant.

'Tea, Albert? Inspector Price?' Mrs Byrne said, nodding towards John, Albert's friend and former colleague. 'Or something stronger?'

Albert nodded at the drinks cabinet. 'Would you join us, Mrs B?'

'I won't if you don't mind. Funerals always exhaust me. If I have even a sniff of brandy I'm likely to fall asleep, and I've still got tonight's supper to prepare. Nice chicken, I thought. And maybe a lemon posset for pudding, if Tom remembers to bring me back some lemons from the greengrocer's. I'll leave you to it.'

Albert and John seated themselves by the fire, each nursing a large glass of brandy. The cold seemed to have permeated Albert's bones, and he dragged his chair closer to the hearth.

'A good send-off, Albert,' John said tentatively.

Albert nodded. 'It was kind of you to come. Particularly as you never even knew her. Work is busy as ever, I imagine.'

John shrugged. 'You know how it is, Albert. Always busy, just some times not quite as bad as others.'

'The Hairpin Killer seems to have gone quiet,' Albert said, grateful to talk of something other than the morning's events.

The Hairpin Killer had stalked the streets of London for the last decade, preying on young women and murdering them with a knife to the thigh and then inserting seven hairpins into their hearts. Hence his moniker.

'Quiet for now,' John said. 'He's done this before, mind. Lain low for a while and then re-emerged.'

'In prison, do you think?'

John nodded as if the idea wasn't a new one. 'That's my theory. I reckon he gets nicked for something minor, spends a few months inside, then he's back out again.'

The two men peered down at their drinks and John shifted in his seat. 'Your father—' he said, then winced as if his thoughts caused him discomfort.

'You can't think worse of him than I do, John. I learned long ago that he has a heart of flint.'

'Did he speak to you at all?'

Albert shook his head. 'Not even today. At my own mother's funeral. I've no doubt he's feeling her loss, but he couldn't bring himself to offer a word of greeting or condolence. Just walked away when I tried to approach him.'

'I liked your sister,' John said. 'Kind of her to take the time to speak to me, particularly when she was taking it so hard. But that husband of hers—' He broke off again, not needing to complete the sentence. Albert had little time for his brother-in-law, Monty Banister, and had never made any secret of his feelings. The man was a pompous, self-serving ass. And that was on a good day.

They sipped their drinks, enjoying the fact that neither of them felt the need to speak. The quiet was broken by Mrs Byrne re-entering the room to hand Albert a small parcel. 'It came while we were out,' she said.

Albert read the card: 'A token of my gratitude – Lord Ballantyne'. He unwrapped the parcel and held out the item to John, who turned it slowly in his hand.

'Are those real?' John asked.

'Oh, yes. Although what Lord Ballantyne imagines I'm going to do with a diamond-encrusted snuffbox is anybody's guess.'

'Well, your investigation did save his only daughter from running off with that dodgy fella with the dicky eye. Although something a little more practical might have been handier. You could always flog it, I suppose. Work's going well, I take it?'

Albert felt relieved to be on the safer ground of his detective agency, rather than discussing his uncomfortable relations with his family. 'Almost too well. I'm having to turn cases away. I've hired Tom Neville – that lad who worked for Lionel Winter, remember? Which reminds me. Any sign of Tom, Mrs B?'

'He was here when we got back, and then he heard me muttering about lemons and he decided I was also running low on tea so he's popped out again. Can't stand funerals, that lad. When he saw me in my mourning dress he went a very strange shade of green. I expect he'll be back in an hour or so.'

'Is that young lady at Fletcher's still sweet on him?'

Mrs Byrne nodded. 'And he's too soft-hearted to tell her no. Still, I imagine it takes his mind off Daisy, if only for a while. God rest her soul.'

She closed the door behind her. John lit a cigarette, offering one to Albert, who declined. Although surely, today of all days, Mrs Byrne could have no objection.

'Been working on anything interesting?' John asked. 'Anything that would explain why I ain't seen you in the ring for weeks?'

Albert winced. He and John had been regular sparring partners

23

for several years now, but Albert knew he was guilty of sometimes allowing work to take precedence over friendship and boxing.

'Next week, I promise,' he said. 'And yes, I have had an interesting case. Or a puzzling one, at least. Client came to see me about her husband's death. William Fowler. He was found hanged. His wife thought it was suspicious and she said there was never any hint he'd been suicidal. I've looked into it, but it's the old problem: I came too late. Didn't see the body when it was first found, and the man was buried before his widow even thought to speak to someone about it. There's nothing to suggest foul play. But also nothing to suggest he was unhappy enough to take his own life.'

There was a knock at the front door. A few moments later, Mrs Byrne entered, a smile playing at the corners of her mouth. In her wake was Minnie, removing her hat and coat as she came in.

'Well, if it ain't *Inspector* Price,' Minnie said.

John grinned and looked mildly embarrassed. His promotion was still very new.

She turned to Albert, took in his mourning suit, noticed his hat on the table, the black band encircling it.

'Who's died?' she asked.

'My mother.'

Her face softened and she reached forward to take his hand. 'Oh, Albert, I'm so sorry. Was it sudden?'

'A short illness,' Albert said, struggling to keep his voice under control. Minnie's obvious sympathy had released an unexpected wave of emotion.

'And the funeral?' she asked.

'It was this morning.'

Minnie frowned, pulled back from him. 'This morning? Why am I only hearing about it now?'

Albert shrugged. 'You didn't know her, Minnie.'

'Neither did John, but by the looks of his suit he's come from

24

the same place as you. Besides, I might not have known your ma, but I know *you*, Albert. You should have told me.'

It had been his first thought on hearing of his mother's death – to tell Minnie. And then he had reminded himself of how cold she was with him these days, pushing him away, refusing to help with the business, although she had promised she would. What were they now to each other, other than two people who had once worked together, once dreamed of something more. He wanted to tell her this, but what was the point?

'You're so busy these days, Minnie. I didn't want to trouble you.'

Her frown deepened. He knew the truth of his words had hit home, but she would never admit it. 'I ain't so busy I wouldn't have time to pay my respects, offer some comfort. And you know that, Albert. So don't go putting it all on me.'

An uncomfortable silence descended on them for a few moments, then Minnie continued. 'Anyway, I didn't come here for a barney, Albert. I need to ask you something. A favour.'

'Anything,' he said. 'You know that.'

'It's Bernard. Or, rather, his brother.' She outlined what she knew of Peter Reynolds's disappearance.

'Has he done anything like this before?' Albert asked.

'Not according to Bernard. He's really worried, Albert, or I wouldn't ask.'

'Tell him I'll look into it, of course I will. Top priority,' Albert said, trying to assuage his guilt for the pain he'd caused her.

'And me,' John chipped in. 'Can't hurt, can it?'

Minnie gave them both a thankful look and then turned away. Her eyes darted round the room, lighting on the snuffbox John had left on the mantelpiece.

She walked across, picked it up and traced a finger over the jewels before holding it up to the light for a closer look.

'Very la-di-da. Surprised you can find time for the likes of me and John these days.'

'It's because of you I have clients like that, Minnie.'

A shadow crossed her face. So fleeting most people would have missed it. Albert didn't. He knew Minnie struggled with any mention of the previous year's events.

'Take it,' he said, as she placed the trinket back on the mantelpiece.

She shook her head, the slightest smile flickering across her lips. 'I've been trying to give up the snuff. Plays havoc with the old nasal passages.'

Albert smiled and the mood lightened between them.

'I passed Fletcher's on the way here,' Minnie said. 'Tom's in there, sitting on a sack of spuds, chatting to some girl.'

'He has an admirer.'

She smiled. 'Is he admiring in return?'

'Mrs B thinks not.'

'Shame. Still, if it—'

'—takes his mind off Daisy. Exactly.'

A loud knocking on the front door made them all jump. A few moments later Mrs Byrne appeared, her lips pursed with anger. 'There's a lady here, Mr Easterbrook. Says it's urgent. I told her this wasn't an appropriate time, but she's insistent. I said we should have put crape on the door. That way, everyone knows and they leave you alone.' She dropped her voice to an indignant whisper. 'She won't take no for an answer. Throwing her weight around, if you ask me. Acts like a fancy carriage and a nice set of furs can get her anything she wants.'

'Show her in, Mrs Byrne.'

John stood and reached for his coat and hat. 'Time I was off. Those criminals won't be catching themselves.'

He looked at Minnie, who had also retrieved her coat and bonnet. The door opened and Mrs Byrne ushered in a woman, introducing her as Mrs Eddings. She was somewhere in her fifties, Albert guessed. Fully attired in widow's weeds. Dear God, was

26

there anyone in London not mourning somebody? Black suited her, though, and Mrs B wasn't wrong: very nice furs. She was tall, statuesque. A handsome face, with intelligent eyes and a generous mouth. She moved with great self-possession, as if it were her home and she had invited Albert in, rather than the other way around. Albert followed her gaze as she surveyed the room. He wondered if he saw her lip curl but couldn't be sure.

John nodded at her as he left. Mrs Eddings ignored him, instead peering closely at Minnie. 'You must be Miss Ward,' she said. 'If the newspapers are to be believed, you played no small part in bringing that rogue Linton to justice. Excellent work.'

Minnie blushed. Albert knew she was uncomfortable when praise was directed at her, and any reference to the gruesome case they'd dealt with the previous year was particularly difficult. 'Thank you,' Minnie murmured, and moved closer to the door. Mrs Eddings took in her coat and hat and frowned.

'Miss Ward won't be staying,' Albert said. 'Her time is taken up with other matters these days. She's an extremely busy woman.'

Minnie cast him a withering glance. 'I can speak for myself, thanks very much. I've got a music hall to run, Mrs Eddings. Full-time job, so I don't really have much time for detecting. That's Mr Easterbrook's domain.'

'A great shame,' Mrs Eddings said. 'It was you I wished to see. I couldn't persuade you to stay?' She reached for the clasp of her bag, and Albert wondered what she would produce in the way of an inducement. It probably wouldn't top a diamond-encrusted snuffbox.

'I think you'll find Miss Ward is immovable,' Albert said, shaking his head with an elaborate show of regret.

He'd found his mark.

'I have time,' Minnie said, staring pointedly at Albert. 'I can always make time for someone in need. Or a friend.'

'But what about the Palace?' Albert looked at his watch. 'The evening performance starts in an hour.'

'Tansie'll be there,' Minnie said, turning away from him as if his comments were of no significance. 'I can send a note, let him know I might be delayed. Besides, Mrs Byrne mentioned she's got a fruitcake needs eating.' She placed her coat and bonnet firmly on a chair, then positioned herself securely on the couch. Mrs Eddings joined her and Albert took his customary place on the staggeringly uncomfortable armchair he had inherited from his Aunt Alice.

Mrs Byrne appeared with tea and a plate piled high with slices of dark fruitcake which she positioned directly in front of Minnie before leaving the room.

'Have you come far, Mrs Eddings?' Albert asked. It was one of his usual openings, designed to put new clients at ease.

Mrs Eddings dismissed the question with a wave of her hand. 'No need for small talk, Mr Easterbrook. We are not friends. This is a business transaction.'

Albert nodded and waited for her to continue. Once upon a time, he thought, Minnie would have leapt in to fill the silence. But she was different now. He wanted the old Minnie back.

'My husband is – was – Mr David Eddings. Judge Eddings.' She paused, as if waiting for a reaction. Albert obliged.

'I'm sorry for your loss. I read of your husband's passing in *The Times*. A tragic accident, I understand.'

He struggled to recall the details. Something about a locked trunk? Asphyxiation?

'No accident, Mr Easterbrook. Our grandson Percy was staying with us for a few days and he and my husband were playing hide-and-seek. After a period of time, it became apparent that my husband was missing.'

'You were not present?'

She shook her head. 'I was having lunch with my sister at her home in Kensington and we went shopping on Regent Street afterwards. I was gone for several hours, during which time my servants searched high and low for my husband. Eventually he was found inside a trunk in the attic. He had suffocated.' She lowered her head, reaching into her bag for a linen handkerchief edged in black.

Albert glanced at Minnie, but she seemed unwilling to say anything. 'You say it was no accident?' he prompted.

'My husband had an extreme fear – a phobia, if you will – of confined spaces. He would never have placed himself inside that trunk. Never. Besides which, he was seeking, not hiding.'

'Maybe your grandson got confused? Maybe it was your husband's turn to hide.'

'Even if that were the case, my husband would never have gone into the attic. Percy is only four years old, Mr Easterbrook. He is expressly forbidden to go into the upper reaches of the house.'

'This trunk he was found in. How did he get trapped in there?'

'It's made of oak. Iron-bound. The police believe my husband must either have climbed into the trunk or somehow fallen into it. The lid fell shut, and the movement knocked some other items off a shelf above. Even if you could open it from inside – which it transpires you can't – the combined weight of the trunk lid and the additional items would have made it impossible to escape.'

'But you ain't buying that explanation?' Minnie said, leaning forward in her seat.

Albert smiled to himself. Her interest was piqued.

'I am not, Miss Ward. As I've explained, my husband had an extreme fear of confined spaces. He would never set foot inside that trunk voluntarily. And I fail to see how a grown man can fall into a four-foot trunk, folding his legs up in the process. The mechanics alone seem impossible.'

'And yet impossible things do happen, Mrs Eddings.'

She gave Albert a long stare. 'They do, Mr Easterbrook. I have lived long enough to know that to be the case. But nothing about this sits right with me.'

Albert thought for a moment. 'Could your grandchild have done it? As a prank, without realising the consequences? You said he was only four.'

'Percy may not be the brightest of children, Mr Easterbrook, but he is exceptionally honest. I believe what he has told me.'

'A servant?'

She shook her head. 'Most of my staff have been with me for years. They say they weren't involved and I believe them.'

'What if I investigate, and it's just as the police have concluded? A tragic accident.'

'Then I shall trust your verdict. Your reputation precedes you, Mr Easterbrook. As does yours, Miss Ward.'

'Did your husband have any enemies?' Minnie asked. 'Anyone suspicious seen near the house in the days leading up to his death? Anything missing?'

'No to all your questions. My husband was respected by his colleagues, loved by his family and friends—' She broke off. Minnie reached for her hand and Mrs Eddings looked down with mild alarm on her face, before her gaze softened and she threw Minnie a grateful look. 'Please find out what you can, Miss Ward,' she said, turning towards Minnie. 'My husband was very dear to me. He has left a considerable absence in my life.'

'We'll do everything we can,' Minnie said softly.

Albert and Minnie stood at the window, watching as Mrs Eddings's carriage pulled away from the kerb.

'*We'll* do everything we can?' Albert repeated, trying to keep the anticipation out of his voice.

Minnie shrugged. 'She was upset, weren't she? And it was me she wanted help from. I couldn't very well tell her I weren't gonna have nothing to do with it, could I?' She turned away, retrieving her coat and bonnet from the chair. 'You'll do an excellent job, Albert. You always do, with or without me. Just make sure you leave yourself time to have a nosy about Peter Reynolds.'

And before he could say anything more, she was gone.

THREE

Peter Reynolds's landlady, a tall, thin woman who put Albert in mind of a human greyhound, had seen nothing of him for over a week. Prior to that, there'd been no unusual behaviour, no visitors, nothing out of the ordinary.

'Mr Reynolds keeps himself to himself,' she said, primly. 'He stays out a bit late for my liking, but he's a theatre gent, ain't he, so it's to be expected. Apart from that, he's a perfect tenant.'

John identified himself as a police officer and the landlady reluctantly showed them into Peter's rooms, muttering under her breath about respectable households and how she'd be having a word with Mr Reynolds when he showed his face again.

The rooms were spotless, with everything tidied away in drawers and cupboards; if ever his theatre career foundered, the man would make an excellent housekeeper. In an old cardboard suitcase, they found programmes from various shows Peter had appeared in over the years. For a spell, he seemed to have been part of a double act and Albert wondered if his former partner might be able to shed any light on his disappearance. Alongside the programmes were one or two props and bits of costume Peter must have smuggled out past a careless stage manager; Kippy would never have let him get away with it.

Drawing a blank at the lodgings, Albert and John made their way to the Fortune Theatre. It wasn't due to open for another day or so but George Nipper, the stage manager, had agreed to meet them there. He was waiting for them at the stage door, a shifty-looking chap, eyes too far apart, and a restless energy about him. Mind you, with the kind of clientele the Fortune attracted, he'd need to keep on his toes.

'I don't know how I'm gonna help,' he said, unlocking the door and grunting as he gave it a sharp heave with his shoulder. 'Peter keeps himself to himself.'

'Steady type, is he?' John asked.

'As steady as they come. Always on time. Always knows his lines and where he's gotta stand. Wish they were all like that.'

Once inside the theatre, George showed them the male dressing room and gestured towards a row of battered tin lockers. 'Peter's is the third one on the bottom.'

The locker contained a few sticks of stage make-up, some old rags and half a loaf of bread covered in mould. Nothing else.

'Anything out of the ordinary you can remember?' John asked, straightening up from inspecting the locker and wincing. His back was playing up again. 'Any changes in his behaviour recently?'

George considered the question. 'There was something, now you mention it. A woman came to the stage door the evening before we closed for the refurbishment. Asked for Peter. Which was unusual, 'cos he didn't normally have much to do with the ladies.'

'A tail?' John asked.

George shook his head. 'I don't reckon so. She was quite soberly dressed. It was half four, mind. Already dark. I couldn't tell you exactly what she was wearing.'

'Description?'

He frowned, trying to recall the details. 'Young, I'd say. Average sort of height. She had a shawl over her head.'

'Like she wanted to hide her face?'

He shrugged. 'Maybe. Or maybe she was just cold. Or shy.

Some women don't wanna be seen hanging around a stage door. She asked for Peter, I fetched him, and the two of them took off. Gone about half an hour or so. Peter came back on his own and cracked on with the run-through.'

'Was he acting any different when he came back?'

He thought for a moment. 'A bit strange, now I come to think about it. Happy, like, but a bit jumpy too.'

'And this woman, she ain't been round here since?'

'Well, we closed the next day, so – no, I'm guessing not.'

'And there's nothing else you can tell us?' Albert said.

'Sorry, no. Although – we could have a look in the cellar. There's a room down there for spare costumes, a few personal effects. Cleaners keep their stuff in there, and there's a makeshift bed. Somewhere for the old boys to sleep it off if they've had one too many the night before.'

'I thought Peter was a steady chap?' Albert said.

'Oh, he is. But his lodgings are a way out. Too far for him to go home between the matinee and the evening performances. Sometimes he kips downstairs. It's a long shot, but he might have left something there that could be of use. Let me just grab a lantern or you won't be able to see your hand in front of your face.'

As they descended the stairs to the cellar, the air grew noticeably colder and damper. John pressed his handkerchief to his mouth. 'What's that stink?' he asked.

'The river,' Albert said, remembering Minnie explaining to him how the Thames ran underneath the Strand.

'Or the sewers,' George said. 'Bit of both, more likely. It's bad at first, but you don't notice it after a while.'

They entered the cellar, the light from the lantern casting long shadows across the brick floor and up the walls. Rats scuttled underfoot back into the dark recesses.

'I wouldn't fancy sleeping down here,' John said.

George shrugged. 'Any port in a storm. It's safe. Usually fairly quiet, too. Unless someone's in here getting stock for the bar.' He gestured towards the boxes of beer and other alcohol piled up against one of the walls.

Albert tried to breathe shallowly. George was wrong. He wasn't getting used to the smell. 'That's not the river,' he said. 'Something's died down here.'

'Rats, most likely,' George said. 'There's enough of 'em. Or a dog, maybe. They get in here sometimes, looking for scraps of food or a warm billet. Maybe one slipped in just before we shut the place up.'

Crossing the floor to a door in the far corner, George turned the handle but the door remained closed. 'Funny,' he murmured, 'door's never locked.' He unhooked a bunch of keys from his belt and sorted through them until he found the right one.

As soon as he opened the door, a wave of warm air was released from the room and the smell intensified immediately. Rank, pungent, like rotting vegetables and faeces and mothballs all rolled into one. And underneath it a sickening kind of sweetness that rested on your tongue so you felt as if you weren't just smelling death, you were tasting it.

If it was a dog, it was a very big one. Albert exchanged a glance with John.

'Best we take over from here, sir,' John said.

George didn't put up an argument.

Albert entered the room first. Illuminated by the lamp, he saw it was more of a cupboard, with mops and buckets piled up in one corner. There was a mattress resting on a pair of trestles and a board.

'I don't think anyone's gonna be sleeping in here for a while,' John said.

On the floor, in the corner furthest away from the door, was a dark shape. Most definitely not a dog.

The man was curled up, his back pressed against the wall. His

35

body had already started to bloat, distorting his features, his skin marked with large blisters; it looked as if it would peel off at the slightest touch.

All the years he'd been a police officer and Albert was still never really prepared for this. The fact of a body. He'd worked with men who'd hardened themselves to the horrors of the job by treating the corpse as a source of dark humour. But Albert never allowed himself to forget this had once been a person, who had loved and been loved.

Behind him, Albert could hear John breathing. Everything was louder, clearer; time seemed to have slowed.

He knelt down. Candlelight flickered across the man's face, which was turned towards him, his eyes open and bulging from their sockets. There was dried fluid around the nose and eyes. Albert looked more closely. There appeared to be some sort of rag in the man's mouth, held in place by a length of rope.

'What's that on his wrists?' John said, placing a hand on Albert's shoulder and pointing.

The man's wrists were bound with the same rope he was gagged with.

On the little finger of the left hand, a gold ring, the flesh swollen around it. Albert held the lamp closer. The ring, with its engraved initials, looked exactly like the one Bernard wore on the same finger.

'I think it's him,' Albert said. 'Peter Reynolds.'

'And it's murder,' John said. 'Unless the man found some way of binding his own hands, locked himself in here and disposed of the key.'

Later, when the body had been removed, the three men sat in the quiet of the empty auditorium while George told them again all he knew. Which wasn't a great deal.

'Ain't you had workmen in all week?' John asked. 'Surely they'd have noticed the smell?'

George shook his head. 'They were refurbishing the upper galleries, going in and out of the building through the front doors. They didn't go anywhere near backstage and certainly not downstairs. More's the pity.'

'The door to that cupboard,' John said. 'You mentioned it was unusual for it to be locked. Who had keys?'

'Me. The caretaker. Mr Walker, the owner of the theatre.'

'Any spares?'

George nodded. 'Ned, the caretaker. He keeps a spare set in a desk in the props room.'

'Not the kind of thing you'd know about unless you worked here?'

George frowned as the impact of John's comment sank in. 'Maybe not. Problem is, we've got people coming and going all the time here. The owner's always trying to save a bob or two, so he has lots of casual workers. Fellas working here for a few days to build a set and then they're gone.'

'I don't suppose Mr Walker keeps any details of their names? Addresses?' Albert asked, already knowing the answer.

'What do you think?' George said.

John finished his questioning and the two of them left the theatre. They stood outside in the fading afternoon light.

'I need to have a bath,' John said, conspicuously sniffing his coat. 'I can still smell it on me.'

'And taste it,' Albert said.

'And then we need to go about finding this mystery woman.'

'But first, I need to tell Bernard,' Albert sighed, reluctantly turning towards the Palace.

FOUR

Minnie stood in one of the snuggeries, three small private rooms running behind the bar in the Palace. She'd felt the need to stay busy since Albert had delivered the news about Bernard's brother. She'd never met Peter but it had stirred up memories of the year before, when she'd been told about Rose. Overseeing the redecoration of the snuggeries seemed as good a task as any to keep her occupied. She leaned forward, squinted, then took two steps back and cast an appraising eye over all four walls.

'Sorry, Jack, but we're gonna need another coat, I reckon,' she said. 'That should do it.'

'I've already given it three,' said Jack, a short, heavyset young man wearing paint-spattered overalls and wielding a paintbrush. 'Whose idea was it to paint it pink? It's been a bugger to cover.'

Minnie gave him a knowing look. Jack Cassidy had been working at the Palace long enough to know that most of the stupid ideas originated with Tansie. Most of the good ideas too, mind. Tansie maintained pink made people drink more. Coupled with gold, though, the rooms screamed 'whorehouse'. Which wasn't far off the truth, in Minnie's opinion. Tansie had always argued that the snuggeries were private rooms for punters who wanted to enjoy a quiet drink in company away from prying eyes. In reality, everyone knew what went on behind the closed doors. As long as none of the girls complained, Tansie had never had any problem with the arrangement.

Minnie peered closely again at the walls, now painted a fetching shade of blue. 'This is much better. You've done a bang-up job.'

Jack gave a half-smile, turning away to hide his delight in the praise. He was a quiet, shy chap. Unassuming. He'd been doing odd jobs for Kippy for about three months, and it was only now that he was starting to emerge from his shell. And he never knew what to do with himself when someone offered him a kind word. Which made a nice change from pretty much everyone else who worked at the Palace, most of whom needed praise like a flower needs water to survive.

Somebody coughed and Minnie turned to see a stoutish man looking at her expectantly.

'Ned. Caretaker from the Fortune,' he said, nodding at her and Jack. 'Although you know that, of course. We agreed I'd pop over for the chairs.'

The Fortune had agreed to buy the old chairs from the snuggeries, so Minnie could replace them with something a little less exuberant.

Between the three of them the chairs were quickly loaded onto the back of Ned's cart. She and Jack had just returned to the snuggeries when from backstage came an almighty roar.

'Where the chuffing hell has he got to now?'

Minnie and Jack shared a glance. 'Tansie,' they said as one.

The shouts grew louder, and Tansie emerged from the door beside the stage. Today he was sporting a teal velvet suit and tartan waistcoat. Much closer to his old swagger. Minnie nodded her approval. You couldn't grieve forever. Then she remembered Bernard's face, ashen and drawn as he had listened to Albert's news, and she pushed the thought aside.

'What is it now?' Minnie asked.

'Monkey. He's gone missing again.'

'You looked up in the rigging?' One of the monkey's favourite pastimes was climbing up way out of everyone's reach and then peeing on any unfortunate soul who happened to be on the stage. Annoying enough at the best of times, but once or twice he'd done it during a performance.

'I've looked everywhere,' Tansie said impatiently. 'He's scarpered.' He turned on Jack with an accusing eye. 'You ain't seen him, have you?'

Jack shook his head vigorously. 'No offence, but he gives me the creeps. Those little hands of his. Like a hairy, shrunken baby. It ain't right.' He gathered together his paintbrushes and pots. 'That needs another hour to dry, I reckon, Minnie. Kippy said you wanted the doors taking off? I could get started on that.'

Tansie frowned. 'Are you sure about this, Min? The snuggeries don't half boost the bar takings.'

She shook her head firmly. 'No more secrets at the Palace, Tanse. Not on my watch. Those doors are coming off and we'll just have to find other ways of getting the punters to drink more.'

Tansie eyed Jack as he left the auditorium. 'I don't trust that fella,' he said. 'You heard what he said about Monkey. What if he left a door or a window open somewhere, accidentally on purpose like, and the little fella got out?'

'Don't you go making accusations. We pay Jack bugger all for everything he does here. And he's bloody useful. Scenery-building, painting, decorating. Wouldn't be surprised if he could show Carlotta a thing or two about plate spinning. If he takes offence and decides to sling his hook, it'll cost us.'

Maybe she could flatter Jack into staying, if the occasion arose. But best not find out.

'You don't trust anyone, Tanse. And the monkey'll turn up.'

She took his arm and led him through the auditorium. 'Nice suit, by the way,' she said, giving his arm a gentle pat.

'You don't think it's a bit – much?' he said, stroking the front of the waistcoat and tugging down the jacket sleeves.

She'd never known him question any of his sartorial choices in the past. Not the velvets, the silks, the tartans and plaids, the colours even a working girl might have drawn the line at. So maybe he wasn't quite back to normal.

She stood back and carefully appraised him from head to toe. 'Not everyone could carry it off, I'll give you that. But, no, you look proper dimber-damber.'

'I just thought, with Bernard's brother 'n' all, maybe it was a bit – lively?'

'I can't imagine Bernard would mind, Tanse. Besides, he ain't here to see it, is he?'

'Any idea when he'll be back?'

She shook her head. 'There'll be a lot to organise. Keep him busy. It's afterwards we'll need to keep a close eye on him. Come on,' she said, punching his arm affectionately, and thankful for the distraction, 'let's find that monkey.'

It was just past midnight. The evening performance had finished and the Palace was almost empty. Tansie and Kippy had offered to lock up and Minnie hadn't put up a fight.

She traipsed wearily up to her rooms at the top of the Palace, just at the rear of the upper circle. Her living room was a tiny space barely big enough to swing a cat. Or a monkey. She lit the lamp, unlaced her boots and pulled the pins from her hair, the dark luxuriance tumbling down over her shoulders. Then she unbuttoned her dress and loosened her stays, before placing both hands on the small of her back and arching backwards to ease the tensions and fatigue of the day.

And that was the moment she realised someone else was in the room.

41

It was the smell that first alerted her: a sickly sweetness that failed to mask something deeply unpleasant. She recognised it immediately, told herself it couldn't be who she thought it was.

But it was him.

She froze, her eyes darting round the room, trying to buy herself enough time to grab hold of something, anything, that could serve as a weapon. Nothing.

She turned slowly, a curse ready on her lips and her hands already clenched into fists. The curse froze in her throat as the sight of him catapulted her back to an autumn evening in a pleasure garden by the Thames.

Seated in her battered old armchair was Freddie Forrester. Better known as Three-Fingers, for obvious reasons, as he was missing the little finger and thumb of his left hand. Instinctively, her hand flew to her right arm, to a scar invisible to everyone but her, a silvery thread left by Freddie's knife over a year ago.

'Well, if it ain't the lovely Miss Ward,' he said. 'What are the chances?'

She stumbled back a step or two, reaching behind to stop herself falling. Her hands found the door and she steadied herself against it. Her heart was thumping so hard in her chest she was sure it must be visible to him. Slowly, her fingers felt across the surface of the door for the handle.

Three-Fingers tilted his head whimsically to one side. 'Now, now,' he said, and placed a gun on the side table, readjusting the weapon so it aligned perfectly with the edge of the table. He leaned forward in his seat, his plump manicured hands resting on his thighs.

Minnie raised her hands in front of her, although what she imagined she could offer in the way of defence was anyone's guess. 'Come a step nearer and I'll scream the whole bleedin' theatre down,' she said, struggling hard to control the tremor in her voice. It was an empty threat and they both knew it. She'd left Kippy and Tansie backstage, and even if they'd moved into the auditorium there was a chance they wouldn't hear her, no matter how loudly she screamed.

Three-Fingers leaned back in the seat. 'Calm down. There's no need for any – histrionics. Maybe you're confusing me with some other chap.'

'I ain't confusing you with anyone. I know what you did to me in the Cremorne. And I know you were involved in poor Rose's murder. Daisy's too.'

He gave an exaggerated shrug. 'Hearsay. Rumour. Besides' – he pulled open the cuffs of his jacket and peered inside before patting down his pockets – 'nothing up my sleeves. Nothing in my pockets. Nothing to be afraid of.' He smiled at her again, a greasy smile. Minnie had forgotten that about him, the pleasure he seemed to take in frightening people. She took a deep breath, told herself to stay calm. Above all, she must try not to show him how terrified she was. That was simply fuel for Three-Fingers.

'How did you get in here?' Minnie said.

'You ain't the only one with impressive lock-picking skills, Miss Ward,' he said, placing a slender pick on the table next to the gun. 'Not that it took much. You should get that lock seen to. Anyone could get in here. Any time they liked.'

'What do you want?'

'Dispensing with the social niceties, are we?' He placed one hand on his chest, as if distressed. 'And there was me thinking we might be chums. Maybe more than chums, now Albert seems to be out of the picture.'

So he'd been watching her. Following her. For how long?

'Given you ain't in any hurry to crack open the fizz and renew our acquaintance, I'll let you know I am here merely to pass on a message. From a mutual friend.'

'Linton,' she said flatly, as if she had always known. Why had she ever imagined she could leave the events of the past year behind her?

'That's *Lord* Linton to you. And, yes, the message is from him. He'd like to see you.'

Her bewilderment must have been evident on her face, and he smiled again. 'Don't worry, Miss Ward. They haven't let him out. Not yet, anyway. He'd like you to visit him in Broadmoor.'

Instinctively, she recoiled, as if he were about to drag her there right away. 'Why on earth would I do that?'

'Well, he's asked you to. And in my experience it's always wise to do what a member of the aristocracy asks of you.'

'I don't give a rat's arse what he wants me to do. I ain't going.'

Three-Fingers winced. 'Language. I feared as much. I told him you might need some further – encouragement. So he asked me to nudge your memory about the ownership of the Variety Palace.'

'Edie—' she started, and then faltered as the impact of his words hit home.

Three-Fingers nodded sagely. 'Exactly. Lady Linton's share passed to her husband on her marriage. Seventy per cent, wasn't it? That kind of money would take some finding if Lord Linton ever needed to – what's the phrase them fancy banking folk like to use? – liquidate his assets.'

Minnie felt the blood thumping in her ears, as the ramifications of what Three-Fingers was telling her sank in. Edie was still in Italy; her latest letter to Minnie had made no mention of ever returning to England, and she certainly no longer seemed to have any interest in the Palace. If Linton sold his share they could be forced to close within days, and no clever bookkeepers or sympathetic dressmakers would save them.

Three-Fingers eyed her carefully, his head tilted to one side. He retrieved the gun and pick from the table, rose from his seat and reached into his pocket. He handed her a business card. 'Lord Linton's barrister. He'll make arrangements for the visit.'

'Why does Linton want to see me?' Minnie asked.

'Oh, you'll have to ask him that. I am merely the messenger.'

He buttoned up his coat and turned to examine his reflection in the looking glass. He seemed pleased with what he saw, giving the image a half-smile and a nod. He turned towards her and she moved swiftly to one side. At the door, his hand on the handle, he turned to her. 'Good night, Miss Ward. Sweet dreams.'

And he was gone.

Panic and relief flooded through Minnie's body. She bent over double, her hand on the back of the chair, as she struggled not to be sick, her blood thundering in her ears, her stomach convulsing. The feeling passed, and she roused herself, turned and ran down the stairs to the auditorium, oblivious of the fact she was in her stockinged feet, her dress unbuttoned, her hair down.

Tansie and Kippy were enjoying a brandy at the auditorium bar before heading home for the night.

'You joining us, Min?' Tansie said. And then he took in her appearance. 'What's up?'

'Three-Fingers,' Minnie gasped, her hands to her chest. 'Where did he go?'

'You what?'

'Three-Fingers. Freddie Forrester. He was here. Just now. In my rooms. He must have gone past you.'

Tansie slowly stood and took Minnie by the arm, leading her to an empty seat. 'No one went past us, Min,' he said, with unaccustomed calm. 'You sure you ain't been asleep? Had a nightmare?'

She nodded at the brandy bottle and glasses. 'How many of them have you had?'

'That's the first,' Kippy said. 'We've barely started.'

'No one went past us, Min,' Tansie said again.

'Then he's still here,' Minnie said. 'And he's got a gun.'

FIVE

They'd stayed up until the small hours, searching the Palace for Three-Fingers but there'd been no sign of him. However he'd managed it, he'd slipped out unnoticed. In the cold light of day, Minnie had to admit his disappearance wasn't quite so miraculous as it had seemed the night before. The chandeliers had been extinguished, and all but one or two of the wall lamps. Tansie and Kippy had been seated in a small circle of light from a handful of candles, but the rest of the auditorium had been plunged into darkness. Providing he'd stayed quiet and kept to the edges of the room, it wouldn't have been difficult for Three-Fingers to slip past unnoticed, then out the back through the stage door.

Tansie had taken one look at Minnie when he'd arrived at the Palace that morning and suggested a visit to Brown's Bakery. Minnie lingered for a moment outside the tea room, eyeing the fruitcake, scones and iced buns arrayed in the window. She thought back to the times she and Albert had used the bakery as a makeshift office, discussing their investigation into Rose's death. She hadn't been back to Brown's in months and wondered if their takings were down as a result.

'So what you gonna do?' Tansie asked, once they were seated and had given their order to the waitress, a blonde slip of a thing Minnie didn't recognise.

'I ain't got much choice, have I? If I don't go, he's gonna pull the plug on the Palace.'

Tansie thought for a moment. 'I could go in your place. It's my business we're talking about, after all.'

'It ain't you he wants to see.'

Tansie frowned, then nodded encouragingly as the waitress appeared with their order. The girl looked as if it might be her first day, and she clearly hadn't carried a laden tray before. Minnie feared for the crockery. Tansie helped the girl unload the tea things and two iced buns, without too much of the tea landing on the tablecloth.

'I don't like it, Min,' he said, after the girl had gone. 'He's a queer cove, and I ain't happy with the idea of you spending any time with him. Never mind hanging out with the loons and the donkey-lovers in Broadmoor.'

'Well, I won't be left alone with him, will I?' She paused, a horrible thought striking her. 'Will I? They wouldn't, would they? Not with what he's been found guilty of.'

'Won't be left alone with whom?' It was Albert. He must have seen them through the window and entered the tea room. Neither she nor Tansie had heard him approaching. Bloody detectives and their stealth. And what was he doing here anyway?

'Nothing. No one,' Minnie said, throwing Tansie a pointed look which he immediately ignored.

'Teddy Linton. He wants to see Min. In Broadmoor.'

'What? You aren't seriously thinking of going, are you?' Albert asked, pulling up a chair. The waitress reappeared, blushing violently at the sight of Albert's muscular frame, coupled with an accent you could cut glass with.

'Nothing for me, thank you,' Albert said.

The waitress grew wide-eyed with alarm. 'You've gotta have something,' she hissed. 'Them's the rules.' She threw a nervous glance over her shoulder at the counter, where a stern-looking

47

woman with an enormous bosom propped up on folded arms was eyeing their table.

'Well, I could have a bite of that iced bun,' Albert said, gesturing towards Minnie's plate.

'You bloody won't,' Minnie said, placing a protective arm around the cake. 'Order your own, you stingy bugger.'

'Tea, then,' Albert said dismissively. The girl skittered away and Albert turned again to Minnie. 'Please tell me you're not thinking of going.'

Minnie bridled. 'It ain't for a social visit, Albert. We won't be sharing cucumber sandwiches on the lawn and enjoying a nice game of croquet.'

'Although they do play croquet there,' Tansie interjected. 'Cricket as well, so I've heard. Choral societies. Amateur dramatics. More like a bleedin' holiday than a punishment, if you ask me.'

Albert swept Tansie's interruption aside. 'Why does he wish to see you?'

'He's throwing his weight around.' She filled him in on Teddy's threat to sell his share of the Palace.

'Can he even do that?' Albert asked. 'If he's imprisoned, does he have control over his finances?'

'Well, if he don't, he can find someone who'll control them for him, surely?' Tansie said. 'Either way, if he sells that seventy per cent, sure as eggs is eggs he's gonna sell it to someone who'll shut us down. He hates us, Albert.'

'He probably ain't that fussed about you, to be fair,' Minnie said to Tansie, 'but you're right. Albert and I ain't his favourite people.'

Tansie shrugged. 'Whatever his feelings about me, I don't like the idea of Teddy having anything to do with the Palace, but I ain't got any other option at the moment.'

Albert turned to Minnie. 'You can't go,' he said. 'I shan't let you.'

48

'I beg your pardon? You shan't *let* me? Last time I checked it weren't none of your business how I spend my time.'

'For God's sake, Minnie. Is there any chance you can just abandon your independence for five minutes? The man is a murderer, remember? A murderer with a penchant for attractive young women.'

'I do know that, Albert,' Minnie replied. 'It ain't something that's likely to slip my mind. But what can he do to me in Broadmoor? There'll be guards. And if I don't go—' She broke off, gazed round the tea room, a feeling of helplessness overwhelming her. She thought back to the last time she'd been there. Out on the Strand, there'd been a fella with a ferret on a length of string, charging a farthing for a chance to hold the creature. A pretty young girl had wanted to pet it and then screamed when she got close. Despite all the horror they'd been investigating, life had somehow seemed simpler then. She and Albert had one job to do: find Rose's killer. All the terrible things that followed hadn't happened yet.

'Minnie,' Albert said, breathing slowly as if to calm himself down and clearly misreading her silence as defiance. 'Please do not go to see that man. He's insane. He's dangerous. He's either prepared to sell his share in the Palace, or he's not. Your visiting him will have no bearing on that decision. He's playing with you, for whatever reason I can't fathom. But if you agree to see him, you're playing straight into his hands. Don't give him the satisfaction.'

Minnie looked over at Tansie, who nodded his agreement. 'He's right, Min. This'll all be some sort of cockeyed game on Teddy's part. I'll see if I can pull in a few favours. Find the money somewhere else.' His words were optimistic but his face told a different story. Tansie knew a few magicians, but not anyone who could pull that kind of money out of a hat.

Minnie sighed. They were right, of course. And there was

49

nothing about her that wanted to see Teddy again as long as she lived. But still. 'So why are you here?' she said to Albert, abruptly changing the subject. 'And don't tell me you just happened to be in the neighbourhood.'

'I wanted a word with Bernard. Is he back at the Palace?'

'He is,' Tansie said. 'Neither use nor ornament, mind. He'd be better off staying at home until after the funeral.'

'Brimming with the milk of human kindness, ain't you, Tanse?' Minnie said. 'It's just flowing through every little vein.'

He grunted, then insisted on paying for their tea, which made Minnie wonder how bad she looked after the previous night's events. She took a quick look at her reflection in a shop window on the way back to the Palace. Not good. She could have ordered anything off the menu and Tansie would have stumped up for it.

Back at the Palace, they found Bernard in the tiny cupboard that passed for Wardrobe. He was making a right dog's dinner of altering his latest costume, and the dark rings under his eyes testified to the fact he hadn't slept much since hearing of Peter's death. There was no way he'd be going back on stage for the foreseeable. When he spotted Albert, he gave a hopeful smile that almost broke Minnie's heart.

'Any news, dear boy?' he said.

'One thing. Your brother had a visitor at the Fortune the day before they went dark. A young woman. The stage manager didn't catch her name and his description wasn't a great deal of help. Nondescript kind of face. Average height. Neither fat nor thin, he said. John and I aren't having any luck finding her. I just wondered if you knew anything.'

'A woman?' Bernard said. 'And you think she might have some part to play in – in what happened?'

Albert shrugged. 'Very difficult to say. It might just be a coincidence. Did he have any lady friends?'

'Friends, yes. But no romance, if that's what you're thinking. My brother was of a more – Uranian persuasion.'

Albert looked confused.

'He liked boys,' Tansie said.

'He liked *men*,' Bernard said, throwing Tansie a disparaging glance. 'This woman, it might be someone he worked with. But then the stage manager would most likely have recognised her. Besides, in the last few years, he's worked alone.'

'But he did have a partner at some point, didn't he?' Albert said. 'The Jollity Brothers, that was his act, wasn't it? Any idea where we might find the other man?'

Bernard flushed and directed his attention back to his costume.

'What ain't you telling us, Bernard?' Minnie asked.

Bernard eyed her carefully, then seemed to make up his mind.

'*I* am the other man you're looking for. Peter and I were the Jollity Brothers.'

'So? That ain't nothing to be ashamed of, is it?' Minnie asked.

Bernard glanced from side to side, as if anxious that he might be overheard, then leaned forward, dropping his voice to a conspiratorial whisper. 'He was a seasonal performer, dear heart. I am a *professionally* trained *Shakespearean* actor. My job is to convey the tragedy, the poetry, the poignancy of the Bard's work. My job is not to humiliate myself for the entertainment of unformed minds.'

'What? Like dressing up as a rhinoceros?' Tansie murmured, nodding at the costume Bernard was holding.

Minnie shot him a look. 'So why did you do it?' she asked Bernard. 'If it was so humiliating?'

'In case you haven't noticed, dearest one, most people are cultural philistines. Demand for Shakespeare in his truest form is not always the highest. I had bills to pay.'

'Well, I shall keep looking,' Albert said, buttoning his coat. 'Anything you can think of, no matter how small, do let me know.'

'I will, dear boy,' Bernard said, and turned back to his sewing. Minnie, Tansie and Albert slowly made their way to the office.

'Any news on the monkey?' Albert asked.

'How'd you know about that?' Minnie said.

'I have my sources.'

'We've heard nothing,' Tansie said mournfully. 'I've put flyers up everywhere, asked around. Not a peep.'

'Does he have any favourite haunts?' Albert asked. Minnie eyed him carefully, but he appeared to be taking the matter seriously.

'Nowhere he went on his own,' Tansie said.

'Wasn't there something about you taking him to the zoo?' Albert asked.

'I did take him a few weeks ago. Regent's Park. Thought we might find him a little lady companion.'

'And?'

'I left him there for an hour. When I came back the attendant just handed him to me without a word. White as a sheet the fella was. Wouldn't tell me what went on, but the lady primates were giving Monkey a very wide berth. I reckon I'd have heard by now if that's where he'd turned up.'

He looked so despondent and lost that Minnie had a sudden rush of blood to the head. 'C'mon,' she said, grabbing her coat from behind the door. 'Let's nip back to Brown's for a pork pie and we'll try wafting it up and down the Strand. He can't be far.'

Tansie gave her a grateful smile and then looked behind her. Standing in the doorway was Dorothy Lawrence, the disapproving bookkeeper with the lovely hair and, Minnie noticed this time, equally lovely skin.

'Miss Ward?' she said, holding out a bundle of tatty papers tied together with some string. 'I'm returning what you optimistically term "the books". Oh, and somebody handed me this on my way in. It's addressed to Mr Tansford, whichever one of you gentlemen that is.'

Tansie put out his hand for the envelope. Dorothy handed it to him, then took two steps back, glancing round the office with a look of mild horror on her face. 'Is this some sort of – props department?' she asked.

'It's my office,' Minnie said.

'Ah,' Dorothy said, nodding her head slowly. 'That explains a great deal.'

A retort flew to Minnie's lips but before she had time to speak, Tansie let out an agonising cry. She turned to him, and he thrust a single sheet of paper at her.

'Fifty spangles or the monkey cops it,' the note read. Glued to the bottom of the paper was a tuft of black-and-white fur and a single claw.

SIX

'Tell me again what happened,' Tom Neville said, leaning forward in his seat at the Dog and Duck and supping the last of his pint, anticipation lighting up his boyish features. 'The bit about the bookkeeper and Tansie.'

Albert could understand Tom's enjoyment. It had been pretty spectacular, even by Palace standards, where histrionics were the order of the day. The ransom note had been received, Tansie was shouting blue murder, Minnie was pouring a stiff one and Albert was trying to convince Tansie the fur and claw might not necessarily belong to Monkey, when the clear voice of Dorothy Lawrence cut through the furore.

'Why is Mr Tansford so distressed?' she asked. 'And what on earth is a spangle?'

'A spangle's a sovereign,' Minnie said. 'Tansie's monkey's been kidnapped.'

'Is that some sort of theatrical euphemism?'

'No. He has a monkey. A real monkey. His pet. And it's been kidnapped. They're asking fifty sovs as a ransom.'

Dorothy narrowed her eyes and gave Tansie a hard stare. 'Is it a special monkey? Surely he can just get another one?'

Tansie had lifted his head with such ominous slowness it warned everyone in the room to duck, except for Dorothy Lawrence, who didn't know Tansie. Or his fondness for the monkey.

'Get another one?' Tansie said, stretching each word to its limits in a performance worthy of Bernard. 'Get. Another. One?'

At which point he had unleashed a string of insults and threats at Dorothy, most of which were anatomically impossible. Imaginative, but impossible. She, in her turn, had responded with remarkable aplomb and lobbed a few choice words of her own. And then she had turned on her heel and left.

'So now Minnie thinks she'll be looking for a new bookkeeper,' Albert said, nodding at the note from Minnie that had arrived that morning.

'You must know someone, surely. Fancy fella like you always has staff,' Tom said, smiling broadly. Albert felt the running joke about his assumed wealth, based largely on his public-school accent, wore a little thin at times.

'You don't need someone to do your accounts if you're not making any money. Which was the case until recently.'

'The only fellas I know who handle money are all in clink,' Tom said. 'But I'll ask around.'

Tom had hinted before about occasional brushes with the law, how he had lived on the fringes of a criminal life until he got the job as Lionel Winter's horse boy, which had, in turn, led to him working with Albert. Occasionally, it crossed Albert's mind to question Tom about his felonious past, but he decided it was probably best he didn't know the details. The lad's contacts had proved useful in more than one case. Albert was hopeful the same would prove true with the kidnapped monkey. He nodded at Tom's empty glass.

'Not for me,' Tom said, pushing back his chair and reaching for his coat. 'People to see. Places to go. Monkeys to find.'

'Any leads?'

Tom shook his head, then screwed up his face in a way Albert was familiar with. 'What haven't you told me?' Albert asked.

'Tansie's acting mighty cagey about the whole thing, if you ask me,' Tom said, buttoning up his coat. 'It sounds crazy, given how much he loves that bloody monkey, but I reckon he knows something about the kidnappers and he ain't letting on. Would it be bang out of order to tail him?'

'Slightly unusual practice to follow the client rather than the suspect, but I can't see any ethical problem with it. He's smart, though. And he knows you. You might want to adopt some sort of disguise.'

A broad grin spread across Tom's face. 'I've been waiting for just the opportunity to wear that fake moustache,' he said, stroking his upper lip, where any facial hair resolutely refused to grow. 'Any news on the dead judge?'

'I went to his house the other day. Looked at the scene of his death. Couldn't spot anything untoward, so it might just have been a tragic accident. I'm interviewing the servants today,' Albert said. 'See if they can provide any further leads.'

'I'll catch you later, then. I'm just off to buy a wig.'

It was a pleasant stroll from Albert's local to the Eddings house in Upper Grosvenor Street, a stone's throw from Hyde Park. The house was impressive. Six-foot-high black railings, behind which lay a broad driveway, and then a double-fronted detached house. Pillars, Albert thought. Pillars always meant money. The front door – glossy black paint and a door knocker you could see your reflection in – was opened eventually by an elderly maid who looked as if she should have retired several decades earlier. She took Albert's hat and coat and led him through to the rear of the house, where Mrs Eddings was sitting in state on a sofa piled high with cushions, a delicate bone china tea service on a table in front of her. Albert accepted the tea, which came out strong and dark. She made him no offer of milk.

'This interviewing of my staff, Mr Easterbrook,' Mrs Eddings said, 'is it entirely necessary? They can't tell you anything I haven't already.'

'My experience is that household staff see and hear a great deal more than we imagine. I've solved several cases with the help of a housemaid's observation. And we do want to get to the bottom of your husband's death, don't we?'

She bridled. 'Of course we do. And I have nothing to hide. Do you wish to have me present during these interviews?'

'No. Best I speak to them alone.'

'Well, then, if you have no objection, I have some calls to make. Mrs Hargreaves will see you out when you've finished.'

'Before you go, Mrs Eddings, I wonder if I might ask you about your husband's financial affairs.'

She looked appalled at the very idea. 'What are you suggesting, Mr Easterbrook?'

'You believe your husband's death was suspicious. Which suggests you think he was murdered. By whom, we don't know. A stranger? An acquaintance? You've said he had no enemies through his work. Might he have made enemies some other way? Money and greed are great motivators for evil.'

'My husband had no *business* dealings,' she said, her lip curling slightly at the word 'business', as if she could somehow be contaminated by the mere mention of such a thing. 'He was a judge, Mr Easterbrook.'

'Any investments?'

She frowned. 'The usual. Stocks. Shares. You'd need to talk to our accountant for the full details.'

'And you have no objection to my doing so?'

Mrs Eddings hesitated for a moment. 'None,' she said eventually. 'Although I can't imagine it will prove useful.'

She crossed to a walnut bureau; probably Italian, Albert thought, and, like everything else in the room, very expensive. All a bit too heavy for his taste. Mrs Eddings removed a business card from the bureau and handed it to Albert. 'Mr Barker was my husband's accountant. I shall let him know you are to be provided with full access to all my husband's financial dealings. Now, if you don't mind, I shall be late for my appointments. Mrs Hargreaves can see to your needs.'

Two hours later, Albert was nearly done. His policy was always to interview staff in the order of their perceived merit within the household: so, he started with the butler if there was one, then the housekeeper and so on. No butler at the Eddings house, which had surprised him, given the ostentatious display of wealth. Starting with Mrs Hargreaves, the staff had all essentially told the same story, one that concurred with Mrs Eddings's account in pretty much every detail. Judge Eddings had been playing hide-and-seek with his grandson and he'd gone missing. His body was discovered several hours later in the trunk in the attic. He was a lovely man, a kind employer, no enemies. Other than all the men and women he'd sentenced to prison or worse, Albert thought, but kept that to himself.

The final interviewee was Lily, the scullery maid, a surly-looking girl who reminded Albert of a white mouse he'd kept once as a child. Her skin and hair were so pale she looked as if all the colour had been bleached out of her, and Albert wondered when she'd last seen daylight. He learned she'd been working for the Eddingses for four months, her first job after moving to London from Norfolk.

'Do you miss it?' Albert asked. 'Norfolk?'

Lily eyed him suspiciously, as if he were trying to catch her out. 'What's it to you?' she asked.

'It must be difficult, that's all. Moving to a big city like this. A long way from home.'

She looked angry, defensive. Albert recognised the look. A way of not letting your real feelings show.

'It's all right, I suppose,' she said. A flush crept up her neck to her cheeks, and she turned her head away from him.

'It's hard work, though. Thankless work, I imagine.'

Lily shot him another suspicious glance, and then seemed to realise he was not playing with her. 'It's a job. There's nothing at home. I didn't have a choice.'

Albert nodded, then asked her the same things he had asked everyone else. Her responses were largely the same and he moved swiftly through his list of questions.

'The other staff have mentioned there was some decorating going on in the house the day Judge Eddings died. Can you tell me anything about that?'

Lily shrugged. 'There was a fella here, painting the dining room. Couldn't see nothing wrong with it myself, but apparently it's a fancy of Mrs Eddings to change the colours in the rooms every few months or so.'

'Did you speak to the decorator? Catch his name?'

She shook her head. 'Don't know nothing about him. Didn't even see him. Only know he was here that day 'cos Nancy, the parlour maid, she was moaning she couldn't get into the dining room to clean the grate.'

Albert thanked her for her time, which drew another suspicious glance from her, and she was just rising to leave when she paused. 'You spoken to the sweep?' she asked.

'The sweep?'

'Chimney sweep. He was here that day.'

'None of the other staff mentioned a chimney sweep.'

Lily shrugged. 'They wouldn't, would they? Probably didn't even notice he was here. I reckon I could grow a second head, and they'd only notice if it interfered with my work.'

'This chimney sweep, do you know his name?'

'Jimmy? Bob? William? I don't have much time for chit-chat and finding out fellas' names.'

'I don't suppose you know where he lives? Or other houses he works in?'

'I think he does most of this road, but he won't be back again for another few months. No idea where he lives.'

'Description?'

'Shortish fella, but quite strong-looking. Fair hair. Clean-shaven.'

'Did you speak to him?'

She gave a bitter laugh. 'No speaking allowed. That's one of Mrs Eddings's rules. Besides, there's not much time for chatting with all they've got me doing. So, no, I didn't speak to him.'

Albert thanked her again, and she dropped him a brief curtsy before leaving. She hadn't curtsied on entering the room, so Albert figured he might have made some headway with her.

A chimney sweep. A painter. Men who might go unnoticed, and the chimney sweep in particular would have access to pretty much every room in the house.

And there was something else niggling at the edge of his thoughts, an itch he couldn't scratch. A memory slowly stirring into life.

SEVEN

The journey from Waterloo had been a pleasant one, through a number of pretty suburbs where the houses had generous back gardens and the air wasn't cloaked with smog. Or the journey would have been pleasant had Minnie not been half sick with worry about what was to come. She had lied to Tansie and Albert about visiting Teddy Linton. She knew one or both of them would have put their foot down, tried to stop her. Failing that, they'd have insisted on joining her, for part of the way at least. And she needed to do this on her own.

'Wokingham,' the train guard called out. 'Wokingham Station.'

Minnie repositioned her bonnet, picked up her bag and left the train. Standing outside the quiet railway station was the Broadmoor omnibus. She looked around her. Half a dozen other people were making their way towards the 'bus, one or two of whom looked as tentative as she felt, while others were clearly seasoned visitors. Minnie climbed aboard and took a seat by the window, pointedly turning away from everyone else to avoid conversation. No such luck. Five minutes into the journey, an elderly couple seated across the aisle unwrapped sandwiches and half of a very fine-looking pie. Leek and potato by the smell of it. They offered some to Minnie, but she politely declined.

'Who you seeing, then?' the woman of the couple asked her, a dough-faced woman with a gentle smile who only unclasped her husband's hand long enough to take a bite of her food. 'We're off to visit our son.'

Minnie thought for a moment. How to define her relationship with Teddy? I'm visiting the murderer of my dearest friend? The man who almost ruined my life? The couple had a timid, giving look about them. Easily shocked, she imagined. 'A relative,' she murmured. 'An uncle.'

After a journey of some miles, down winding lanes and through the village of Crowthorne, the 'bus began to climb, leaving the carefully tended fields behind. They entered thick woodland, finally stopping high up on a ridge with magnificent views of the countryside below. So this was where Linton spent his days. It didn't look like much of a punishment to Minnie.

As they alighted from the omnibus they were greeted by an officious-looking chap in a suit that was too big at the collar and too short in the sleeves. Minnie gave her name and the man made heavy weather of consulting a sheet of paper, running one skinny finger down the list of names. 'Ah, yes,' he said eventually. 'Lord Linton.' He rolled the name around his tongue, stressing the title, as if it would confer some particular status on him. 'He don't get many visitors. Apart from that Mr Gillespie. You know him? Gillespie?'

Minnie shook her head. She remembered Albert mentioning him, but she'd never met the man.

'So you a friend? Relative?'

Christ, why did everyone need to interrogate her about her relationship with Teddy? 'Acquaintance,' she murmured.

'Well, he's expecting you. Block Two. The privilege block. What with him being a lord and all. You'll find him on the terrace.' He gestured for her to follow an attendant, a huge wall of a man who Tansie would have hired as a chucker-out if he'd been there. Ahead of them lay a tall archway topped by a large clock, and a pair of enormous green wooden doors, then a further set of gates.

Something about him told Minnie the attendant didn't want to engage in conversation, so she didn't bother. What would she have said anyway? He slowed his pace for her to keep up, but still she found herself trotting after him, like a stray dog after someone with half a pound of scrag.

They entered Block Two and went up to the first-floor terrace. Teddy was waiting for her, his hands resting on a railing, his body angled towards the landscape. Everything about him told her he was anticipating her arrival, had chosen his pose of indifference with care. Her footsteps tapped across the floor, but he did not turn even when she stopped a few feet away from him. Close enough to catch the aroma of his expensive cologne.

'You came,' he said, without turning his head away from the magnificent views of the Blackwater Valley. 'I thought perhaps you wouldn't.'

His voice was clear, bold. Entitled. He was wearing a dark-navy suit so exquisitely cut she suspected it would move Albert to tears. Judging by the look of the other inmates she'd passed on the way in, Teddy wasn't getting his clothes from the Broadmoor seamstresses.

'You didn't give me much choice,' Minnie said, speaking slowly to control the tremor in her voice.

'We always have a choice,' he said, finally turning to her, and she was reminded of the exaggerated blinking that marked him. Funny how she'd forgotten about that, when she'd remembered so much else.

He looked at her appraisingly and then frowned. 'Dear me. You're not looking your best, Minerva. A little rouge would help, don't you think? Some colour to the lips? Or are they no longer selling cosmetics on the Strand?'

'I ain't here for beauty tips. You asked to see me. Tell me what you've got to say and then I'll be on my way.'

He made an exaggerated moue of disappointment. 'But I've got so much planned. A gentle stroll in the grounds. Some refreshment. A little visit to my cell – apologies, we're encouraged to call them *bedrooms*, not cells.'

He was going to make her wait, that much was certain. 'My train's at three,' she said.

'Best we embark on our little tour, then.' He offered her his arm, and she instinctively flinched away from him. 'Too soon?' he said. 'Maybe on your next visit.'

She did not rise to the bait. Teddy glanced over her shoulder at the burly attendant who had accompanied her. 'Ralph here will have to escort us, I'm afraid. But he can be very discreet, can't you, Ralphie?'

The attendant said nothing, merely moved his hand to some sort of truncheon hanging from his belt, alongside a set of handcuffs.

Teddy looked up at the sky, then ran his eye over Minnie, wincing a little at the sight of her plain shawl and workaday bonnet. 'I rather fancied a stroll in the grounds,' he said. 'Will you be warm enough?'

Minnie nodded, and the unlikely trio headed outside.

'Do you know I'm referred to here as a "pleasure man"?' Teddy said as they started to walk away from the main building. 'I was found not guilty by reason of insanity, and I am detained at Her Majesty's pleasure. Don't you feel it's rather an appropriate title? Perhaps that's what I should have called the members of the Godwin. Pleasure men. Any pleasure in your life these days, Minerva? How is the lovely Albert?'

She dug her nails into her palms. His words, his lingering looks, his enquiries into the private areas of her life felt as if he was placing his hands on her. Invading her. She breathed slowly, told herself she would be leaving here soon. It had been a mistake to come. What on earth had she thought she'd achieve? He was just playing with her, and his decision to sell or keep the Palace would happen regardless of what she said to him today.

Teddy carried on, seemingly unfazed by her lack of response. 'They tell me I am morally insane. My mind is unable to think and behave as it should. But who decides what "should" looks like? My mind works perfectly well. It just doesn't want exactly the same things other men want. Or not what men admit to wanting, at least.'

He nodded towards an elderly man who was walking quietly on his own. 'One of our more famous inmates. Richard Dadd. Heard of him?'

Minnie shook her head.

'Killed his father. People say he's a great artist but I've seen some of his stuff. Dadd's daubs, I call 'em. Fairies and suchlike. Can you believe it? Total and utter loon. What's wrong with a decent painting of a horse, for God's sake? Or a nice bowl of fruit?'

They strolled on further, and Teddy gestured towards a small group of men huddled under a copse of trees. The other patients seemed to be avoiding them. 'Those with an unhealthy interest in our four-legged friends,' whispered Teddy, leaning in close to share the information, as if Minnie had asked a question about them.

He stopped suddenly and turned towards her, a smile illuminating his face. 'Would you like to know how I spend my days, Minerva? Or would you rather hear about the food? Or our cells? Or—'

'I'd like to know why I'm here,' she interrupted. 'What exactly it is you want.'

'Is it not enough that I might have just wanted to see you? You are rather – delicious.'

She flinched, couldn't help herself. He smiled at her discomfort.

'Oh, very well. Although I am hopeful this little outing will have piqued your curiosity enough to trigger a second visit. I've got so much more to show you. For today, though, I have a simple request. Orange, the chief here. Decent enough chap, I suppose.

My release rests with him. He determines if I'm unlikely to reoffend, and then petitions the Home Office. He's a great believer in redemption. Forgiveness. Repentance.'

'And are you? Repentant?'

He said nothing for a moment, just eyed her closely, a gentle smile playing across his lips. 'They never ask us in here, you know. About the acts that brought us here.'

'Never?'

'When you're first admitted, they ask you a few questions but that's all. After the first day or so, it's never mentioned again.'

'Why not?'

He shrugged. 'I imagine it's born of sensitivity. This is a hospital, after all. Do you dream of her?' he asked suddenly, tilting his head inquisitively to one side.

'Who?'

'Rose.'

She raised her eyes skywards, to hold back the tears.

'Me too,' he said, his voice low and gentle as a caress. 'And not just dreams. She comes to me. Every day.' He must have registered her disbelief. 'I know, remarkable, is it not? Every day at roughly the same time, she appears in my cell. We talk. Well, I talk, she listens. An exceptional woman. I rather wish I'd kept her.'

A tear escaped from between Minnie's lashes, and she brushed it away angrily.

'You were saying. About Orange and petitioning the Home Office.'

'Ah, yes. Forgiveness goes a long way with him. If you could be persuaded to tell him – or write to him; I could help you write it – that you have witnessed the change in me. That you feel I'm not the man I was, some such nonsense. It would help. To get me out of here.'

Minnie said nothing, struggling to comprehend what he was asking of her.

'And the girl's mother. Never caught her name.'

'Ida,' she said, her voice flat and dull. She felt as if she were tainting Ida just by mentioning her name in Teddy's company.

'Yes. Ida. No father? No, thought not. Well, if Ida could be persuaded to say a kind word or two. All grist to the mill.'

'And if I won't?'

He pulled an exaggerated grimace of disappointment again. 'How much was Edie's investment in the Palace? Seventy per cent? All of which passed to me on our marriage. I'm not sure whether mathematics is one of your many talents, but you're clever enough to work it out, surely?' He turned and walked away from her, as if confident in the knowledge she would follow him. She looked at Ralph, the attendant, but his face was a blank. Cursing herself, she hurried after Teddy.

They called it the privilege block, but Minnie couldn't see any difference between Block Two and the others. Dark-red brick, bars at every window, surrounded by a huge wall topped with iron spikes and broken glass. It didn't scream privilege.

Ralph led the way, unlocking a door which opened onto a long corridor. A guard was sitting at a table, a single candle lit beside him.

'This,' said Teddy with an exaggerated show of politeness, 'is Brian. And this is the candle from which we are allowed to light our cigarettes or pipes. No naked flames left unsupervised, eh, Brian?' He gave the guard a wink, but Brian ignored him.

Teddy showed her his cell. Or, rather, his cells. Three adjoining rooms: a bedroom, some sort of day room and then a smaller cell which housed his books on shelves which extended from floor to ceiling and covered three of the four walls. Teddy followed her gaze. 'I had to have the shelves built,' he explained.

The rooms were comfortable, with touches of luxury, but it was impossible to forget you were in a gaol. The doors were unlocked during the day but bolted from the outside at night, by

67

Brian or one of his co-workers. The door housed a long, narrow slot which the guards and doctors could look through at any time and there were iron bars at all the windows. And yet, look beyond the bars and there were lovely views from Teddy's rooms: a long valley, with cows clustering beneath a copse of oak trees. And, closer to home, the tennis courts and cricket pitch.

'You seem to be allowed anything you want,' Minnie said, her eyes darting from the books to photographs, a paintbox and sketchbooks, a flute and a violin, and several nice-looking bottles of claret.

'Anything money can buy,' he said, his eyes never leaving her face. 'Provided it doesn't impinge on my safety or the running of the asylum. I even have staff. I don't believe you've met Andrew?'

She looked at him, incredulous, as he gestured over her shoulder for someone to come forward. The man was young – probably in his early twenties, like Minnie – with large, doe-like eyes and a generous mouth. He smiled tentatively at Minnie. 'Andrew Bryant,' he said, his voice low and melodious. 'Lord Linton pays me to work for him, run errands, deliver his post to the main lodge, minor things really. I've told him time and time again, I'd do it for free. He's such a remarkable man, don't you think?'

'No,' Minnie said baldly. 'I don't find him remarkable at all.'

Andrew looked puzzled. 'You clearly don't know him very well. Give it time and you'll see just what a unique individual he is. I feel blessed to call him my friend.'

'Well,' Teddy said, visibly wincing, 'I'm not sure I'd go quite that far, Andrew. Now, run along until suppertime.'

Andrew bowed and almost backed out of the room.

Teddy gazed after him, the tiniest frown creasing his brow. 'Murdered his parents when he was eighteen. Butchered them in their bed.'

Then, after a brief shake of the head, he told her about the food, the activities they were allowed, the structure of the day.

He showed her the clay he used for model-making, the programme for the evening of dramatic performances he had lately been involved in. The words poured out of him as if this were his last and only chance to speak. Finally, it was time to leave.

'Will you come again?' he asked. And there was a weakness, a desperation in his voice that took Minnie by surprise. 'Time passes slowly here, Minnie. I have few visitors, little correspondence.'

'Edie?'

He shrugged. 'She writes. Her letters provide little consolation. No mention of when she might return. I rather fear my darling wife has abandoned me.'

'You can hardly blame her.'

'And yet I do.' He broke off abruptly, turning his head away. If it were anyone else, Minnie would have felt moved by their unhappiness. But this was Teddy.

He turned back to her, forcing a smile. 'Your presence today has been – a delight.'

She said nothing, went to turn away. Teddy grabbed her hand and, quick as a flash, Ralph tapped him on the wrist with the truncheon and was reaching for the handcuffs with his other hand.

'No touching, Minnie,' Teddy said, rubbing his wrist. 'Can you imagine? Not the slightest human touch. Day after day. A man could die of such cruelty.' He looked at her, all artifice stripped from his face.

Rot in hell, she thought. But the words stopped in her throat. She took her skirts in her hand, turned and swept off down the long corridor. Behind her she heard Teddy call her name. Once. Twice. But she kept on walking, out of the building and onto the waiting omnibus to take her back to the station.

EIGHT

Albert was enjoying a last cup of tea and a read of the newspaper before heading up to bed, when a loud knock on the door pierced the quiet. Mrs Byrne had already retired for the night, so he went to the door.

Minnie.

She was out of breath, and the street lamps caught a sheen of sweat along her hairline. Instantly, as if assailed by the recollection of a bad dream, a thread of panic ran through his veins.

'What is it?' he asked. 'What's happened?'

She held up a hand to stop him before he could say anything more. 'Nothing's happened. At least, nothing terrible. I just needed to talk to you. I thought it could wait until morning, but it can't.'

'So come in,' he said, standing back from the door. 'It's freezing out there.'

She shook her head. 'No, I need to say it all now. And then you can decide what you wanna do.'

Albert nodded, bewildered.

'I went to Broadmoor today,' Minnie said, 'and, yes, I know. I shouldn't have gone. You were right. But I did go. Seeing Linton, it all came back to me. Everything I'd pushed away so I could tell myself I was coping when I weren't. Rose. Cora. Daisy. And him. Teddy. That man scares the hell out of me, Albert, I've gotta be honest.'

'He scares me too.'

'He's in there. Banged up. But he ain't exactly suffering. He's got backhanders going left, right and centre. Stays in what they call the privilege block. Little chums inside and outside Broadmoor. Luxury items that are making his life easy. Did you know he's learning to play the violin? That they put on little plays and choral evenings that the locals get invited to?'

Albert shook his head.

'No, well, why would you know that? Sorry, I'm rambling, ain't I?'

'A little. It might help if you came inside?' he suggested again.

She shook her head. 'No, let me finish. After I'd left him, as I was coming back home on the train, it struck me that one day, with all his money and his fancy connections, Linton's gonna get out of that place. I'll be walking down the street one day, and he'll be there, right in front of me, with his weird blinking and his way of making you feel like he's got his hands on you even when he ain't. He'll appear, just like Three-Fingers did the other night.' She paused, shuddered, and pulled her shawl tighter round her body. Albert waited for her to continue.

'And that thought, knowing he was gonna get out one day – it felt like' – she took a deep breath – 'it was like being at home, thinking you're all snug and safe and, just like that, the walls collapse and fall away. And I'm standing there. Exposed. Like anyone could just walk into my house and get me. Am I making any sense?'

'You are. Keep going.'

'I realised that all the things I'd been doing to make myself feel safe, moving into the Palace, staying there as much as I could, hiding myself away – none of it was really gonna help. And then I thought of you, and how I've hidden myself away from you more than anyone else, and I felt so—' she faltered, and Albert instinctively reached towards her, but she took a step backwards and swiftly shook her head as if to ward off whatever he was about to say. Then she raised her eyes to his, and he swore for a moment his heart stopped beating. 'I felt so *ashamed*, Albert. All you've ever done is look after me, and I've treated you like you were part of the problem. You didn't even tell me about your poor ma. Hiding away ain't gonna do any good, is it? I've been trying it for nine months, and all it's done is make me bloody miserable. There's bad stuff out there, and the only way I think I can deal with it is by fighting it. So,' and she inhaled deeply again, 'if the offer still stands, I'd like us to work together.' She fumbled in her bag and withdrew a small piece of dog-eared card which she handed to Albert. He recognised the business card he'd given her all those months ago.

'Glad to see you've been taking good care of it,' he said after a few moments, gesturing to the worn edges and the trace of what looked like face powder on the back.

The merest flicker of a smile crossed her face. 'I kept it, didn't I? What more do you want? And we'd have to change it, like I said. "Easterbrook and Ward" just sounds better, don't it? And I'll still have the Palace, so it can't be full-time, but I thought maybe – maybe I could start with Bernard's brother? Bernard's in a right state, although he's doing his best to hide it. I could ask a few questions, have a bit of a nose around. But if you don't want to – I'll understand. Truly, I will—' Her voice broke.

Albert took a step forward, pulled her towards him, led her into the morning room and guided her to the couch. He sat beside her while she sobbed, so hard he worried she was going to hurt herself. And inside he cried too. For Rose and Cora and Daisy. For all those poor dead girls and the people they had left behind who could never sit again like this with their loved ones. Who could never hold them and tell them all would be well. Even if that was a lie.

Finally she stopped, blew her nose loudly in the handkerchief he'd given her and gave him a weak smile.

'I imagine you're hungry,' Albert said. 'You usually are.'

'Well, I wouldn't say no to—'

'—a slice of cake? I suspected that might be the case.'

Together they went to the kitchen and found a slab of fruitcake and a few bottles of beer. Minnie eyed the heel of a loaf of bread with interest, so Albert grabbed that too, along with some cheese, and a few apples. They took their provisions back to the morning room, sat side by side on the couch and ate, washing it all down with the beer. Albert kept the fire high. They talked, and fell silent, and talked again. Hours passed. The first time Minnie laughed Albert felt maybe there was some hope after all.

He woke to the early-morning sun peeping through the curtains. Outside, the birds were ecstatic with the excitement of a new day. The fire had died out and there was an unwelcome chill in the air. His back was killing him, and he realised he must have slept in his Aunt Alice's chair, a seat so uncomfortable the Spanish Inquisition could have found a good use for it. Mrs Byrne stood over him. He went to speak, but she raised a finger to her lips and nodded towards Minnie, who was deeply asleep on the sofa, curled into a ball, her legs pulled up against the cushions. She had a blanket tucked round her, and Mrs Byrne handed another one to Albert. She left the room, returning a few minutes later with a cup of tea which she placed on the table next to him before creeping out again.

The sun rose slowly in the sky. The shadows crept across the floor. His tea went cold. At some point he fell asleep again, and the morning slipped gently into afternoon.

NINE

Mrs Byrne showed John into the morning room just as Albert was starting to despair of ever finding his wallet.

'It'll be where you left it,' John said. 'That's what my Mary always tells me. I don't find it the most helpful advice, to be quite honest.'

'It was on the mantelpiece. Your bedroom,' Mrs Byrne said curtly, before handing him the wallet and leaving the room without another word.

'What's up with Mrs B?' John asked.

'She's worried I'm turning into some sort of Lothario.'

'You?' John said, unable to hide his amusement. 'You sure she's using the same dictionary as the rest of us?'

'Minnie ended up staying over last night– entirely innocently, might I add.'

'Shame.'

'It happened before. Once. But Mrs B knew about it in advance; it was her idea, as I remember. This time, she was happy enough with it initially, but now she keeps muttering about Minnie's reputation and how I used to be such a nice young man.'

'So what happened? How did Minnie end up here?'

Albert recounted brief details of Minnie's visit to Teddy Linton in Broadmoor, the effect the man had had on her, and her decision to start working with Albert again.

'She's got pluck, that girl,' John said. 'You wouldn't catch me visiting anyone in that madhouse unless I had to.'

'I don't imagine it was the highlight of her week.'

'And is he going to leave his money in the Palace?'

Albert shrugged. 'Who knows? Linton enjoys playing games. He'll leave his money in there for as long as it suits him, I imagine. I told Minnie she shouldn't visit him again.'

John laughed. 'I'd like to have seen her face when you told her.'

Albert smiled at the memory of Minnie's indignant response. 'I don't know why I bother, I really don't. Telling her to do something usually results in her doing the exact opposite.'

'Still, it's good you two will be working together. And who knows? Maybe something more, Casanova?'

'She was very clear the last time we spoke about it. I'm not holding out a great deal of hope. Now,' he said, pocketing his wallet, 'I believe there was some mention of beer.'

The two men made their way through the chilly streets to Albert's local, the Dog and Duck. Nat, the barman, whose belly suggested he might be sampling his own wares a bit too often, nodded a greeting as they entered the steamy fug of the pub's interior and started pulling a pint before Albert even got to the bar. 'Same?' Nat asked John, who nodded.

They found an empty table and quietly enjoyed the first few mouthfuls of beer. Then John wiped the foam from his moustache and leaned back in his seat, the wood creaking gently as he moved. 'Any more on the judge in the box?' he asked.

'There is something. It might be nothing, of course. There were two men in Judge Eddings's house on the day he died. A decorator and a sweep. No one seems to know anything about the sweep.'

'And the decorator?'

'Peters. Gordon Peters.'

John frowned. Albert went to say something, but John held up a warning finger to stop him. 'That name. It's ringing a bell, but I can't – got it! Fella I copped a couple of years ago for burglary with assault. Gordon Peters. Might be the same fella. Any description?'

Albert pulled out the small notebook he kept with him at all times, a legacy from his days as a police officer. 'Tall. Thin. Dark hair. Not a great deal to go on.'

John shook his head. 'Sometimes I wonder how we ever catch anyone. What I wouldn't give for a nice distinctive-looking criminal. Someone with a diamond-encrusted eyepatch, or one leg three inches shorter than the other. Tall and thin with dark hair could describe half the fellas in London. Although it does match what I remember of Peters. I could make a few enquiries, see what he's been up to since he got out? If he's out.'

Albert nodded. 'There's something about him that's been bothering me. Not the name, but something about him.'

'I find a second pint is a great memory aid.'

'Shouldn't it be the reverse?'

'You'd think, wouldn't you? But if ever I've got a little nugget of an idea rattling around at the back of my mind, a couple of drinks often coax it into the light.'

John went to the bar and returned with the second pint. They talked of his wife and his eighth child, a girl they had christened Elizabeth and who was waking half a dozen times every night.

'It's Mary's job, of course, feeding her. But the other night, she must have slept on. I woke up, sitting by the window, Lizzie's on my lap, fast asleep, sucking my finger. As if that was gonna do her any good. I don't even remember getting up to her. It was five o'clock. Too late to go back to bed. So I just sat there, figuring out if we needed a new coat of paint in the girls' room before we move Lizzie in—'

'Damn, I nearly had it!' Albert interrupted, slamming his fist down on the table. 'You talking about painting the girls' room.

There's something about that decorator at the Eddings house. Something I'm not seeing.'

'Give it time. You'll get there.'

'Your theory of the second pint doesn't appear to be working.'

'Because this is clearly a three-pint problem, Albert. And it's your round.'

The third pint hadn't brought the solution to light. Neither had the fourth. Now, the following morning, Albert's head was thumping as he sat in Dorothy Lawrence's office, watching her rifle through the business documents he'd brought her. His visit to Judge Eddings's financial adviser had proved useful, and surprising. Buried among various share certificates and letters pertaining to other business matters, he'd found the name William Fowler. The man whose hanging Albert had been hired to investigate had been Judge Eddings's business partner.

Mrs Lawrence was certainly easy on the eye. Her hair was a dark blonde and elaborately dressed. Albert imagined the weight of it in his hand. She peered up at him, noticed him looking at her.

'Yes?' she said, her manner reminding Albert of his censorious Latin master at school.

'Nothing,' Albert said, shaking his head vigorously. 'Nothing at all. I was just – lost in my thoughts for a moment. Have you found anything?' He gestured towards the documents spread across her desk.

She inhaled sharply, as if collecting her thoughts and considering how to frame them. 'There's something here, Mr Easterbrook, but it requires a bit more investigation. A trip to Companies House might be in order. I'd be happy to go. I rather enjoy the investigative side of bookkeeping. Your Mr Eddings and Mr Fowler were both founder members of something called Capital Holdings. There's nothing here to tell me what the company traded in. It seems to have achieved moderate success for a short period of time, but three years ago it collapsed, with what looks like no warning. I suspect people lost a great deal of money.'

'Including Eddings and Fowler?'

'Not necessarily.' She sighed and gazed out of the window. Her office was a quiet oasis in the midst of all the activity out on the street. The books and files on her shelves all looked to be meticulously organised and Albert felt he'd be able to lay his hands on anything with very little guidance. There was the odd feminine touch of some pretty cushions, some framed tapestries on the walls, but the room felt quite robustly masculine in its organisation.

'In my experience,' Dorothy continued, 'when a company collapses like this, it impacts on all sorts of people. Some wealthy enough to swallow the loss. Others not. It's often those who can least afford it who end up losing the most. I'll do some further investigation and let you know what I find.' She shuffled the papers into a neat pile, placed them to one side, then steepled her fingers under her chin and stared directly at Albert. Lovely skin, he thought. Nice hands. Long, slender fingers. Like Minnie's. God, he needed to stop thinking like this. Maybe he had too much time on his hands. Perhaps he should cultivate a hobby, or take up another sport alongside boxing.

'So now perhaps we might discuss the other reason you're here, Mr Easterbrook.'

'Sorry?'

'There are any number of accountants operating within a mile of my office. Your choosing to see me, might it have something to do with the Variety Palace? With Miss Ward, perhaps?' she asked, raising one quizzical eyebrow. As a child, Albert had spent an entire summer trying to perfect the technique of the single raised brow. He'd been beside himself when he finally mastered it. He remembered rushing to show his parents: his mother had given him a distracted smile and then hurried off to dress for a dinner engagement. His father had suggested there might be better uses of his time.

'Well, now you mention it,' Albert said, 'I did wonder if you might consider going back to work for the Palace. Minnie – Miss Ward – is having great difficulty securing the services of another accountant. Some of them are very reluctant to associate themselves with a music hall. But mainly they are resistant to working with a woman. And besides – I think she likes you.'

Dorothy suppressed a smile. 'And I her. She has what my Jewish friends would call *chutzpah*. Despite the somewhat reckless way she seems to have been operating that business. As for Mr Tansford—'

Albert shook his head vigorously. He'd been expecting this objection. 'He is an acquired taste, I do appreciate that. But you wouldn't need to have any dealings with him. Minnie could come here, to your offices. You'd never need to set foot inside the Palace again. Unless you wished to, of course. Myself, I've become very fond of the place.'

'The Variety Palace have an act on their billing called the Mexican Boneless Wonder. Some sort of contortionist, I imagine. Some of the insults Mr Tansford hurled at me, the things he suggested I do might be beyond the capabilities even of our Mexican friend. Mr Tansford seemed to mistake me for someone much more – supple.' She broke off, no longer attempting to suppress the smile. 'He's imaginative, I'll give him that.'

'As I recall, you delivered a few choice words yourself, Mrs Lawrence.'

'I'm a woman operating in a man's world, Mr Easterbrook. I've had to learn to take care of myself.'

Sometimes, Albert wondered if he'd led an exceptionally sheltered life. Prior to making Minnie's acquaintance, almost all

79

the women he knew had been quiet, submissive. Dull, even. Or they'd appeared to be at least. Now, he seemed to spend all his time running up against formidable women. Even Mrs Byrne had become more outspoken since she'd got to know Minnie.

'So you'll continue working with the Palace? It would mean a great deal to Minnie.'

'Tell her I'll see her at the Palace on Friday. And make sure she has the books to hand. I'm in need of some amusement.'

As Albert went to leave, he noticed a large glass display case against one wall. 'Is that – what *is* that?' he said, drawing closer and struggling to make sense of what he was seeing.

'My father's work. I like to think of it as morbid whimsy.'

'Are those—'

'—baby rabbits? Yes,' she said, in so matter-of-fact a tone she almost made it seem normal.

The case contained about half a dozen tiny stuffed rabbits, arranged in a classroom. They were sitting on little benches, grasping tiny pencils and tiny exercise books. One was holding up his work for the teacher's approval. Another appeared to be copying the answers from his classmate while, at the rear, one frustrated individual had thrown down his pencil in despair.

Albert leaned in closer. They were doing mathematics. Quite complicated long division. No wonder some of them were struggling.

He turned to Dorothy. 'I am literally at a loss for words.'

She laughed. 'I don't blame you. Among his other interests my father was an enthusiastic if somewhat unconventional taxidermist. My mother still has his other work. A kitten's wedding party. A croquet match for squirrels. The funeral of Cock Robin, with pigeons as pallbearers.'

'Do you – like it?' he said, choosing his words carefully.

'I used to think it was ghastly and it gave me the most terrible nightmares when I was a child. But now it reminds me of my father.' She smiled fondly. 'And also serves as a reminder that people find beauty in the strangest of places. I think the main reason I like it though,' she said, running one elegant finger along the top of the glass case, 'is that it confounds expectations. People expect bookkeepers to be rather dull individuals.'

'And you like that? Confounding expectations?'

'I do,' she said, smiling.

Albert cast his mind back to Teddy Linton's collection of anatomical models. This seemed positively benign by comparison. But it was certainly changing his opinion of Dorothy Lawrence.

When Albert got back home, Tom was waiting for him. Albert had appraised Tom's disguise before the lad went off to follow Tansie, and he wasn't holding out a great deal of hope that Tom had gone unnoticed. But he was wrong.

'I followed him to a house on Oakley Street,' Tom said, excitement lending his face a warm glow. 'Number 24. He went inside, and I was just figuring out if there was a way I could get in there after him when he came out again, quick smart. Manhandled by two fellas who looked like they could give Gypsy Mace a run for his money. Tansie was shouting the odds, as you can imagine. Hurling abuse at a third fella. Looked like it was the third fella's house, and the two heavies were his men.'

'I don't suppose you recognised the third man?'

'That'd be handy, wouldn't it? But, no. He looked to be around forty. Maybe a bit older. Shock of dark hair and a very impressive beard. I reckon a bird could nest in it and you'd never know.' Tom's inability to grow even the slenderest moustache left him permanently envious of other men's hirsuteness.

'What was Tansie shouting at him?'

Tom shook his head regretfully. 'I was having to keep my distance or Tansie would've spotted me. I couldn't catch any details. Something about murder, and having Beardy's guts for garters. I reckon they didn't part as friends.'

'How did Beardy respond?'

'Just laughed, like it meant nothing to him. Mind you, he did have his two heavies there. I ain't so sure he'd be laughing if he met Tansie alone down a dark alley one night. Tansie's short, ain't he, but I reckon he'd make a tidy fighter. Particularly if he was proper riled.'

'And then what?'

'Tansie went in the Traveller's Rest on St George's Road. Downed a few and went home.'

Albert took an empty clay pipe from the mantelpiece, rolling it distractedly between his fingers. 'It might have nothing to do with the monkey,' he said. 'Tansie strikes me as a man who's made a few enemies in his time. Maybe the argument was about something else entirely.'

Tom nodded. 'I thought that too. But there was just something about Tansie. He's all bluster normally, ain't he? But, I dunno, he looked really upset to me.'

'Keep an eye on him, Tom. And let's see if we can find out who lives at 24 Oakley Street.'

TEN

Minnie had spent the morning trudging round the West End and several rather alarming streets further east, trying to find out something – anything – about Peter Reynolds that would explain why someone might have wanted to kill him. So far, she'd spoken to his landlady and some of his fellow performers from the Fortune Theatre. She'd learned he was a very nice man. Kind and generous. Much quieter offstage than on, which made her fleetingly wish Tansie had hired Peter all those years ago and not his more flamboyant brother. And that was it. Nothing salacious or surprising. No enemies. Nothing in his financial affairs that might arouse hatred or envy. Bernard inherited everything, and there was precious little to inherit.

Nothing to kill a man for. Although, in Minnie's experience, you didn't always need a reason.

Andrew Wright, the manager of the Fortune, showed her the room where Peter's body had been found. The room was empty of all the paraphernalia that had been there when Albert and John had made their gruesome discovery.

'Cleaners won't use this cupboard no more,' Wright said. 'Reckon it's haunted now, but I can't imagine Peter would have the wherewithal to scare anyone. Bang-up fella he was.' He pointed to the far corner. 'That's where they found him.'

'He was locked in here, weren't he?' Minnie said.

Wright nodded. 'The caretaker's spare set of keys have gone missing. Must have been what the killer used.' He paused. 'The worst of it is, the doctor reckons he might have survived if he'd stayed away from that far wall. There's a furnace on the other side of it. It weren't on while the workmen were in, but it would have stayed warm in here for a while, 'cos it heats the bricks. The doctor wondered if Peter curled up against that wall for warmth. It might have been his undoing. If he was warm, he'd have dehydrated quicker.'

Minnie peered into the darkness, imagined ending her days in a tiny space like that, not even realising your actions were speeding you closer to death. She shuddered. Wright gave her a sympathetic look then rifled in his pocket. He held out a sheet of paper, crumpled and stained. There were markings on it, more like scratches.

'We found it underneath the mattress when we removed the bed. I was gonna take it to the coppers, but seeing as you're investigating the case – don't know if it means anything.'

Minnie looked at the markings. Were they letters?

'You reckon Peter did this?'

He shrugged. 'Who knows? Might be something. Might be nothing.'

She thanked him, made her way back outside into the rain and turned towards the Palace. They weren't getting anywhere. The only clue was a scrap of paper that might have been there for years. But the more she heard about Peter Reynolds, the more determined she became to find his killer. Minnie could think of a few people the world would be better off without: Teddy Linton and Three-Fingers just for starters. But they continued to thrive, and poor Peter Reynolds had died a lonely and horrendous death.

Minnie slipped in through the rear of the Palace and walked wearily to her office, shaking the rain off her coat and umbrella. On the way, she popped her head into Wardrobe. Bernard was there, holding the head of his animal skin and deep in conversation with Frances Moore, the dressmaker.

When Bernard had first proposed the idea of the magical menagerie, Minnie had suggested he play the part of a cat, recycling an outfit from a production of Dick Whittington a few years back. Bernard had decided this was not enough of a stretch. The costume had been problematic from day one.

'What are you doing here, Bernard?' she asked gently.

'I am seeking the expert opinion of the lovely Frances. As you know, I am a professional, Minnie. When Mr Charles Davey is undertaking a new animal mime, he acquires the animal and keeps it in his home for at least a month to study its behaviour, its mannerisms. He has a team of seamstresses on hand to create a facsimile of the animal's skin. I, on the other hand, have received no assistance with my costume. And I have had to resort to visiting the Zoological Gardens to study the creature. In November, might I add, when they are remarkably reluctant to venture into the open air.' Every sentence was punctuated by a stab at the costume with a needle and thread that seemed to be making matters worse with every stitch. Frances made nervous motions to intervene with each thrust of the needle, but she was clearly reluctant to distress Bernard any further.

'You're playing a rhinoceros, Bernard. I'm not sure even Mr Charles Davey would consider housing a rhino in two small rooms in Bermondsey. They ain't known for their hygiene.'

'Be that as it may, Minnie, I am an *artist*. This' — and here he held up the rhino head, which Minnie had to confess looked like a coal sack stitched by a blind man — 'this *monstrosity* is simply not good enough. "I waste my light in vain, like lamps by day."' He threw her a questioning look.

'*Much Ado?*' she ventured. Most of Bernard's favourite Shakespearean quotations came from *Much Ado about Nothing*. It could be worse. His favourite play could be *Titus Andronicus*.

Bernard shook his head, grimacing as if she had committed the most shameful faux pas. '*Romeo and Juliet,* dear heart,' he said. 'Had you but followed the arts, you would know that. But I am – as I have long suspected – surrounded by vulgarians. Thankfully, Frances has a degree of expertise sadly lacking elsewhere in this establishment.' He gave her a grateful smile. 'She has offered to wield her needle and work some magic.'

'Well,' Frances said, looking at the costume with undisguised alarm, 'I'll do my best. I can't promise miracles.'

'That's very kind of you,' Minnie said. 'Bernard, don't take this the wrong way, but should you be here at all? Ain't you got nowhere else to be?'

He lowered his head and said nothing for a few moments. Then he turned to her, all his bravado stripped away, his eyes brimming with tears. 'Don't ask me to go home, dearest one. That way madness lies.'

She pulled him to her, held him close. It felt as if he'd lost weight, and there was something else. It took her a moment to realise. He hadn't applied his goose-grease pomade. His hair was hanging loose and unkempt and this, more than anything, made her heart catch in her throat.

'Let's have a cuppa,' Minnie said. 'Tell you what, let's go to Brown's and I'll treat you to a slice of cake. You too, Frances. Then, when we come back, you can have a look at that thing,' she said, gesturing towards the rhinoceros head and wondering if she could persuade Frances to lose it in a bin somewhere.

'Tansie says you're looking for a room,' Frances said, removing her coat and bonnet from one of the rails.

'News to me,' Minnie said sharply.

'Oh, I must have got it wrong. I just thought – after that fella got in the other night. Forget I said anything.'

Despite Minnie's best efforts to keep Three-Fingers' visit quiet, word had spread quickly. Tansie and Kippy insisted it wasn't safe for Minnie to live in the Palace. Minnie had put on a brave face, maintaining that a change of lock was all that was needed. But, deep down, she knew they were right. She certainly hadn't been sleeping as soundly since Three-Fingers' visit.

She softened at Frances's discomfort. 'Sorry. It ain't you I'm annoyed with.'

'Tansie?'

'Who else?'

'He's got a point though, Minnie. I wouldn't feel safe sleeping here after what happened. And I reckon I could squeeze you in at my place. I've got a spare room. It's tiny, but there'd be room for a bed once I've moved out my fabric and bits and pieces. And it's only on Wellington Street, no distance from here. I thought it might work until you find yourself something more permanent.'

Minnie considered the proposal. Even before Three-Fingers' midnight visit, she'd been thinking about moving out of the Palace. And this would provide a short-term solution. Besides, she liked Frances. There was a quiet, calm air about the woman that Minnie found restful.

'You could come round and have a look?' Frances said.

'All right. Let's go to Brown's first, and then I'll pop round for a butcher's.'

As they turned to leave, the entire fabric of the building shook from a thunderous din beneath their feet.

'Christ! What the hell is that?' Minnie cried.

'Tansie's latest project,' Bernard said. 'There's been the most horrendous racket coming from below stage all morning.'

Swallowing a curse, Minnie ran down the stairs, following the sound of raised voices.

'And what exactly is that?' she said as she reached the area below the stage. Whatever the answer, she had a feeling it wasn't going to be good.

A pile of metal sheets was taking up most of the area directly

below the stage, with a rack of costumes and newly delivered stage
flats pushed to one side to make room. Each sheet looked to be
about six feet high, maybe three feet wide, and there were at least
a dozen of them. Jack was using a block and tackle to lift one of
the sheets upright, while Kippy and Tansie were fastening it to
those already assembled. Once the thing was fully built, Minnie
figured you'd need to edge sideways to get round it. With the way
Tansie's waistline was expanding, he might not manage it at all.

'This, my dearest Minnie, is the future of the Variety Palace,'
Tansie said. His use of 'dearest Minnie' told her immediately that
he knew he'd done something wrong and was desperately hoping
to forestall her wrath.

'You still ain't answered my question,' Minnie said, struggling
to remain calm. 'What is it?'

'It's a water tank,' Tansie said, as if the answer were obvious,
'and this little beauty is going to deliver us from our financial
distress overnight. The punters'll be piling in, just you wait and
see.'

'That,' Minnie said, measuring her words carefully as she
watched Jack struggling to haul another of the panels upright, 'is
neither little nor beautiful. It is a bleedin' monstrosity.'

'It is a little larger than I anticipated, I'll give you that,' Tansie
said, stepping swiftly to one side to avoid a collision with the
panel, which had developed a life of its own.

'And – assuming you bought it from Handy Mick – it will
almost certainly end up drowning someone. Or flooding the
audience. Or both.'

'Now, that's where you're wrong,' Tansie said, smiling broadly
in a way she found very ominous. 'Handy Mick swears blind
there's nothing wrong with it. And' – he paused for dramatic
effect, punching her lightly on the arm to reinforce his point – 'if
we ain't one hundred per cent happy with it, he'll take it back.'

'And you believed him? This being the same Handy Mick who

cheated you out of all your marbles when you were kids, and has still never replaced them? The same Handy Mick who stole your girl and then stood her up at the altar? The same Handy Mick who sold you a pigeon and convinced you it was a rare African dove? You've got a history with that man and you're the loser every time. You are seriously telling me he's gonna take this back if we ain't happy with it?'

'He will,' Tansie said, his voice dropping to a disturbingly soothing level.

'If we can ever get it out of here,' Kippy interjected. 'Given that it's taken half a dozen of us to get it in here, two of whom are sitting out in the lane suffering from exhaustion, and one of whom is now on his way to hospital. My advice is that we make it work, 'cos I reckon the only way we'll ever get it out is if we dismantle the Palace around it.'

Jack nodded his agreement. 'Seriously, Minnie, I'd rather spend the day with Tansie's monkey than have to move this bleedin' thing again.' He looked over her shoulder, to where Frances was standing behind her. A noticeable blush crept up his neck into his cheeks. Frances didn't seem to have noticed. Or, if she had, she wasn't interested. Minnie looked again at Jack. Good-looking lad. Stocky. Nice hands. Frances could do worse. Although Minnie wasn't sure she could take another Palace romance; if it followed their usual track record, Frances or Jack would end up dead.

'Well, we ain't moving it today, that's for certain,' she said. 'If you can make it work, Tansie – and I mean *if* – then maybe we'll think about keeping it. But if there is the slightest problem, I'm holding you personally responsible for getting rid of it. Now, if you can all get out of here quick smart, I'm treating everyone to a Chelsea bun at Brown's.'

Two hours later, everyone's sugar levels suitably replenished, Minnie and Tansie were seated in her office. Minnie had spent the last half-hour listening to Tansie's ambitious plans for the water tank, including renaming the music hall the Water Palace. In an effort to shut him up, she handed him *The Era*, while she opened the post.

A few minutes of blissful quiet ensued, then Tansie passed her the newspaper, tapping an article halfway down the page. 'Remember him?' he asked her. 'Freddy Graham?'

''Course I do. He was the caretaker when I started here. Bit of a grumpy bastard, but he was kind once you got on his right side.' She scanned the article, read of the man's sudden death by heart attack and immediately regretted calling him a bastard.

Tansie nodded. 'It was a bit of a step down him working here. He'd been a stage manager before, the Adelphi at one point I seem to remember, but then I heard he hit a hard patch.' He mimed drinking from an imaginary glass. 'Must be what done for him in the end. Still, he was no age. Nice fella. No family. Makes you think, don't it?'

'About what?'

'Well, say I dropped the cue tomorrow, I'd leave no one behind. My ma and pa are both gone, no brothers or sisters, no wife. No kiddies.'

'That you know of.'

'You know what I mean, Min. Who would care?'

'Christ, fetch me my violin. We'd care, wouldn't we? All of us here?'

'It ain't the same though, is it? I thought – with Cora – I really thought—' He tailed off.

'I know, Tanse. I thought so too. But there'll be someone else. You're still a good-looking fella. And lots of girls like a short chap. Gives them someone to look down on.' She opened another envelope, glanced at the contents and tossed it in the bin. 'No news on Monkey, I take it? Not that I'm suggesting he's an alternative to a wife and children.'

His face darkened. There was no getting away from it, he loved that monkey. 'Nothing so far, although I'm pursuing a few leads, as Albert would say.'

'Such as?'

He tapped the side of his nose conspiratorially. 'That's between me and Jinks the barber at this precise moment.'

'Meaning?'

'Meaning I have my informants, and I am investigating some lines of enquiry. Much like you and Bert.'

Minnie grunted. He'd tell her soon enough. There was no point in trying to wrestle a secret out of Tansie; he only held on to it tighter. She tore the brown paper off a small box and opened it.

At first, she couldn't understand what she was seeing. Then she screamed, hurling the box and its contents onto the floor.

'Christ, Min, what is it?'

She pointed at the floor, her other hand over her mouth. She wasn't sure if she was going to scream again or throw up.

Tansie bent down to retrieve the contents of the box. As realisation dawned on him, he emitted a long, low keening. In his hand lay one tiny monkey's paw.

ELEVEN

Minnie handed Albert the slip of paper she'd been given by the manager of the Fortune Theatre. Albert crossed to the window and held it up to the light while Minnie sipped her tea and tried to suppress her disappointment at the lack of cake. Mrs Byrne had apologised when Minnie had arrived, said she could nip out for some. Minnie had insisted she was fine and now she was regretting it. A cuppa hardly seemed worth bothering with if there wasn't a nice slab of fruitcake to go with it. Maybe a scone. At the very least, a slice of plain sponge.

'It could be letters,' Albert said. 'Possibly a name?'

'It'd be handy if it was the name of his killer, wouldn't it? But if it's letters, I can't decipher them.'

'Or maybe it's nothing,' Albert said, handing Minnie back the paper. 'We've no idea how long it's been there, even. Never mind if it's a message Peter left about the identity of his killer.'

'I know,' Minnie sighed. 'Clutching at straws. But it feels like we're getting nowhere. And I have to face Bernard every day, watch the anticipation die in his eyes as I tell him we've got nothing new.'

'Give it time, Minnie,' he said, finishing the last of his tea. 'Lots of murders take months, sometimes years, to figure out. You think you've hit a dead end, and then a tiny little clue emerges, and the whole thing opens up in front of you like a Chinese puzzle.'

Minnie gave him a sardonic look. 'Ain't you the poet this morning. Making headway with the Eddings case?'

'No, I'm not as a matter of fact. John had a quiet word with the decorator, Gordon Peters.'

'And?'

'He's kept his nose clean since he was released, working with his brother. He was at the Eddings house that day, but he ran out of paint and was done by two o'clock. He met his brother and a friend for a bite to eat and then they had a few at their local. Plenty of people saw him there.'

'And Judge Eddings was still alive at two o'clock, you said.'

Albert nodded. 'According to everyone I spoke to, he was. So it's not Peters. But I swear, there's something there.'

He crossed to the writing desk and removed his notebook. He read aloud his notes from the interviews at the Eddings house. Nothing. Idly, he flipped back a few pages, then slammed his hand down on the desk so hard it made Minnie jump.

'It's the sweep,' he said. 'Fowler's widow told me she hung back that morning because she needed to speak to the sweep. The fire in the back bedroom wasn't drawing properly and she wanted to ask him if there might be anything blocking it. But he was late and she had to leave.' He handed Minnie the notebook: 'Sweep late.'

'Who's Fowler?' Minnie asked.

'A case I had before Eddings. Fowler hanged himself. His wife thought there was something suspicious about it all, but I couldn't find anything. It turns out both Fowler and Eddings were owners of a company called Capital Holdings. And now it turns out there was a sweep at both their houses on the day they died.'

'Easy way to get inside someone's house. You'd have access to pretty much every room. And no one really notices you.'

Albert rang a bell by the side of the fireplace. Moments later, Mrs Byrne appeared.

'Our sweep,' Albert said. 'What's his name?'

She gave him a bemused look. 'Why? Are you thinking of adding him to your stable of detectives?'

'His name?' Albert said, betraying a hint of impatience.

'Henry.'

'And what does he look like?'

She frowned, then saw he was serious and took a moment to consider. 'Dark hair. Middling height.'

'Anything else?'

'I don't pay him a great deal of mind, Albert. I've got a lot else to do.'

'Exactly,' Albert said. 'No one ever notices the sweep.'

'Or the housekeeper, much of the time,' Mrs Byrne murmured as she cleared away the tea things and left the room.

'She forgiven you yet?' Minnie asked. 'For the other night? I did tell her it was my fault, but she weren't having none of it.'

'Mrs B has a long memory,' Albert said. 'When I was four I accidentally broke a china ornament in her bedroom. I swear she's never forgiven me to this day. Now, I need to track down this sweep, but first I need to pop in on Dorothy Lawrence. She sent me a note this morning. Said she's found something at Companies House about Capital Holdings, the company Eddings and Fowler launched.'

'I'm meeting her back at the Palace in twenty minutes,' Minnie said, glancing at her watch. 'I need to ask her a few questions about insurance. Tansie's bought this bleedin' water tank that's a disaster waiting to happen and I need to know if we're covered for flooding. You're welcome to join us.'

The pair of them left the house. It was a beautiful morning, bright and crisp, and they opted for the slightly longer route through St James's Park. As soon as they entered the park Minnie wondered if this had been such a good idea. The last time they'd been here, skirting the tea stall and the lake, she'd told him the secrets of her past, and the reasons why they couldn't be together. She looked up at Albert, but if he had made the connection he was keeping it well hidden. They walked without speaking for a while. She'd missed this.

'You'll be pleased to know I've moved,' she said finally, explaining her new arrangement with Frances. 'The room ain't that big, but it's near the Palace. It'll do until I find something else.'

'And Frances? You like her?'

Minnie smiled to herself. 'I do. This is gonna sound strange, but I like watching her do stuff. You know me, I rush at everything like a bull in a china shop. But Frances, she takes her time. Lays all her stuff out nicely and then calmly completes the job. Won't let nothing go out unless it's perfect. I find it very restful, sitting in an armchair, watching her work.'

'You wouldn't think to help her?'

'Have you seen my sewing? I'm all right at pinning stuff, and turning up a hem, but the kind of work she does? It's like art.'

They left the park, turning onto the Mall.

'Have you heard anything more from Teddy?' Albert asked.

Minnie shook her head. 'Not yet, although I suspect he ain't gonna give up. And sometimes I get this feeling that Freddie Forrester's there, in the shadows. The other day I was buying a newspaper, and I swear someone came up behind me and blew on my neck. When I turned round, there was no one there, but I'd put money on it, it was Freddie. If Teddy asks me to visit him again, what do I do? I don't reckon I could bear to go back to that place, but if I say no he's gonna try and shut down the Palace. I'm like a cat on hot coals every time the letter box goes. What with Teddy's invitations and random bits of monkeys that some nutter's been popping in the post.'

'Have you spoken to Ida?' Albert asked. 'He wanted her support too, didn't he?'

'How do I tell her? The fella who had her child murdered wants her forgiveness or he's gonna put all her daughter's friends out on the street? It ain't easy, Albert.'

They walked on in silence, past Trafalgar Square and then reached the ceaseless bustle of the Strand.

Dorothy was waiting for them in Minnie's office, dressed in a delicious dove-grey silk, trimmed with burgundy at the sleeves and collar. Not a combination Minnie would have thought to put together, but it looked striking: conspicuous and yet somehow classy. Minnie reminded herself to get the name of Dorothy's dressmaker. Although, now that she was living with as good a seamstress as Frances, maybe her own clothes would improve somewhat. She looked down at her dress. A rather unflattering brown. A dress designed to disappear into the background. With what looked like a soup stain halfway down the front.

Dorothy's face lit up when she saw Albert. 'How convenient,' she said. 'I happen to have the information here about Capital Holdings. I spent a very productive afternoon at Companies House,' she continued, extracting a bundle of papers from her bag, neatly tied with a length of ribbon, 'and then afterwards with Mr Pemberley, an acquaintance of mine who writes for some of the financial publications.' She paused, smoothing out the papers on the desk. 'Messrs Fowler and Eddings ran into a spot of bother a few years ago. Have you ever heard of Adelheid Spitzeder?'

They both shook their heads.

'She was brought to trial in Germany around five years ago. She'd been running a private bank, encouraging people to invest money and promising them a healthy return on their investment.'

'Nothing illegal about that, surely?' Albert asked.

'Except she wasn't actually investing the money. She was simply paying older investors with money from newer ones. The phrase "robbing Peter to pay Paul" is the easiest explanation. It all works fine until Peter wants a return on his investment. There was no actual growth, just a circulation of funds that was bound to collapse one day. Which it did. She was convicted of mishandling customers' money and received three years in prison.'

'And Eddings and Fowler were doing something similar?'

'It appears so. They established a company called Capital Holdings, allegedly investing in titanium mining in Russia.'

'They were convicted?' Minnie asked.

'Fowler. Not Eddings. Connections, I imagine, with him being a judge and all. Fowler did two years and was released last year. Eddings got away scot-free.'

'So their deaths might be down to a disgruntled investor?'

'When Spitzeder's bank collapsed, thirty-two thousand people lost their money. The equivalent of thousands of pounds in some cases. Fowler and Eddings were never so successful. They were caught very early on in the scheme. But Mr Pemberley reckons there were about fifty investors, most of whom lost money. And there were suicides.'

'How many?'

'Difficult to determine. Some deaths were passed off as accidents, unsurprisingly, but he remembers one in particular. Hugh Littleton. The man posted a letter to all the newspapers just before he died, blaming it all on Fowler and Eddings.'

'How did this Mr Littleton die?' Minnie asked.

'He hanged himself.'

'So your father, or husband, or son loses their life savings to these two swindlers and kills himself. That is a motive to seek revenge,' Albert said.

'Indeed, Albert.'

Minnie frowned. It had taken Albert weeks to get comfortable with Minnie calling him by his first name. He'd known Dorothy five minutes and he seemed perfectly happy with the arrangement. Dorothy beamed at him. Nice teeth, Minnie thought.

'Now, Minnie, I believe you wanted to see me about a water tank and whether or not your insurance will cover you?'

Albert started to say his goodbyes.

'A quick word before you go?' Dorothy said.

Albert nodded and the two of them left the office. After a moment or two, curious as to what they could be talking about, Minnie stuck her head out into the corridor. They were standing by the stage door, deep in conversation, their heads almost touching. Dorothy looked up, saw Minnie, and made an elaborate show of seeing Albert out of the building. She turned back to Minnie, smiling broadly.

'What was that all about?' Minnie asked.

'Oh, nothing,' Dorothy said. 'Just some further details about Capital Holdings. Now, explain to me about this tank.'

Minnie took Dorothy below stage and showed her Tansie's latest acquisition. Dorothy felt it would almost certainly result in an increased premium. Yet more money.

'Any news on Mr Tansford's missing pet?' Dorothy said, as she prepared to leave. 'Anything I could help with?'

'No offence, but you're a bookkeeper, ain't you? I don't really see how you can help with this one.'

'I have an interest in animals.'

'The kind of interest that means you know how to fashion a new leg for a monkey?'

Minnie explained about the item they'd received in the post. Dorothy raised a hand to her mouth. Minnie thought at first she was horrified but then realised Dorothy was fascinated and trying to conceal it.

'There was another ransom note with it,' Minnie said. 'This time asking for a hundred sovs.'

'Have you still got it?' Dorothy asked. 'The paw?'

'Why? You wanna have a look?'

'Well – yes. As I said, I have a strong interest in animals. Inherited it from my father. I might be able to tell you if it was definitely Mr Tansford's monkey, at the very least.'

'I told him to throw it out,' Minnie said, rifling through piles of sheet music behind her desk. 'But he's got some harebrained idea we might be able to sew it back on if we get Monkey back alive. I was gonna give it another day, then accidentally throw it in the bin.' She retrieved the box and handed it to Dorothy. 'Funnily enough, it should be smelling by now, but it ain't.'

Dorothy opened the box and leaned in for a sniff. 'You're right. No smell at all. That's because it's been stuffed, although very poorly.' She removed the paw and peered at it. 'Mr Tansford's creature. A capuchin?'

'That's what he was told by the fella he bought it off. Mind you, Handy Mick would have told him it was a giraffe if he thought he'd get a few bob.'

'Black and white. About so high?' Dorothy said, holding her hand a foot or so above the desk.

'That's the one.'

'Well,' Dorothy said, peering closely again at the paw, 'this doesn't look like it's from a capuchin. Maybe a colobus? Black and white but much larger than a capuchin.'

Minnie eyed the other woman carefully. It seemed a little convenient that this beautiful bookkeeper, all curves and hair, was also able to identify a breed of monkey from a single paw. Dorothy caught her eye. 'My father was something of a natural historian and a hobby taxidermist. I'll show you some of his work, next time you're in my office.'

'Tanse'll be relieved. I'll fetch him and you can tell him the good news yourself.'

Dorothy baulked. 'Mr Tansford and I didn't exactly hit it off when we first met.'

Minnie dismissed Dorothy's qualms with a wave of her hand. 'Bluster. Bluff. You learn to ignore it.'

Bobby, the stagehand, passed her office and she sent him to fetch Tansie. 'Tell him it's about Monkey.'

Moments later, Tansie appeared, anxiety written all over his face. 'What now?' he said. 'Not another paw? Or – dear God – not his tail?'

Minnie shook her head and gestured to Dorothy, who explained her findings.

'So it ain't him?' Tansie said.

'No,' Dorothy said, trying and failing to restrain a smile. 'It's not Monkey. I rather think the claw you received in the post wasn't Monkey's either, given that this paw is missing a claw. It's been stuffed for some time and badly at that. I suspect the animal or maybe just its skin might have been shipped over here, but they didn't do a good job of preserving the skin. See, it's rotted in places. They should have covered it in alum salt, or arsenic soap. That would have helped. And it's an old paw, I suspect. The skin's been draped over what was probably rather a clumsy metal frame and stuffed with hay. Rather shoddy work.' She looked up from the paw at their aghast faces and laughed. 'I'm sorry. I know far more about this than anyone should, and I tend to let my mouth run away with me a little. The long and the short of it is, I don't know what unfortunate creature this once belonged to, but it's not Monkey.'

Tansie took a step towards Dorothy as if he were about to embrace her. The woman looked slightly alarmed and took a step backwards, so Tansie contented himself with grabbing her hand and shaking it a little too vigorously.

'You're an angel. A bleedin' angel is what you are – sorry, I didn't catch your name last time.'

'Lawrence. Mrs Lawrence.'

Tansie grimaced and shook his head. 'This is the Palace. We don't stand on formalities here. What do your chums call you?'

'My *friends* call me Dorothy, but—'

'Dot it is, then. Very pleased to make your acquaintance, Dot. Now, Min, open that bottle of brandy you've got hidden in the bottom drawer and let's celebrate the first bit of good news we've had in ages.'

TWELVE

William Fowler's widow had agreed to meet Albert at her home. A pleasant-looking woman in her forties, she looked as if, under normal circumstances, her face might fall readily into a smile. But not any more. To Albert's eyes, she'd lost weight since the last time they'd spoken and she'd developed a nervous habit of squeezing the tips of each of her fingers in succession. He wished he had better news to bring her. He asked her about the sweep.

'The fella who was coming that day,' she said, 'we'd only used him a couple of times. Terence, our usual fella, had been a bit poorly – he's getting on a bit, to be honest – so he'd fixed us up with a replacement. I wanted a word with this new chap 'cos the fire in the back bedroom had been belching out smoke and I wondered if maybe there was a dead bird or something up the chimney. But he was late, so I had to leave. My employer is a stickler for punctuality, and we needed the money.'

'It can't have been easy for your husband, finding work when he got out.'

She flinched at the mention of her husband's prison sentence. 'You know about that, then,' she said, a hint of bitterness entering her voice. 'You're right. It didn't make life any easier. He had some daft idea when he got out that he'd write a play and make us a fortune. You can doubtless guess how that turned out.'

'I imagine this was probably the last thing on your mind that day, but I don't suppose you noticed if the sweep had been or not?'

She frowned. 'Didn't cross my mind. Betty, the kitchen girl, she might know. But it's her half-day off today. She always takes it in the morning, goes to the shops with her ma.' She paused. 'Mind, it was her half-day on the day William died as well. She wasn't here that morning.'

It was as he'd expected. She'd come home to find her husband swinging from the ceiling. She was hardly likely to have checked the state of the chimneys.

After he left her, Albert knocked on the neighbours' doors. No one had seen anything that day, although one elderly gent remembered seeing someone arrive at the house that morning. Or maybe it was another morning, he couldn't be sure. A man, or maybe it was a woman. Whatever day it had been, he couldn't remember anything about the visitor.

Albert was starting to share some of Minnie's frustration. He just needed a tiny break, a little chink of light.

Terence Godfrey, the Fowlers' original sweep, lived in Montague Road, in a modest but tidy set of rooms. He was a neat, dapper chap with a clipped moustache, although Mrs Fowler hadn't been wrong when she said he was getting on a bit. He looked as if he was well into his seventies and so thin Albert wondered how he managed to carry all the rods and brushes he'd need for his job.

Albert gave him the dates of Eddings's and Fowler's deaths. Terence frowned and held up a finger. 'One moment, sir,' he said and crossed to a cupboard, from which he removed a large leather-bound journal. He opened it, flicked through several pages, then ran a finger down a column, humming to himself all the while. 'Ah,' he said eventually, 'not me. Lookie here,' and he pointed to an entry in the journal. 'Ridley Road, 22nd October, Danny,' the entry read. 'And what was that other date?' he asked.

'The second of November, Upper Grosvenor Street,' Albert

said. Terence flipped forward a few pages, found the correct entry and, once again, the name Danny was there.

'Danny Webster,' Terence said. 'Young fella. Not exactly my apprentice, but I pass work his way when I'm too busy to see everyone. Or when the old joints are playing up. I'm not getting any younger—'

'Do you know where I might find this Danny?' Albert interrupted. Terence was a nice old chap, but Albert didn't really want to hear the man's life story.

'Why, of course,' the man said, apparently bemused at the question. He turned to the back of his ledger and read out an address to Albert. The man's record keeping was meticulous. Perhaps Albert should introduce him to Minnie.

'And what does Danny look like?' Albert asked.

'Young fella, like I said. Fair hair. Clean-shaven. Nice kind of face.'

A description that fitted half the young men in London. Albert thanked him and gave him a few coins for his trouble.

The house on Mare Street was grim, and Albert could only conclude the rent must be very low. The windows were grimy, the curtains that had once been white were now almost black with dirt, and paint was peeling from the windowsills and the front door. The woman who opened the door was of a piece with the building. Albert asked for Danny and drew a suspicious look from her.

'He ain't here,' she said, eyeing him carefully. 'You a copper?'

'No. Quite the reverse. I was hoping to put some work his way. But if he isn't available—' He tailed off, turning away.

'I didn't say he weren't coming back,' she said hastily, taking in the cut of his suit, the shine on his shoes.

Albert slipped her a shilling. 'Might I wait in his room?'

She pocketed the coin and gestured with her head to the room on the ground floor, at the front of the house. She made heavy weather of finding her keys, then hovered at the doorway of Danny's room, as if reluctant to leave. Albert gave her another shilling.

'If you need me,' she said, 'I'll be out the back.'

Left alone, Albert examined the room. Whatever rent Danny Webster was paying was almost certainly too much. Dark patches of damp were creeping up the walls, and the floorboards felt decidedly spongy in places. As Albert moved tentatively across the floor, there was an audible scuttling in the corners of the room. Rats or cockroaches. Probably both. The whole place needed to be pulled down. And yet, in the midst of the squalor, Danny had tried to impose some sort of order. Every surface was clean, and Albert was fairly certain the landlady played no part in that. It was a room that spoke of a desperate need to maintain order in the face of hopeless circumstances.

He parted the curtains, which almost fell apart in his hands. Approaching the house was a young man. His collar was up, his hat pulled down low. A muffler was wrapped tight across the lower half of his face, keeping out the cold. It was hard to tell from a distance, but it looked as if there were tufts of fair hair peeping out from under his hat.

The man looked up at the movement of the curtains, his eyes met Albert's and he froze. Before Albert had time to register what was happening, the young man had turned and was tearing back down the street in the direction he'd come from. Cursing, Albert took off after him. The landlady was standing in the hallway and took a step forward to block the door before taking a look at Albert's face and moving swiftly to one side. As he ran down the front steps, she called something after him, but he couldn't catch it.

Danny was fast and had made some progress. Mare Street was

lined with shops, and teeming with people, carriages, bicycles and the odd omnibus. Albert cursed again. Just the kind of street to get lost on. Trying desperately to avoid running into anyone, he managed to keep the lad in sight. Occasionally, he disappeared from view, but then reappeared. Already Albert felt his breath tightening and he cursed the fact he'd chosen to wear a new pair of brogues that day. Danny was younger than him, had a head start and was more familiar with these streets than Albert was. And for whatever reason he was intent on getting away.

Ahead, the crowds parted for a moment, and Albert spotted Danny ducking right, slipping down an alleyway between a greengrocer's and an ironmonger's. Albert followed him, wondering for a moment if he might be gaining on the lad. As soon as he turned into the gap between the shops, the stench assaulted him. In such a confined space, tall buildings louring on either side, the smell had nowhere to go. The uneven cobbles underneath his feet were wet, and Albert suspected it wasn't rain. He didn't allow himself to think where the moisture was coming from and concentrated on keeping his wits about him, and his balance, to avoid tripping or treading in something unmentionable. Lining the alleyway were bins overflowing with rotting food. The smell was almost unbearable. Two young children, not much more than toddlers, were kicking what looked like a stone, half wrapped in a piece of old rag. A third child was watching their progress, perched on a filthy mattress lying in the gutter. They looked up blankly at Albert, then turned away.

The way ahead looked like a dead end, and Albert braced himself for a confrontation, praying Danny didn't have a knife. Or, worse, a gun. Just as the lad seemed to be about to run into a brick wall, he ducked to his left, through an even narrower alley. So narrow in places, Albert had to turn sideways to ensure he could get through.

The passageway ended in a high brick wall. Danny took one

look behind him and hurled himself at the wall. He was agile, Albert had to give him that. With one deft motion, he was over, and had disappeared from sight. When Albert reached the wall, it took him three goes to get over, and he cursed the weight he carried. Useful in a boxing ring, but a definite hindrance in a situation like this. When he finally made it over, he was in someone's garden. A young woman was sitting on a stool, scraping the mud off the soles of a pair of boots. Mutely, she pointed to the passageway running down the side of her house. Albert briefly nodded his thanks and shot down the alleyway, finding himself back out in a main street, busy with street sellers and customers lingering at shop doorways. He scanned left and right and swore under his breath.

The lad was gone.

Albert took a cab to John's station, and half an hour later they were back at Danny's lodgings. The landlady wasn't happy to see them, but there was nothing she could do once John had shown his warrant card.

The room didn't take long to search. A mattress on the floor that passed for a bed, a wardrobe, a chest of drawers and a rickety table with a single chair. Danny's few clothes were hanging neatly from hooks in the wardrobe or folded in drawers. The upper drawers housed tobacco pouches, cigarette papers, a comb, moustache wax, a handful of letters and some official-looking documents. The letters were addressed to a number of different people, all with the same address: Danny Webster, James Thompson, John Thomas. Either Danny was sharing the room with someone else, which Albert didn't imagine would have gone unnoticed by the landlady, or the man had a number of aliases, which the landlady presumably knew about but was turning a blind eye to. In Albert's experience, people who operated under more than one name tended to be up to no good. But was that enough of a reason for the lad to run the minute he'd spotted Albert in his room?

'Looks like he might be our fella,' John said, 'given that he scarpered as soon as he saw you.'

'It doesn't make sense, though,' Albert said, placing the letters back in the drawer as he'd found them. 'If Eddings and Fowler were killed because of Capital Holdings, why would a sweep be connected to it? No sweep I've ever met had money to spare on investments.'

'Maybe his father lost all their money. Danny – or whatever his name really is – was on his uppers. Had to find work somewhere. Or maybe Danny worked for Eddings and Fowler in some way. When it all went south, he was left without a job.'

'Maybe. Or maybe this is just a dead end. Danny – we'll call him that for convenience' sake – saw me in his room, and just assumed I was a copper or something worse. Debt collector, perhaps. There are a lot of people whose instinct is always to run first and ask questions later.'

John picked up the letters and documents, all of them addressed to different names. 'I'll see if any of these ring a bell with the lads back at the station. I'll let you know what I find.'

THIRTEEN

'So I did a bit of sniffing around,' Tom said, as Albert let him into the house. 'Followed that fella from Oakley Street who Tansie had the run-in with. Turns out he ain't the kind of chap I'd have thought Tansie would have much time for.'

'Why not?'

'Fella's name is Jem Blount.'

'Should I know that name?'

'Depends what you like to do in your spare time. He's a big name in the more unpleasant end of gambling. Dogfights, bear baiting. Illegal, of course, but that don't seem to stop it. I followed him to the Westminster Pit last night. What they call a blood sports arena.' Tom shuddered. 'Hate to imagine what goes on inside there.'

'So are you thinking Tansie owes this Jem Blount some money, and Blount's taken the monkey until Tansie pays up?'

'I dunno. My gut tells me there's something more to it. Anyway, there's a fight on there tonight. Thought maybe we could both go and see if we can spot anything.'

When he was a police officer Albert had tried to avoid anything involving animals. It wasn't that he didn't like them. He liked them too much. Once he'd found a dog lying in the gutter, run over by a carriage and left to fend for itself. He'd sat with the creature for an hour while it died, and then he'd gone home and cried like a baby. He was not looking forward to visiting the Westminster Pit.

Neither, apparently, was Tom. 'I know this was my idea, but we ain't gonna – see anything, are we?' he asked later that day as he buttoned up his coat and secured his muffler. 'I mean, we're there to find out if this Blount fella knows anything about the monkey. We don't need to watch the fight, do we?'

Albert shrugged. 'I have no desire to see it. But we're going to be in a fairly small space, Tom. Everyone else will be there for only one reason. It might look a little strange if we're looking elsewhere during the fight.'

Vere Street was a mile or so from Albert's house in Bury Street, but it felt like a world away from the quiet gentility of his home. It always surprised him how in London you could be in the midst of luxury and yet no real distance from squalor and poverty. The Westminster Pit was a flat-fronted building nestled between a second-hand bookseller's and a tobacconist's. Inconspicuous, until you noticed the decidedly suspicious-looking men entering the premises.

Inside, Albert nearly choked on the dense fog of tobacco smoke. He bought a beer for himself and Tom, then surveyed the room. Men, all of whom had bottles and glasses in hand, were milling around the fighting arena, a pit about the same size as a boxing ring. A raised gallery ran above it, so everyone could get a decent view.

'Why is no one betting?' Albert murmured to Tom.

'I was wondering the same thing. Fella I spoke to just now said it's a special event tonight. There's a wager of forty sovs that a dog can kill a hundred rats in twelve minutes.'

'Whose dog is it?'

'His.' Tom nodded towards a very tall man in his forties, with hair so dark Albert suspected the colour might come from a bottle. Tom had been right: the man was sporting the most impressive beard Albert had seen in a long time. He was dressed in an immaculately cut purple plaid suit and flanked by men who Albert wouldn't fancy his chances against in the ring.

'Jem Blount,' Albert said.

'The very man,' Tom replied.

'Right, gents,' a skinny man covered in tattoos bellowed above the noise. 'As advertised, a special event. We are graced tonight with the presence of the rat-killing phenomenon known as Bullet.' A cheer went up from the crowd. 'Mr Blount' – the tattooed man nodded at Jem – 'has been wagered forty of the Queen's finest sovereigns that the aforementioned Bullet will fail to kill one hundred rats in twelve minutes. Mr Blount, you are confident in Bullet's abilities?'

Blount nodded briefly and murmured something under his breath. He seemed impatient to get started.

'Gentlemen,' the tattooed man continued, clearly sensing Blount's impatience, and glancing nervously at his henchmen, 'without further ado, bring forth the dog.'

A door to one side of the arena opened and a young lad emerged. He was struggling to hold the lead on a bull terrier.

'Ugly thing, ain't it?' Tom whispered.

Albert wasn't so sure. True, they'd never win any beauty contests. But there was an honesty about them that he liked. And they were often surprisingly friendly creatures. At first glance there was nothing special about this one, the usual egg-shaped head and tiny, triangular eyes almost disappearing into his head. He was all white, his ears cropped and tail docked.

'Why'd they do that?' Tom whispered. 'With the ears and tail?'

'Gives the opponent fewer areas to grab hold of in a fight,' Albert said, surprising himself with the knowledge.

There wasn't an ounce of fat on the creature; he was pure

muscle and looked to weigh a couple of stone at least, with strong muscular shoulders and short legs that made him look squat and ready for battle. When Albert peered more closely, he could see the dog's lower jaw appeared unnaturally big, even for a bull terrier. He'd heard stories of men hanging their dogs by the mouth from trees, to strengthen their jaws. It wouldn't surprise him, given the money involved.

Bullet was straining at the leash, desperate to get into the ring. Albert didn't want to think about what Blount did to the dog to make him so desperate to kill. Not long after he joined the force, he'd been involved in a raid on a house where they were breeding dogs for fighting. Half a dozen of the animals were kept in the yard, secured on short, heavy chains that left them close enough to lunge at each other constantly, but not close enough to actually do any harm. The worst were the bait dogs, weaker, smaller animals with their jaws wired shut so they couldn't fight back and cause injury to a creature that had the potential to make a lot of money for its owner.

The young lad released Bullet into the arena, and exited quickly. Two men appeared with large weighty-looking coal sacks, with something live writhing inside. They tipped the sacks over the edge of the arena, and the entertainment began.

Albert had no fondness for rats, but he would have paid good money to stop this. The rodents, as soon as they realised what was happening, tried frantically to climb up the sides of the pit and a few crouched beneath Bullet, perhaps hoping they'd escape his notice. But he dispatched them by twos and threes, flinging their corpses across the arena, some so high they flipped out into the audience.

It was all over in five minutes. Bullet looked as if he could have dispatched another hundred with ease. His head and jaws were covered with blood and gore. The young dog handler appeared again with a bucket of water. Bullet took a long drink from the bucket, then the lad used the rest of the water and a rag to wipe him down. A hatchet-faced man handed over forty sovereigns to Jem Blount, spitting on the ground as he walked away. A young woman sidled up to Blount, a conciliatory smile on her face. With barely a glance in her direction, Blount raised a hand and struck her hard across the face, then moved on as if nothing had happened. Albert sprang forward, then reminded himself he needed to keep his powder dry. He was here to help Tansie. Any other scores he wished to settle with Blount would have to wait.

Behind him, Albert heard mutterings. 'I reckon half of them rats were dead before they even got out of the sack.' 'And look, some of them are still moving.' 'So they ain't dead, are they?' Albert was turning away in disgust when he noticed a movement in the crowd near Jem Blount. There were shouts, raised voices, and he recognised one of them. Beside him, Tom swore and they moved quickly towards the source of the noise.

It was Tansie. Albert hadn't spotted him in the crowd, but now here he was, squaring up to Blount. In normal circumstances, this might have been comical, given Tansie's diminutive height, and the fact Blount had about eighteen inches on him and was flanked by two bruisers. But Tansie was livid and seemed unaware this wasn't going to be a fair fight. As Tom and Albert drew closer they heard him shouting at Blount, spit flecking from his mouth.

'Give him back, you bastard,' Tansie said. 'I know you've got him.'

Blount gave a broad grin as he pocketed his winnings. He said something to Tansie, too quietly for Albert to hear. Whatever it was, it incensed Tansie further and he lunged at Blount, fists clenched. One of the bruisers placed himself between the two men. There was only one way this was going to end. Albert sized up Blount's thugs. Both of them well over six feet and each as broad as he was tall. He could match them for height, but certainly not for weight. Albert had fought men like that in the ring and often beaten them. Skill, and knowing your opponent's weaknesses could often outsmart brute force. But there were two of them and God knows how many others in the crowd who might be happy to spring to Blount's defence.

Albert bent down and whispered instructions to Tom, who ran straight at Blount's man and then appeared to trip, chucking beer over the man. Distracted, the bruiser turned to Tom and, while his attention was elsewhere, Albert grabbed Tansie by the arm.

'Get out of here,' Albert hissed. 'Now, Tansie, or it won't just be Blount's men who'll be taking a swing at you.'

Shocked, Tansie looked at Albert wide-eyed and then seemed to decide that Albert might have a point. He nodded and let Albert lead him away. Tom, feigning drunkenness, was offering heartfelt apologies to the bruiser and had slipped him a couple of notes by way of apology. The three of them made their way quickly to the door and stepped out into the night.

Ten minutes later, they were sitting in the Nightingale, a quiet pub three streets away from the Pit. As soon as they'd entered the pub, Tom realised how close he'd come to being pulverised. He'd gone an interesting shade of green and had to sit down rather quickly. He was now working his way through his second whisky. Tansie had a full pint of beer in front of him that he hadn't touched, Albert the same.

'You wanna tell me what you were doing there?' Tansie asked.

'I might ask you the same question,' Albert said. 'Given that I suspect you weren't there to watch Bullet's impressive achievements. This is about the monkey, isn't it?'

Tansie narrowed his eyes and thrust out his chest in a show of belligerence. Then his shoulders dropped and he gave a large sigh before taking the first sip of his pint. 'It is about Monkey, yeah.'

'You think Blount's taken him?'

'Oh, I *know* Blount's taken him. When I got that first ransom note, it had Blount written all over it. I asked a few questions and I was right.'

'I don't get it,' Tom said, his voice already starting to slur with the whisky. 'Why would Blount steal your monkey?'

Tansie shook his head. 'Business matters. Least you know about it the better.'

'Except it's our business too,' Albert said. 'Tom's been trying to find the creature, and all along you've known something you aren't telling us. More to the point, Minnie's worried about you. And if Minnie isn't happy, nobody's happy.'

'She's worried about me?' Tansie said, his face softening.

'Of course she is,' Albert said. 'Now you'd better tell us what you know. If you carry on confronting Blount like you did tonight, you're going to end up in hospital. Or worse. And I don't want to face Minnie's wrath if anything happens to you, because she'll blame me, whether it was my fault or not.'

Tansie hesitated, clearly thinking about how much he should tell them. 'All right,' he said eventually, 'but you can't tell Min.'

'Why not?' Tom asked.

'Because I'm – I'm ashamed of what I was up to, all right? It seemed like a good idea at the time, but watching that tonight, with Bullet and them rats, I don't know how I could even have thought of it.'

'Thought of what?' Albert said. Getting this story out of Tansie was like pulling teeth.

Tansie took a long swig of his beer, wiped his moustache and leaned forward in his seat. 'You ever heard of Jacco Macacco?'

Albert and Tom shared a glance, both shaking their heads.

'Jacco Macacco,' Tansie said, 'was a bleedin' marvel. Fifty-odd years ago, he was the talk of the sporting world. Earned his owner a small fortune, he did.'

'Doing what?'

'Killing rats,' Tansie said, as if the answer was obvious.

'Jacco Macacco,' Tom said, slowly rolling his tongue over the words as if they held some special meaning. 'The rat-killing dog. What of it?'

'Ah,' Tansie said, a broad smile revealing the glint of a gold tooth, 'here's the thing. Jacco weren't a dog. He was a *monkey*.'

'Please don't say what I think you're about to say,' Albert said.

'Jacco was a walking goldmine,' Tansie said. 'I figured if I could get Monkey to do the same, I could make a tidy sum of money. Enough to get us out of the hole Minnie managed to dig for us. Maybe even enough to get Teddy bleedin' Linton and his three-fingered crony off our backs.'

'And how was that plan working out for you?' Albert said sarcastically. 'Before Monkey was kidnapped, I mean.'

Tansie winced. 'Not brilliantly, to be fair. Monkey has a natural talent for public urination and giving himself one off the wrist, but he didn't exactly have what you'd call the killer instinct. So that's when I came up with my ingenious plan.'

He stood up, reached into the inner pocket of his coat and laid a small claw hammer on the table. Clumsily carved into the handle was the owner's name: Kippy.

'You were training Monkey to kill rats with a *hammer*?' Tom said.

'I was,' Tansie said. 'There ain't nothing in the rules that says the animal can't use a tool.'

'That is bleedin' genius,' Tom said, downing the last of his drink and staring mournfully at the empty glass.

'Well, it's not that genius, is it?' Albert said. 'The creature's been taken now, presumably so that Blount can make money out of him the same way you were planning. How did he find out about it anyway?'

'One night in the Traveller's, I might have had one too many,' Tansie said. 'Got a little boastful about my plans.'

'And I thought you loved that creature, Tansie.'

Tansie's eyes filled with tears. 'I do, Albert. I really do love him. I thought I could train him so he'd be safe. He'd be the best little rat-killing monkey in town. And every night, after he'd earned me a packet, he'd come home with me, have a bit of pork pie, curl up in his little bed. But now he's gone. And Blount's taunting me, sending bits of fur and paws through the post. He won't give him back, no matter if I pay the ransom or not.'

'Then we'll have to get him back another way,' Tom said, pushing back his chair and nearly keeling over. 'But first: more whisky.'

FOURTEEN

Minnie pulled her scarf tighter and secured her bonnet more firmly on her head. It didn't seem possible, but the weather had turned even colder.

'Why'd you need me?' she asked Albert, raising her voice above the wind, which felt as if it could strip the skin off your face.

'Hugh Littleton left a widow, two daughters and a son. It's mainly women, Minnie. And you're better with women than I am.'

Minnie wasn't so sure that was true, but she'd take the compliment. 'And how exactly do we go about this? I mean, what do we say? Sorry Hugh lost all your money, killed himself and you're now living in poverty, but is there any chance one of you – possibly all of you – have taken a bloody revenge on Eddings and Fowler?'

'That wasn't precisely the line of questioning I had in mind,' Albert said, lowering his head against the wind. 'The Littletons have agreed to meet us, which was more than I expected, given the circumstances of Hugh's death. Think of this as an exploratory visit. A chance to see what kind of people they are.'

The house was a modest affair. Two-up two-down. But the windows were clean, the step immaculately scrubbed, and the street was filled with similar houses. People who didn't have much but were taking care of what little they had. Not a bad place to live, Minnie thought.

A pleasant-looking woman in her twenties opened the door.

No servants, although that was hardly surprising with two daughters and not a great deal of money to splash around. The woman introduced herself as Agnes, and led Albert and Minnie to the living room. Seated around the fire, as if preparing themselves for a family portrait, were Mrs Littleton and her other daughter Anne, with an empty chair filled by Agnes. The son, William, stood behind his mother's chair. Agnes and Anne were similar-looking, both dark-haired and modestly dressed. They resembled their mother, with large eyes and full lips.

William must take after his father, Minnie thought. He was in his early twenties, fair hair. Minnie recalled the description of the sweep at the Fowler and Eddings residences. It could be him. But then he would recognise Albert, surely, and that didn't appear to be the case. Unless he was a very good actor.

The living room was sparsely furnished but clean and neat. Hanging on the wall was a simple wooden crucifix and one of those pictures Minnie was convinced were the stuff of nightmares: Jesus with his heart on show and a miserable look on his face. On a table next to the window were piles of fabric, and Minnie guessed the women of the family were making a living taking in sewing. By the looks of it, they were nowhere near as skilled as Frances. They wouldn't be making a great deal from piecework.

Agnes poured them all tea.

'I'm very sorry to have to bring this up, but it's in connection with your husband's death,' Albert said, addressing Mrs Littleton.

Her two daughters shared an uncomfortable glance. William stiffened and laid a protective hand on his mother's shoulder. Mrs Littleton went to speak, but William got there first. 'What about Father's death?' he said. The hostility in his voice was unmistakeable but it failed to hide what sounded like nerves to Minnie, his voice pitched a little higher than felt right.

'We understand it was a consequence of the collapse of Capital Holdings,' Albert said.

'That's one way of putting it,' William said. 'I prefer to say Eddings and Fowler killed Father.' Again, the nerves, Minnie thought.

'Now, son,' his mother intervened, dabbing nervously at her lips with a handkerchief, but speaking with a degree of firmness that belied her actions. 'We've discussed this. What's done is done. Mr Easterbrook and Miss Ward have questions, and we will answer them as best we can.'

Albert nodded his thanks. 'You may not be aware that Mr Eddings and Mr Fowler have both died recently.'

'We read of Mr Eddings's passing in the newspaper,' Mrs Littleton said. 'I was unaware Mr Fowler had also passed, God rest his soul.' Almost imperceptibly, her hand moved across her chest and Minnie assumed she was making the sign of the cross.

'Good riddance,' William murmured, glancing shiftily at his mother as he did so, like a child pushing his luck and anticipating a clout from his parent.

'William, I won't have talk like that in this house. Two men have died and, no matter our personal feelings towards them, they have left loved ones behind. And we all know what it is to grieve.'

William bit his lower lip and said nothing.

'Mrs Littleton,' Albert continued, and Minnie could sense the tension in him. This wasn't going to be easy. 'Mr Eddings and Mr Fowler both died in somewhat suspicious circumstances. Mr Eddings's death at first glance appeared to be a terrible accident. Mr Fowler appeared to have taken his own life.'

Agnes and Anne flinched noticeably at this mention of suicide. Their father had hanged himself, and Minnie wondered who had been the one to find him.

'Appeared?' Mrs Littleton asked. 'You're saying that's not how they died?'

'We think not,' Minnie said. 'We can't go into the details, I'm afraid, but it looks like both men may have been murdered.'

Quiet fell on the room. Agnes refilled their cups.

'If you don't mind my saying so, none of you seem very surprised at that idea,' Minnie said tentatively.

'Why would we be?' Anne said. 'A number of people were ruined by Eddings and Fowler. We suspect more than one person took their own life. Our father left a note, so there could be no mistaking it, but there may well have been others. My mother will not like to hear me say this, Miss Ward, but I find it no surprise someone harboured murderous intentions towards Eddings and Fowler.'

'Nor I,' Agnes said.

Mrs Littleton turned away, dabbing at her mouth again with the handkerchief. It was a strange affectation, Minnie thought. It made the woman look hesitant, unsure of herself. But Minnie was starting to suspect she was anything but.

'We were raised to believe in Christian forgiveness,' Anne said. 'To turn the other cheek. But the actions of those two men is beyond the limits of my forgiveness. They were neither inept nor unlucky. They set out deliberately to defraud people of their money. If somebody killed them, I say good luck to them.'

'And you?' Albert said, turning towards William. 'Do you share your sisters' feelings?'

William gave a pained smile and glanced again at his mother before speaking. 'If I'd known where to find the pair of them, I'd have done it myself.'

Minnie had limited experience of criminal investigations, but she guessed the guilty party rarely admitted to their crimes or their intentions this readily. She looked questioningly at Albert.

'I understand your feelings, truly I do,' he said. 'And I'm reluctant to ask you this question, given all you've gone through, but I do need to establish where you all were when Mr Eddings and Mr Fowler died.'

'You're not a police officer, are you, Mr Easterbrook?' Mrs Littleton said.

'No. Miss Ward and I are private detectives.'

'Well, if someone wants to know where we were when those two men died, they can send a police officer round here and do it properly. My family have been perfectly civil to you. We've welcomed you into our home and answered your questions. But if you are suggesting we might have had something to do with two murders, you clearly don't understand the kind of people we are. So unless you've got some authority to be here, asking us questions like this, I suggest you leave.'

There it was. The hard core of steel running beneath the gentle, unassuming surface.

Minnie went to say something, but the set of Mrs Littleton's jaw told her it was pointless. She and Albert made their apologies and left.

'Well, that went well,' she said, when they were safely out of earshot of the Littletons' house.

'I've seen worse,' Albert said. 'No raised voices. No punches. A reasonably successful interview, I'd say.'

'In what way? All we did was upset four perfectly nice people.'

'Oh, we did a bit more than that. The lad, William, was hiding something. Something he didn't want his family to know about.'

'I thought that, too. He was edgy, weren't he? Like he weren't sure how much he should say?'

'Or how much his mother would allow him to say. A formidable woman, despite the apparent docility.'

'If he is hiding something, it could be anything, surely?'

'Indeed. It doesn't necessarily tie him in to Eddings's and Fowler's deaths. I'll have to see if John can pay them a visit. Extract their alibis from them.'

'If Eddings and Fowler were murdered, and if it was connected to the collapse of Capital Holdings, there could be any number of suspects. It could be someone who lost money, or a loved one of someone who did. It don't have to have been suicide to trigger the killings.'

'No,' Albert sighed, wrapping his scarf tighter around his neck against the chilly wind. 'But until I get a full list of everyone who lost money, the Littleton family are the best place to start.'

The second showing at the Palace had finally ended, and everyone had disappeared into the night. Sometime after midnight, closer to one o'clock than she would have liked, Minnie mounted the stairs to Frances's lodgings. She opened the door as quietly as possible, unlacing her boots before she entered the rooms. To her surprise, Frances was still up, sitting close to an oil lamp and finishing a piece of smocking.

She looked up at Minnie's entrance. 'You look done in. Fancy a drink?' She crossed to a small cupboard and took out a bottle of gin and two glasses, holding them up expectantly.

'I could murder one,' Minnie said. 'I've had Tansie in one ear, trying to get that water tank included in an act, and Kippy in the other ear telling me it ain't safe. I can't think of anyone less suited to a career as a plate spinner than Carlotta, and the Mexican Boneless Wonder's been hitting the brown again. Strangely, though, his act always goes better when he's buffy.'

'Maybe it loosens his joints.'

'Maybe. And then, to top it all, I get a message at the end of the night that Tom, Albert's partner in crime, wants to see me and can I not mention it to Albert. I love Tom, but I've really had enough of secrets.'

'And there was me thinking *you* were Albert's partner in crime,' Frances said, pouring two glasses almost to the brim. 'Sit yourself down and get your feet up,' she said, gesturing to an armchair with a crocheted blanket slung across it, before crossing to the fireplace and adding some more coal.

'Oh, someone delivered this for you earlier,' Frances said, handing Minnie a small brown envelope. 'Odd fella. Smelt funny.'

Minnie's stomach lurched at Frances's words. 'What kind of funny?'

'A bit sickly, like the smell of a sweet shop.'

'Three fingers on his left hand?'

Frances's hand flew to her mouth. 'Christ, it weren't the fella who came to the Palace, was it?'

Minnie nodded. She looked down at the envelope. Her name and her address with Frances clearly printed. So he was still following her. Knew where she'd moved to.

'Ain't you gonna open it?' Frances asked.

Minnie briefly closed her eyes, letting the day's exhaustion flood her body. 'No need,' she said. 'It'll be a message from Linton or one of his cronies. *Requesting* the pleasure of my company at Broadmoor, and by "requesting" you can read "demanding".'

She slumped into the chair and Frances handed her a large glass of gin. It burned as it went down her throat, but almost instantly she felt more relaxed than she had done in days. Maybe the Mexican Boneless Wonder had the right idea.

'Jack was in tonight,' Minnie said, as Frances topped up her glass. 'Kippy wants me to take him on permanently. He's a nice lad.'

'He is,' Frances said, a touch dismissively.

'He likes you.'

'He does. But not in the way you're thinking.'

'How'd you mean?'

'I've made it clear enough that I'm interested, but he never takes the bait.'

'He's shy, Frances. He might need it spelling out for him.'

'Oh, I've spelled it out for him. In six-foot-high letters. I just ain't his type, I reckon. He sees me as his chum and nothing more. And maybe it's for the best. I mean, he's lovely to look at, but sometimes he seems like a little kid. He's only a few years older than me, but there's something about him – it's like, when he first started working at the Palace, when I first met him, he was always filthy. His hands in particular. Like a little kid who needs his ma nagging at him to wash his hands. Not like a man – a nice clean man.' She paused for a moment, clearly thinking about nice clean men. 'Problem is, I like him. We get on, y'know, and you can't say that about all fellas. Got any suggestions as to how I might change his mind?'

Minnie laughed. 'No good coming to me for advice on fellas. I'm a walking disaster when it comes to men.'

Frances narrowed her eyes and gave Minnie a long look. 'Why's that, then?' she said eventually. 'You're a lovely-looking girl. Smart as a whip. You should have them queueing up.'

'It ain't that,' Minnie said, staring into the bottom of her glass and realising she felt quite tipsy all of a sudden. She couldn't remember when she'd last eaten, which might have something to do with it. 'It ain't that,' she repeated. 'It's me. I don't want a fella disrupting my life. Breezing in, messing everything up and then breezing out again.'

'I can't see Albert doing that,' Frances ventured. 'I mean, that is who we're talking about, ain't it?'

'You're right. Albert ain't like that. It's just—' She paused, looking round the room. 'Look at all this, Frances. You've made a lovely home here. All your nice bits and pieces.' She fingered the crochet blanket and nodded at the embroidered cushions and footstool. 'You've got a good business going, making your own money. But that didn't come overnight, did it?'

Frances gave a half-smile. 'It certainly didn't.'

'Exactly. And neither did the life I have. I don't wanna fall for someone and then something goes wrong and they ain't around any more. It's easier to stay away from all that.'

'Bit lonely, ain't it? And what about kids?'

Minnie shook her head abruptly. 'That ain't on the cards. I don't talk about it, so don't ask me, but kids ain't gonna be in my future. So, that being the case, I don't need a fella, do I?'

'They're nice to cuddle up to on a cold night, though,' Frances said, clumsily refilling their glasses and slopping gin onto Minnie's dress. Minnie waved aside her apologies and wiped down her skirts. If it left a stain, it would match the one she'd spotted the other day when she was feeling decidedly dowdy next to Dorothy Lawrence. 'You couldn't make me a dress, could you, Frances? I'd pay you, of course. Proper rates, not what you charge the Palace.'

'What you looking for?'

'Something less—'

'—shabby?'

'Well, that weren't exactly the word I was hunting for. But, yeah, less shabby. Something to maybe catch the eye.'

'I've got just the thing,' Frances said, crossing the room to one of her fabric piles and withdrawing a length of navy fabric covered in tiny sprigs of flowers. 'Got it yesterday. Lovely weight. It'll sew up beautifully, and the blue'll bring out the colour of your eyes.'

Minnie squinted, imagined Dorothy in a dress of the same fabric. 'That'll do it,' she said.

Frances moved unsteadily back to her seat. She had a limp, which Minnie forgot about most of the time, but it was more noticeable tonight, and Frances rubbed her leg as she sat down.

'How'd that happen?' Minnie asked, nodding at Frances's hip. 'Oh, crikey, that's really rude. Forget I said it. It must be the gin talking.'

Frances smiled. 'I don't mind. I broke my leg when I was a nipper. Proper tomboy I was and I jumped off a wall.'

'They didn't set it right?'

'Oh, they did. But not long after I was in another accident. My leg got a bit crushed, and it was never the same since.'

'Blimey, that's bad luck. What happened with the accident?'
Frances looked away.

'I've done it again, ain't I?' Minnie said. 'Me and my big mouth.'

Frances waved her hand dismissively. 'It ain't you, Min. The accident, it was awful. I try not to think about it. It's a bit like you and kids,' she said, giving a gentle smile. 'It's something I don't talk about.'

'Then I propose a toast,' Minnie said, clinking her glass against Frances's and managing to spill even more gin. 'Here's to the things we don't talk about.'

FIFTEEN

Albert could have navigated the route in his sleep. Sometimes, in dreams, he did just that, crossing Piccadilly, past the shops on Regent Street, then onto Portland Place and left onto Devonshire Street. His mother would be waiting for him, flinging the door open wide and folding him into a warm embrace.

Which just goes to show how ridiculous dreams are, Albert thought. He couldn't remember his mother ever hugging him, not even when he was a child and had scuffed his knee or had a fight with another boy. All the affection had been left to Mrs Byrne to administer, as his nanny. Or Hetty Paul, the scullery maid whose murder had shaped Albert's future.

The house looked no different. Double-fronted, set back from the road behind iron railings. A rowan tree in the front garden, now retaining only the last few of its leaves and with almost all the scarlet berries pilfered. Thrushes, Albert thought. His mind was full of these nuggets of information: thrushes eat rowan berries; fighting dogs have their ears clipped so there's less for their opponent to grab hold of. He assumed he had read about these things – he was a prodigious reader, would read a bus ticket if nothing else was available – but he was always surprised when a tiny scrap of knowledge swam to the surface, something he hadn't even known he knew.

He stood on the front step and took in the highly polished door furniture, blinds pulled down in all the windows facing the road. He noted the crape tied round the front door, which would have earned Mrs Byrne's approval. It was a house that brooked no interference. A house that kept its secrets.

When Albert had received the note from his father, requesting a meeting, he had been filled with a sudden optimism he knew was pointless and likely only to cause him unhappiness. His father had made his feelings known long ago, but there was still a small part of Albert that was hopeful of a reconciliation. Why else would his father want to speak to him now? In the intervening days, Albert had entertained notions of his father, marked by grief and the loss of his wife, realising how important family was to him, and how much he needed his son in his life.

The maid who answered the door was unfamiliar to Albert. But then, it had been years since he'd last visited his parents, so why would he imagine the staff had stayed the same. She was young, and reminded him of a field mouse he'd found once. Dark eyes, permanently nervous. She seemed surprised when he gave his name, and he wondered if she even knew her master had a son, or had his father removed all traces of Albert from his life? It wouldn't surprise him.

Taking his coat and hat, she showed him into the drawing room at the front of the house. It faced north, and got no sun all day. It was cold, with a half-hearted fire alight in the grate that was badly in need of more coal. The maid followed his gaze to the fireplace.

'I can ask——' she offered, a tremor in her voice, presumably at the thought of requesting more coal from Albert's father.

'It's fine,' Albert said, forcing a half-smile. 'I doubt I'll be here long.'

She scurried out of the room, and Albert took in his surroundings. Nothing had changed. The walls were still hung with the same pictures, chosen out of convention rather than because they satisfied any aesthetic sense on the part of his parents. The furniture – the two leather chesterfield sofas and accompanying armchairs, the mahogany bureau inlaid with walnut panelling, the occasional tables – were all items the Easterbrooks had inherited over the years and never seen fit to change. He remembered, as a child, sharing the confidence with his mother that his favourite colour was blue, and asking her what her favourite colour was. She had looked confused and then said, in an admonitory tone, 'I have no favourites, Albert. Why on earth would I?'

Someone cleared their throat behind him, and he turned. For the first time in more than ten years he was alone with his father.

The passage of time had not been kind to Godfrey Easterbrook. He had not gained any weight as he aged, and this had given him the appearance of something withered and desiccated. It would suit him to put on a few pounds, Albert thought. As it was, he now resembled nothing so much as a hawk, with his beaked nose and prominent dark eyes. His clothing, as always, was conventional and extremely expensive. It was like camouflage, Albert thought. It enabled him to fit in, disappear into the ranks he hadn't been born into.

Godfrey gestured towards a chair, then sat opposite. Albert waited for his father to speak, and then wondered if he ever would, the quiet punctuated by the ponderous ticking of the grandfather clock in the corner of the room. Eventually, his father cleared his throat again.

'Thank you for coming, Albert,' he said, his voice a little hoarse as if he hadn't spoken in some time.

He'd forgotten this about his father's manner of speaking; as if he were reading from a script and permanently afraid he'd forget his lines. When he was very young, Albert had received elocution lessons to remove any trace of Bermondsey from his accent. His parents must have done the same, because to hear them speak you'd never have guessed their humble origins. But sometimes, when he was tired or particularly stressed, those London streets would sneak back into his father's voice.

'It was your mother's dying wish that we discuss this matter face to face,' Godfrey continued.

And that's the only reason you're speaking to me, Albert thought. 'Are you well, Father?' he asked.

Godfrey gave a dismissive shake of his head, as if Albert's question were fanciful in the extreme. His father had always enjoyed robust good health, and felt that sickness in others was a sign of moral weakness. He must have found it very difficult to deal with his wife's illness. He didn't even offer a reply to Albert's question, instead charging on as if afraid his memory would fail him before he reached the end of his lines.

'Your mother was left a substantial inheritance when her brother died, two years ago.'

Albert remembered his sister, Adelaide, informing him of his Uncle Paul's death. He also remembered not being invited to the funeral.

Godfrey ploughed on. 'Her brother's legacy left your mother independently wealthy, but she never touched the money. There was never any need for her to do so.' He paused, as if waiting for Albert to congratulate him on how well he'd provided for his family all these years. Money isn't everything, Albert thought and sat out the silence until his father started speaking again. 'Your mother left you some money in her will. Not an insubstantial sum.' He rose, went to the mahogany bureau and withdrew a single sheet of paper from one of the drawers before handing it to Albert. Albert looked at the figures. His father was right. It was a substantial amount of money. Life-changing.

Albert laid the sheet of paper on the small side table. 'It's extremely generous,' he said, 'but I don't feel comfortable taking it. Could it not go to Adelaide?' Money like that would enable Adelaide to leave her unhappy marriage, or afford her a degree of independence at least, so she wouldn't have to go cap in hand to her loathsome husband, Monty, every time she wanted to buy a new dress.

Godfrey nodded slowly. 'Your mother anticipated your sentiments. She was very clear in her will that the money was to go to you and you alone. What you choose to do with it is entirely at your discretion. Although—' For the first time since Albert had arrived, his father seemed uncertain of his lines.

'Although?' Albert prompted.

Godfrey rose from his seat. For a moment, Albert thought he was going to ring for tea, but then he realised this would only prolong the visit, and his father was visibly uncomfortable being in the same room as him. Godfrey crossed to the window at the front of the house. The blinds were down, so he had moved purely to avoid the risk of eye contact. With his back to Albert, he continued speaking. 'Your mother's inheritance, wisely invested, would offer you a comfortable existence. One which would remove the necessity of employment.'

Albert smiled grimly to himself. So this was what it was all about. Both his parents had been horrified by his decision to become a police officer. He still remembered the arguments in vivid detail. How they hadn't worked so hard all these years for him to turn his back on a life of wealth and privilege; how he'd be shaming the family by embarking on a career as a common thief-taker. They had disowned him, and if he had believed the passage of years would soften their resolve, he had been wrong. His decision to leave the police force and become a private detective was simply further cause for embarrassment and shame as far as they were concerned. They had never understood that his desire to solve crime was not motivated by money but by a need to do some good in the world. To stem the tide of fear and horror that threatened to engulf him at times, and that had started all those years ago when, aged eight, he had learned of the murder of his beloved friend, Hetty, the scullery maid, and watched as the police had failed to catch the killer. And his parents had failed to care.

'I don't work for the money,' Albert said patiently. This was a conversation whose paths were well trodden. They had had the same discussion multiple times when Albert first announced his plans, the same well-worn phrases and arguments, the same outcome of pursed lips and turned shoulders.

'So you've told me. Many times,' Godfrey said. 'Your mother and I were both well acquainted with your altruism. But you have done some good. Earned yourself a degree of notoriety and success. I simply thought—'

'—that I'd be done with it all now?' Albert interrupted. 'That helping to catch Teddy Linton would be "enough"?'

Godfrey turned back to face Albert and shrugged. 'As I understand it, that was largely due to the efforts of what the newspapers termed your "female accomplice". A certain Miss Ward? The newspapers enjoyed themselves greatly with their descriptions of her. She sounds quite a character,' he said, his voice dripping with sarcasm.

'I'm surprised you deigned to read such things, Father. But, yes, I would say it was almost entirely due to Miss Ward that we managed to catch that particular killer. But there are other killers. Other crimes.'

'And other police officers. Other detectives. You've played your part, Albert. You can retire with a clear conscience. Live a comfortable life. Hopefully marry and have children. I would like grandchildren, and Adelaide seems to have failed in that area.'

Albert wondered what his father would say if he were to tell him that the only person he wanted to marry was his female accomplice. And children were not on the cards for Minnie. But that was a conversation he couldn't ever imagine having.

'I'm not retiring,' Albert said, 'despite this inheritance. And I know you will never be happy with that, but I had hoped

– foolishly, as it turns out – that your inviting me here today might be the start of some sort of reconciliation between us. I'm willing to try.' He held out his hand to his father.

Godfrey looked at the offered hand and then raised his eyes. His face was shadowed by a look of genuine sorrow and, for a moment, Albert thought he was going to take his hand. Then Godfrey's face hardened, as if the man had willed himself to banish any softer feelings towards his son. He crossed to the fireplace and rang the bell for the housemaid.

'My solicitor will be in contact with you to arrange payment,' Godfrey said, each word clipped and precise. He was back on script.

The housemaid entered with Albert's hat and coat. Albert knew as he left the room that he might never see his father again. It seemed like a moment weighted with such significance it should be marked in some way. With noble words, or a means of leaving the door open between them. But his father was already sifting through some other papers, and Albert turned and left the house without another word. As he passed the rowan tree, the breeze caught it and the last of its leaves fluttered to the ground.

SIXTEEN

Minnie brushed down her black dress and rummaged in the top of the wardrobe for her black bonnet. She stood in front of the mirror to position it and wondered how many more times in her life she'd be dressing for a funeral. At least this time it wasn't a close friend; she didn't feel as if someone had ripped out her heart. Freddy Graham had been a miserable old bastard much of the time, but he'd been kind to her when she was starting out. She wanted to say her goodbyes.

Frances was sitting by the window, finishing off some silk-covered buttons in a vivid purple colour she'd told Minnie was called aniline violet. The colour was so intense, it almost hurt to look at it. Frances lifted her head and appraised Minnie's outfit. 'Maybe I should make you a mourning dress after I've finished that navy cotton,' she said. 'That one's seen better days.'

'I've worn it too often,' Minnie said. 'And much as I appreciate the offer, I'm hoping I won't need to wear mourning again for many years.' She nodded at the buttons. 'That ain't for the Palace, is it?'

'No one at the Palace could afford this. Special order for Lady Beaufort.' She nodded towards the dressmaker's dummy in the corner of the room, where the rest of the dress stood waiting, a vivid confection of peplums, ribbons and bows. Even the sleeves were elaborate, punctuated with little eyelets, white silk peeping through each one.

The two women stood for a minute, appreciating the beauty and unattainability of the dress.

'Right,' Minnie said eventually, 'you done?'

Frances nodded. She swept a few random violet threads off her mourning dress and grabbed her coat and bonnet. 'You don't think it'll be a bit odd, my being at the funeral?' she asked. 'I mean, I ain't seen Freddy in years. Not since I was a kid, really.'

'Nothing wrong with paying your respects, Frances. Besides, it's a theatre funeral. There'll be all sorts there, and at the wake. Speaking of which, I was hoping to be out of there by about four. We could grab a cuppa at Brown's if you fancy?'

'No gin?' Frances said, disingenuously.

'Not after the head I had the other morning. I'm off gin for the foreseeable.'

The funeral went as well as these things ever do. There'd been a good turnout for Freddy, which had been pleasing. Now they were all crammed into the back bar at the Rising Sun and Minnie was reminded, not for the first time, of how small and intimate the theatre world was. Kippy was there, Jack too. Bernard had sent his apologies but just couldn't face a funeral so soon after the loss of Peter. Tansie looked as if he might be settling in for the rest of the day, nursing what she reckoned was his third pint and telling dirty jokes to a handful of his mates. Minnie looked at her watch and calculated how soon she could slip away. Not yet, unfortunately. She looked up and saw Jack waving at her across the crowded room. He mimed raising a glass to his lips with a questioning look. She mouthed back 'beer'. They must have got on extra staff behind the bar; people were getting served very quickly and within a few minutes Jack was by her side with her drink.

'You seen Frances?' he asked, having to shout above the raised voices and laughter. Nothing like a wake to bring out people's more raucous behaviour.

'She's here somewhere.' Minnie scanned the crowd, but there was no sign.

Jack frowned. Frances might be convinced he wasn't interested in her romantically, but he always made a beeline for her nonetheless.

'If I see her, I'll tell her you're looking for her,' Minnie offered. Jack's mood visibly lifted at her words. Frances had it wrong; the lad was interested, he just needed a nudge.

They stood uncomfortably for a few minutes, Jack looking down at his shoes and then glancing desperately round the room. They'd never spoken to each other outside the Palace; at work, their conversations usually consisted of her giving him instructions and him following them. Funerals and weddings, she thought. Throwing people together who aren't really friends.

She leaned in to make herself heard. 'I've just seen someone I know over there,' she lied, pointing to a far corner of the room. 'Mind if I go and have a word? And here' – she pressed some money into his hand – 'get yourself another drink.'

He gave her a relieved smile and navigated his way back to the bar. As if by magic, Tansie appeared at her side.

'Good turnout, Min,' he said, his words already slurring a little. 'D'you reckon I'll have this many? When I chuck up the old bunch o' fives?'

'Christ, we're not starting this again, are we?' Minnie said.

She was interrupted by a commotion near the bar. It was a bit early for the fights to be starting, but you never knew with a funeral. People did funny things.

A tall, thickset man suddenly cried out and fell to his knees. Minnie turned away, not interested in watching someone make a fool of themselves over drink. But there was a subtle shift around her, and Minnie turned back. Something about the man's movements told Minnie he wasn't drunk. The crowd seemed to have picked up on the same thing, as people moved back a step or two, leaving a space around him. The barman was wiping his hands on a towel, and just lifting the hatch to come round from the bar when the tall man's body locked into a hideous spasm.

'Fits,' someone murmured behind her, but Minnie wasn't so sure. This didn't look right.

'That's Lennie Thomas,' Tansie said. 'Illustrator for the newspapers.'

Someone ran past her out of the door and she heard a voice shouting for help out on the street. Inside the air grew still and heavy as all eyes were turned on Lennie. The pub, which had been so full of life just a few moments ago, was now deadly quiet, as if they were all watching a show and waiting for the finale.

Somebody knelt down to try to help Lennie, and then pulled away, as if unsure of what to do. Outside, someone was still calling for help, a doctor. Frances appeared in the crowd, her mouth open, eyes wide with alarm. Jack was beside her, frowning. Was no one gonna do anything? But what could they do? This was like nothing Minnie had ever seen.

Lennie lay on the floor, his body arching backwards with each fresh wave of – what was it? Pain? Fits? Had he eaten something? Drunk something? His body was bending backwards in a way Minnie didn't think was possible. He looked as if his feet and head were almost touching. Across from Minnie, a woman had covered her eyes and was hiding her face in some fella's chest. Beside her, another woman was sobbing, staring at the man on the floor as if unable to turn away.

And then, somewhere away to Minnie's left, she heard someone murmur a single word.

Strychnine.

She tried to take a step forward, but Tansie held her arm and shook his head. What could she do anyway? Lennie's eyes were huge in his head, darting round the room for help, but she wondered if he even knew where he was any more. One arm was stretched full out, the other reaching for his throat, grabbing at his collar. Somewhere in the crowd, a woman screamed and was silenced.

Then a light seemed to go out in his eyes. An audible sigh passed round the room, as if everyone had been holding their breath and now they could let go. Too late, an elderly gent came banging through the pub doors, doctor's bag in hand. Somewhere near the bar, a glass got knocked over and smashed on the floor.

The doctor started to check Lennie's pulse, loosened his collar. Minnie watched him closely and then it was as if she suddenly realised what she had just witnessed. Tiny dots danced in front of her eyes as a wave of nausea swept up from her stomach. The sounds around her receded into the distance. She was so hot. Why was she so hot? She reached out to grab hold of something, anything, to stop herself fainting. A firm hand slid round her waist and caught her in time, guiding her to a chair.

'Lower your head, Minnie,' a voice said. 'Put your head right down between your knees. Deep breaths,' the voice said. It was Jack.

She did as he told her, and slowly the light-headedness passed. She lifted her head, her eyes smarting with tears. Tansie and Jack led her slowly out of the pub and into the sunlight. She looked at her watch. Four o'clock. She'd been right. It was all over by four o'clock.

'And he *died*?' Bernard said for what felt to Minnie like the hundredth time since Tansie and Jack had recounted the story to him. 'Just like that? In the middle of a wake for someone else? The man *died*?'

Tansie nodded his head wearily and leaned back in his chair.

They were all seated in the empty auditorium at the Palace. The brandy bottle had made the rounds more than once, the story retold in gruesome detail, and Minnie just wanted everyone to stop talking. But they wouldn't. Couldn't, maybe. She understood it, the desire to relive the scene, to make sense of it with the retelling.

'The gentleman who died,' Bernard said, 'you're sure it was Lennie Thomas? Used to do the illustrations for *The Graphic* and the *Illustrated London News*?'

'That's the one,' Tansie said. 'I recognised him straight away. He had that funny laugh, remember? It was definitely him.'

Bernard fell silent, staring into the darkness of the auditorium. Despite her desire for everyone to just shut up, Minnie felt something was wrong. 'What is it, Bernard? Something bothering you?'

'Probably nothing, dearest one. Just those names together – Freddy Graham and Lennie Thomas. It stirred a memory, that's all.'

A door banged in the backstage area. Footsteps echoed down the corridor towards Minnie's office, stopped, and then came towards the auditorium. Minnie recognised the tread, and she looked up with relief to see Albert.

He took one look at the group and frowned. 'What's wrong?' he asked.

Tansie filled him in on the afternoon's astonishing events. When he reached the point where Lennie Thomas passed away, Frances whimpered and Jack slid an arm round her shoulders. She didn't push him off.

'And they think it was strychnine?' Albert asked.

'That's what people were saying,' Minnie said. 'The doctor who arrived seemed to think the same. I heard him saying as much to the police.'

'God, what an awful thing to see,' Albert said, and a stillness descended on the group as each of them who had witnessed the death relived it.

'Please tell me you're here with some good news,' Minnie said after a moment, with a weak smile.

'Not particularly,' Albert said. 'John checked out the alibis for the Littleton family. They all hold up. It turns out William Littleton has been seeing a girl his mother wouldn't approve of.'

'Girlfriend not a dolly worshipper?' Minnie guessed.

'Indeed. So that's all he was hiding. It couldn't have been one of them who killed Eddings or Fowler.'

Bernard's head shot up. 'Eddings and Fowler?' he said.

Albert nodded. 'Two deaths I'm working on that look like they might be connected. Judge David Eddings and William Fowler. Why do you ask?'

All the colour seemed to drain from Bernard's face. 'Judge Eddings. William Fowler. Freddy Graham. Lennie Thomas,' he murmured to himself. 'And Peter. Dear Peter.'

'What is it, Bernard?' Minnie asked.

Bernard's eyes were darting round the room, as if he were trying to make sense of a difficult puzzle. Then his gaze locked on Frances. Her eyes, wide with horror, were staring into the distance.

'Frances?' Bernard said.

She turned to him.

'Do you know?' he said. 'Were you there?'

'Would one of you pair tell us what the chuffing hell is going on?' Tansie said. 'Or are you gonna spend the rest of the day just staring at each other?'

'It's the Trafalgar Theatre,' Bernard said quietly, his voice so low they had to crane forward to catch his words.

'What Trafalgar Theatre?' Minnie asked. She looked at Albert, but he seemed just as confused. 'And what's it got to do with what happened today?'

'You must have heard of it, Min,' Tansie said. 'Although – maybe not. It was, what, twelve years ago?'

'Fourteen,' Frances said, her voice flat and dull. 'December 1863.'

A glimmer of some distant memory stirred at the edges of Minnie's mind. 'Was this that awful thing where those children died?'

Frances nodded slowly, her mind clearly elsewhere. 'There were nearly two hundred killed.'

'One hundred and eighty-three,' Jack said quietly. Everyone turned towards him.

'Were you there?' Minnie asked.

He dropped his eyes, blushing at the attention, and slowly nodded his head.

'And those children, they were—' Minnie said.

'—suffocated,' Frances said. 'All of them, crushed to death at a children's show at the Trafalgar Theatre.'

'You were there too?' Minnie said quietly, instinctively reaching for Frances's hand. Frances nodded and Jack pulled her closer. She let herself be held, like a rag doll.

'It's the thing I don't talk about,' Frances said to Minnie. 'How I damaged my leg.'

'But you and Jack—'

'We didn't know each other at the time,' Jack said, 'but we were both there that day.'

'I still don't understand,' Albert said. 'What's the Trafalgar Theatre got to do with what happened today, and the cases I'm investigating?'

'Judge Eddings oversaw the inquest,' Bernard said. 'William Fowler wrote about the tragedy and the aftermath. Freddy Graham was the stage manager. Lennie Thomas worked for the *Illustrated London News*. It was front-page news for weeks. He did all the illustrations.'

'So he drew a few pictures, what's that gotta do with it all?' Minnie asked.

'It caused quite a stink at the time because some of the parents felt he'd portrayed the children in a very negative light,' Tansie said. 'Made them look like little animals. As if they'd caused their own deaths. It was made worse, of course, because the inquest concluded no one was to blame. All innocent.'

'And Peter?' Albert prompted. 'You mentioned your brother as well.'

'He was on stage when it all happened,' Bernard said. 'He saw the whole thing unfold before him. He could do nothing about it.' Bernard spoke falteringly, his eyes locked on some point in the distance.

'So,' Minnie said slowly, her brain racing to make sense of what she was hearing, 'these five fellas. Are we saying they were all murdered? And by the same person?' Even as she said the words, they sounded far-fetched.

'I don't know about that,' Tansie said, 'but it's a bit of a coincidence, ain't it? We know Peter was murdered and, Albert, you're saying there's something suspicious about Eddings's and Fowler's deaths. Thomas was poisoned this afternoon, I'm guessing.'

'And Freddy Graham?' Albert asked. 'How did he die?'

'Heart attack,' Tansie said. 'He'd had a dicky heart for years and it finally gave out on him.'

'Or maybe it was made to look like a heart attack,' Minnie said.

'So – what are we saying? Someone's taking revenge? Working his way through everyone who was somehow involved in the disaster?' Albert said.

'If that's the case, there's something else you need to know,' Bernard said.

They all turned towards him expectantly.

'Peter wasn't alone on stage that afternoon. I was there too.'

SEVENTEEN

The attendant at the Public Records Office was gone for some time, finally reappearing with a folder of documents. The fine layer of dust told Albert nobody had looked at it in a long time, and he could understand why. The inquest into the Trafalgar Theatre disaster made depressing reading. There was a lengthy preamble about the legal problems of one coroner speaking in the jurisdiction of another, which Albert had no interest in. And then the different testimonies, laden with poignancy or tragedy in the light of what happened.

He read of the small yellow tickets that had been handed out to schools, tickets which would admit any number of children for a penny each. Each ticket stated that presents were to be given out at the end of the performance, one for every child. Teachers were given free passes. The headmaster of a local school said he had been sent tickets like this for children's shows for years.

'In distributing the tickets were you in communication with the parents?' he was asked.

'Not at all,' was his reply.

'You made no enquiries as to the conditions of the entertainment?'

'None. I simply gave out the tickets.'

'And when you gave the free passes to the teachers, did you expect them to take charge of the children?'

'No. There was no expectation the teachers would be in charge of the children. The show was on a Saturday afternoon, outside of school hours.'

Bernard and his brother gave testimony. They had appeared that day as the Jollity Brothers, part of a touring theatre company headed by a Clive Williams. They were asked about the gifts they distributed at the show's finale, and admitted they had given no thought as to how those gifts would be shared fairly among the children. They had assumed the management of the theatre would see to it, or Williams. The management of the theatre had assumed Williams, or Bernard and his brother would take responsibility.

An architect, asked to consider whether the theatre was perfectly safe, replied that it was rather hard to say. 'Prior to the accident, I should not have seen any danger.'

And within all the testimony an endless stream of numbers. Meaningless, except for the enormous significance they acquired in the light of what happened. Twenty-three steps from the gallery down to the first landing, which was fourteen feet ten inches by seven feet six inches. Then another fifteen steps to the dress-circle landing, twenty-eight feet long.

But the only detail that really seemed to matter was twenty-two inches. A door that led from the stairs into the ground floor had been bolted part-closed to slow down the flow of ticket holders entering the auditorium. Once all the children were inside, the door had remained bolted. A gap of twenty-two inches. Just wide enough to let one person through at a time. A child with a broken arm said he had seen a man put his foot on the bolt to ram it home. When he was asked if the man was fair or dark, the child wasn't sure. Dark, he thought. Another child swore the man was fair.

Albert wasn't surprised to see Jack's name as a witness. What did surprise him was that Jack was not a member of the audience. He had worked at the Trafalgar. Ten years old, and a runner, just like the lads Tansie employed. He'd been backstage. The first he'd known of events was when he heard the screams. He'd played no part in any of it. But still, he could be the killer's next target.

The children's testimonies were the worst. The nine-year-old boy who saw a man with black curly hair rake the muck out of the hole with an old stick, and then push the bolt down with his hand. The little girl who got a ticket from her teacher and a penny from her aunt. The lad who escaped by creeping through a bigger boy's legs. When he got outside, he told a man on the door that he had better get help or people were going to die.

All of it made painful reading, but Albert was particularly moved by the testimony of Inez Shepherd, eight years old. She had got buried under a heap of bodies, somehow finding enough air to breathe. Her little brother had lain beside her, dead. She told the court of her nightmares, how her brother visited her in her sleep, only now he wasn't dead but asking for her help, always remaining just out of reach.

The jury concluded that one hundred and eighty-three children met their death by suffocation on the stairs leading from the gallery, caused by the partial closing of a door fixed in position by a bolt in the floor. There was insufficient evidence to determine who had secured the bolt. The manager of the theatre was to be censured for not preserving order in the hall. Censured, Albert thought. Not the same as punished. The jury recommended that children ought not to be encouraged to attend entertainments or excursions except under proper supervision or control. As if it were the children's fault. Or their parents'. The jury called for legislation to improve the safety of places of entertainment. No one was to blame. Effectively, they were all found innocent.

In among the witness testimonies was a list of names, ages and addresses. One family lost four children that day, aged six, eight, nine and eleven. None of them came home.

Albert looked through the documents one more time, making a note of everyone named who worked or was associated in some way with the theatre. It was a long list. Management, the owner of the theatre, other acts, backstage staff. All of them potential victims.

He closed his notebook, replaced all the papers in the folder and handed it back to the attendant, a different man now. The other one was probably on his midday break, perhaps sitting in a quiet pub, enjoying a pint and a bite to eat. Albert would have liked to do the same, but he wasn't finished. And he suspected his next visit would prove just as difficult as this one.

From Chancery Lane he walked to the offices of the *Illustrated London News*. The archivist wore small, round glasses and a benign smile, his back permanently hunched from leaning over documents. He was enormously helpful and seemed delighted to have anyone interested in the archive. He led Albert into a small reading room, then disappeared for about half an hour, returning with an armful of newspapers.

'Now,' he said, carefully placing each of the editions on a table, 'my advice is that you start – well, at the beginning!' He giggled, as if he had said something very amusing. 'Or,' he pondered, 'you might want to look at the edition marking the first anniversary of the tragedy. It provides a most excellent overview of events.'

'Thank you,' Albert said firmly, taking hold of the first edition the archivist had laid on the table. 'I'll work my way through.'

'If you need any assistance, I'm right there.' The archivist pointed to a tiny desk wedged between two towering bookshelves. 'Anything at all. Right there.'

Albert nodded politely. He suspected the archivist didn't have many dealings with the public. If he gave the man an inch he'd take a mile, and Albert would be there all day.

The reporting of the event was much as Albert expected. Sensational coverage in the days immediately following the accident, then a drier retelling of the inquest. It was the illustrations he was particularly interested in. They weren't all signed, but it was clear they had all been done by the same person: Lennie Thomas. The style was lacking the *ILN*'s usual sophistication, but Albert reminded himself that this was fourteen years ago. All the children looked identical, except for minor changes of clothing or hairstyle. He peered closely at one particular drawing, a reimagining of the children stampeding down the stairs towards the bolted door at the bottom. At this point, they did not know what awaited them, so they should have looked excited. But these children all looked fierce, feral. They were frightening, not frightened. Their hands were reaching forward, fingers curling over as if ready to grab. Not a sympathetic portrayal.

He examined the image more closely. It was a reimagining of what had happened, but he had a fanciful notion that perhaps, in one of these images, he was looking at Frances. If he was, there was no way of knowing. All these children looked the same.

Albert returned the old editions to the archivist, thanked him and managed to extricate himself from what promised to be a lengthy conversation. He started walking slowly back to Bury Street. He'd done nothing but sit at desks all afternoon, he felt weary and his head ached. Near his house, he passed the Dog and Duck. A pint would help, but then he remembered how much work he needed to do and he kept walking.

EIGHTEEN

Minnie placed the bottle of gin and two glasses on the table.

'We need to talk about that thing you don't talk about,' she said to Frances. 'I figured a drink or two might help.'

'You're gonna need a much bigger bottle if you want me to talk about that day.'

'Then we'll get another bottle. And another. But you need to tell me what happened.'

'Why? You can read it in the newspapers. It's all there. All the gruesome details.'

'But you were there, Frances. You saw things—'

'I didn't see nothing. I was trapped under a pile of bodies and then I was rescued. If you want details about what went on, I'm the last person you should ask.'

'I don't need to know the mechanics of it all. Like you say, that's all in the newspapers. But you might have seen something, heard something that can give us a clue as to who's doing this. And who might be the next victim. You could save someone's life, Frances. Maybe several lives.'

Frances sighed and pushed the glass away. 'I drink gin when I'm happy. I ain't gonna drink it if I've gotta relive that day.'

'Cuppa?' Minnie offered.

Frances shook her head. 'I'll tell you what I remember. And then that's it, I ain't talking about it again.'

Minnie nodded and crossed to the fire to add a few more coals. Sometimes people found it easier to start talking if no one was looking at them.

'It was a special treat,' Frances said. 'A few weeks before, I'd broken my leg jumping off a wall and I was like a caged bear, having to stay inside when all I wanted was to be playing out on the street with the other kids. That day, December 12th, it was my eighth birthday, and Ma and Pa had got me a ticket. They couldn't take the time off work to come with me, so I was going with Rosa, our next-door neighbour's daughter. She was to take care of me.'

'Rosa. Do you remember her last name?'

'You won't be able to talk to her. She didn't make it. Her and the other hundred and eighty-two.' A note of bitterness, anger, had crept into Frances's voice. 'I remember she got the needle with me 'cos I couldn't keep up with her, given I was using a crutch. When we got inside the theatre, she spotted some friends of hers and sat with them. She was older than me, and I suppose it was a bit embarrassing being seen with me. The other kids had started calling me Peg Leg, which they thought was hilarious. I found a seat on my own a few rows from Rosa. And once the show started I didn't mind much that I was alone. They were good, all the acts. Bernard and his brother were brilliant.'

'And then what?'

'They started throwing the presents out into the stalls. Some big lads started shouting that we weren't gonna get nothing if we were up in the circle. Rosa appeared, got hold of my hand, she was leading the way, but then there was a surge forward and I slipped free of her. I didn't realise at first what was happening, just thought there was a bit of a scrummage at the bottom of the stairs. I was scared, though, 'cos of my leg. I was afraid of falling, hurting myself more. There were kids rushing past me on all sides, shouting and whooping like it was all a giant game. I managed to

150

wedge myself into a corner, where the stairs turned. Rammed the crutch in front of me, in the bend of the wall. Then it seemed like all in a flash there were kids piled up around me. Dead. Or dying. So quick, Min. All so quick. I shut my eyes, turned my face away. I didn't want to look at them. And then I heard a grown-up. Swearing, he was. I thought he was having trouble breathing, but then I realised he was crying. Ma and Pa had always told me to ask a grown-up if ever I got lost or needed help, so I opened my eyes, and I could just see him, above the bodies piled in front of me. Mr Graham, our neighbour from two doors down.'

'Freddy Graham?' Minnie asked. 'The stage manager?'

'That's him. I called out and he got me, moved bodies out of the way to reach me, lifted me out. Carried me outside into the rain. I looked for Rosa everywhere. Found her in the end. They put the bodies outside the theatre, all laid out in straight lines. I remember thinking they needed covering up, 'cos it was raining, and they were getting wet.'

'And do you remember anything else? Anyone, anything that stood out in your mind?'

Frances gave Minnie a long, almost vacant look. 'You went through some pretty awful stuff last year, didn't you?'

Minnie nodded, images flashing unbidden into her mind. Cora's cry. A body ripped open. A gruesome discovery in an ice house. A fight for her life.

'So you know how it works. Things come back to you in flashes, don't they? You don't see the day as a whole, with one event following another. You remember moments. Like photographs. And then, after a while, you wonder if it really happened like that at all, or if you just read about it that way. And things that stick out in your mind? It all sticks out, don't it? Or none of it. I could tell you about the sounds coming out of the mouths of parents as they held their dead children. I could tell you how, for months afterwards, I could spot another child who'd been there that day 'cos there was something dead behind their eyes. I could tell you about the nightmares I had for years – I still have 'em now. But if you want me to tell you I spotted someone in the crowd who looked like, fourteen years later, he'd go on a killing spree? Like I said, you're asking the wrong person.' She unstoppered the gin bottle. 'Turns out I do fancy one, after all. Funny how reliving the worst day of your life will do that to you.' She poured a single large measure and downed it in one gulp before refilling her glass and passing the bottle to Minnie.

'You know the worst thing, Min? No one really cared. I mean, the parents, the families, they cared. But the people who could have done something about it – *should* have done something about it? They were all too busy trying to make sure no one pinned the blame on them. No one was found guilty. No one went to prison. And the rest of us were just left to get on with it, as if nothing had happened.'

The two women sat quietly for a while. Anything Minnie could think of to say seemed pointless and irrelevant in the light of what Frances had just shared with her. Eventually, it was Frances who broke the silence.

'You gonna talk to Jack?'

'He was there. He might have seen something.'

'Not from what he's told me. Said he was backstage. Didn't know nothing until everyone started rushing out into the auditorium.'

'Still. Sometimes people know something and they don't even know they know it.'

Frances drained the last of her glass, then slowly rose to her feet. She moved more slowly, as if the act of discussing the past had aged her. 'Well, if it's all the same to you,' she said, 'I'm done in. I'm just gonna grab myself forty winks and then I've got that job to finish for the Alhambra.'

Later that same day, Minnie was seated close to the fire in Albert's morning room. Perhaps a little too close, because the heat and the gentle crackle of the logs, and possibly the gin she'd had earlier with Frances, were making her sleepy. But she was here on business, and if she fell asleep at Albert's one more time she suspected Mrs Byrne would never speak to her again.

'This arrived this morning from Dorothy,' Albert said, handing her two sheets of paper. 'It's the list of investors in Capital Holdings who lost money when the company collapsed.'

Minnie scanned the list and gave a low whistle. She didn't know which was worse: having no suspects or too many.

'There are fifty-three names on that list,' Albert said, 'any one of whom might be behind Eddings's and Fowler's deaths. And each of those fifty-three people most likely had relatives and close friends who were angry about what happened.'

'Angry enough to kill?'

'Well, that's the question, isn't it?'

'And there's the other list,' Minnie said. 'One hundred and eighty-three children who died at the Trafalgar Theatre. Losing your child through someone else's greed or negligence. I'm pretty sure that would be motive enough for most people.'

'And then we have Danny Webster, our athletic sweep.'

'Any sign of him?'

Albert shook his head. 'I've paid a boy to keep an eye on Webster's lodgings, but there's been no sign of him. He might not be involved at all, just a lad who was in the wrong place at the wrong time.'

'Why did he run, though?'

'Didn't like the cut of my jib, as you might say. I still look like a police officer, or so I've been told.'

'Copper or prizefighter,' Minnie said, gesturing at his flattened nose, broken more than once in the ring. 'Either way you look like trouble. Finding someone who looks like you waiting in your room – maybe his quick exit ain't such a surprise.'

Albert sighed, his eyes running over the two lists. 'We've got the collapse of Capital Holdings, with a direct link to Eddings and Fowler. And we've got the Trafalgar Theatre disaster, again with links to Eddings, Fowler and three other victims.'

'Assuming Freddy Graham was murdered,' Minnie said, 'which we've got no proof for.'

'True.'

'What's your gut telling you?' Minnie asked.

'It's telling me the answer lies with the Trafalgar Theatre. There's something so – personal about these killings. But I can't yet dismiss the disgruntled investors of Capital Holdings. If I could just be certain the killings were motivated by one event or the other, it would be a start.'

'Right,' Minnie said, standing up, taking the papers and placing them in a drawer of his bureau. 'Let's ignore the numbers and go back to what we know. How were our five victims killed?'

'Eddings was locked in a trunk. Fowler was hanged. Graham had a fatal heart attack. Thomas died by strychnine poisoning, and Reynolds was left locked in a room.'

'So, assuming it's the same person who killed all five, why don't they stick to the same method each time? Ain't that what killers normally do?'

Albert shrugged. 'Sometimes. Sometimes not. The killer may be choosing what's most expedient. Or maybe he almost gets caught and decides it's too risky to do it that way again.'

'Eddings was locked in a trunk, yeah? So, what did he actually die of? What made his heart stop beating?'

'Lack of oxygen. The trunk was airtight and he couldn't get out. Eventually he'd run out of oxygen.'

'So he suffocated, right?'

Albert nodded.

'And when you hang someone, what is it that actually kills them?'

He thought for a moment. 'Their neck breaks.'

'Yeah, but that ain't necessarily enough to kill you. It might put you in a wheelchair but not kill you. And when they hang criminals, they try to get the drop right, don't they, so the neck breaks and they die quickly. But they don't always get it right, do they?'

'No. In which case, the person dies from—'

'—lack of air,' Minnie interrupted. 'So that's two murders, both involving suffocation. What about Peter?'

'Dehydration, probably. That's what the doctor seemed to think had done it in the end.'

'But he was locked in a tiny room with no way of getting out. Bit like being locked in a trunk, wouldn't you say?'

'Freddy Graham died of a heart attack. And we've got no way of knowing if that was murder or just natural causes.'

'Either way, I ain't no doctor, Albert, but I once saw a fella have a heart attack in the intermission at the Palace. He looked to me like he couldn't breathe.'

'What about Lennie Thomas?'

'Again, he was gasping for air, grabbing at his collar.'

'So all five of these men were somehow connected to the Trafalgar Theatre disaster and suffocated in one way or another,' Albert said.

'But were they all connected to the financial scam?'

'Dorothy has looked into that. There's no mention of Graham, Thomas or Reynolds in any of the documentation relating to Capital Holdings.'

Dorothy, Minnie thought. There it was again: Dorothy and Albert.

'So all five connected to the theatre,' Minnie said. 'All dead within a few weeks of each other, and each death has involved some sort of suffocation.'

'Like the children at the theatre. They all suffocated.'

Minnie leaned back in her seat. 'What's your gut telling you now?'

'My gut still says it's the theatre. But what if I ignore Capital Holdings, and it turns out that's the key?'

'Maybe Dorothy needs to do a bit more digging,' Minnie said.

'She's been very thorough. If Graham, Thomas and Reynolds were connected to Capital Holdings, they've kept themselves invisible.'

'Or they're somehow related to someone who was part of the scam?'

Albert shook his head. 'I've spoken to Bernard. His brother had no connection whatsoever with the company.'

'So listen to your gut and maybe you'll have your answer, Albert.'

He sighed. 'Well, it narrows down the suspect list, but not much. A hundred and eighty-three children. Even if we narrow it down to just their fathers, that's an awful lot of people we need to talk to.'

Minnie fell quiet, frowning as she stared into the fire. Eventually, she raised her head.

'What is it?' Albert said.

'What if it ain't a parent we're looking for?'

'If we're extending the suspect list to uncles and grandfathers we'll never get to the end of it.'

She shook her head. 'You ain't got it. What if it ain't a parent, or an uncle or a grandfather. What if it's a child?'

He frowned. 'You mean, a survivor from that day?'

She nodded. 'The Trafalgar Theatre disaster took place fourteen years ago. Why such a long gap between the event and the killings? Why not take your revenge straight away?'

'Maybe you couldn't. Or you didn't feel the need to, and something's triggered that response in you.'

'Or maybe you were a child at the time of the disaster.'

Albert said nothing for a few moments, as if he were turning over the idea in his head.

'There were children who survived, but who went through terrible things on that day,' he said eventually. 'The inquest details make for very grim reading. One child, Inez Shepherd, she talked about how long she was trapped, how she thought she was going to die, couldn't breathe.'

'Exactly. If you went through something like that, I don't reckon you'd ever get over it, would you? Frances don't wanna talk about it. She went to Freddy Graham's funeral with me and never once mentioned that it was him who saved her that day. What if one of the children – maybe more than one – who'd now be, what, twenty? Twenty-five? They've grown up with this terrible experience in their past, they know no one was punished for it, and now they're adults and they can do something about it. And another thing,' Minnie said, her voice speeding up, 'you keep talking about fathers and uncles and suchlike. Who's to say it ain't a woman doing this?'

Albert shook his head. 'Highly unlikely.'

'Why? She could have a gun, make the victims do what she wants. Fowler puts his own head in the noose 'cos she threatens him with something if he don't. Maybe she says she'll hurt his wife if he don't do as she asks. Eddings something similar; his grandson was there that day, weren't he? Graham already had heart trouble; his friends all said so. She does something to anger him, bring on the attack. Thomas was poisoned – well, everyone says poisoning's a woman's game—'

'And the woman,' Albert interrupted. 'A woman came looking for Peter the night before they closed the theatre. It could be, Minnie. I still think it's unlikely.'

'But possible. The only problem is, if it's a woman, that's an even bigger list of suspects. Where do we even start?'

'We start with what we've got. There's no record of who bought

157

tickets for that particular show. The only record we have of audience members is the children who died.'

'And the children who gave evidence at the inquest. That would bump it up to about two hundred or so, I reckon, from what you've said.'

Albert nodded. 'You find out everything you can about the children who gave evidence. Tom and I will start with the children who died, tracking down family members. Particularly siblings.'

'Excellent. Best we get started.'

NINETEEN

A few days later, Albert was wishing he'd never taken on the Eddings case. He and Tom had only managed to interview five families of the dead children and each interview had been worse than the last. Stirring up old memories, hearing tales of that day in December, witnessing the light dying in a parent's eyes as they recalled the moment when they had to identify their child; the pain was almost unbearable. And the numbers were huge; at this rate, it was going to take weeks, maybe months, before they could speak to everyone. By which time, the killer might well have struck again. Albert's analysis of the inquest testimony and his perusal of the newspaper archives had revealed at least half a dozen other names of people who were working at the Trafalgar that day. He'd sat down with Bernard as well, who seemed to have kept every piece of publicity material from his entire career, and they'd come up with a list of names: runners, stagehands, ushers, front of house, backstage, the owner of the Trafalgar, the manager. He'd spoken to Jack and Bernard about the danger they might be in. Jack was unconvinced he'd be a target for the killer and said he could look after himself either way. Bernard was considering Albert's offer of a bed until the killer was found.

Minnie's job was proving equally traumatic. So far she'd spoken to three adults who'd been children at the time and had given evidence at the inquest. One of them was Inez Shepherd, the young girl whose testimony Albert couldn't erase from his mind. The previous night, Minnie had turned up on Albert's doorstep, her face drawn and pale, a bottle of gin in her hand. Silently, he'd let her in, and the pair of them had consumed the best part of the bottle before Mrs Byrne intervened and dispatched Minnie back home in a cab.

Albert's head was throbbing as he took a sip of tea that was closer to water than anything else, and directed his next question to Mrs Turnbull. She was a pale, shadowy type of woman, her voice high and tremulous as she relived the worst day of her life. Her daughter had been six years old on the day of the disaster.

'You live alone, Mrs Turnbull? No other children?'

She shook her head. 'Polly was my only child. We tried for more, but we weren't fortunate.'

'And your husband?'

She dropped her head and started playing with the ring on her wedding finger. Albert waited quietly.

'Clive found – what happened—' She broke off, extracted a handkerchief from her sleeve.

'He left you?' Albert prompted.

'Oh, nothing like that. Well, not in the way you mean. He struggled, well, we both did. You have your child, and you protect her from everything that might harm her. And then something like that happens. Neither of us was with her, see? She went with some other children who lived down our road. The oldest of them was twelve. They all died. Clive couldn't forgive himself. Felt if he'd been there he'd have saved her. I tried telling him, but he weren't having none of it. Tormented himself with the feeling he'd let her down. In the end—' She broke off again, blew her nose and refilled his cup. 'He was committed. Finsbury Asylum.'

She rose, crossed to the mantelpiece and took longer than necessary to coax some more heat out of the fire. 'I used to visit him every week, but it got so I was making things worse. "Visibly distressing the patient", that's what they said. "Marked decline in his progress." So I stopped going. I wrote him letters, but he never wrote back.'

'Is he still there?'

She shook her head. 'He was released after three years. He came to see me, collect his things. Said he still loved me, but couldn't bear to look at me.' She fingered a mourning brooch at her throat. 'Polly looked just like me,' she murmured.

The woman's pain was like a physical presence in the room, sucking out all the air. Albert didn't know how he was going to conduct any more of these interviews. And he didn't see how he could ask Tom to do something he was incapable of doing himself.

'Do you know where your husband is now?' he asked.

'With his brother. The two of them emigrated to New York not long after he was released.'

'And he never returned to England?'

'Never.' The brevity of her answer couldn't hide her pain at what must have felt like abandonment.

Albert thanked Mrs Turnbull for her time and apologised for the distress he'd caused her. It was becoming an all-too-familiar litany. As she showed him to the door, she asked the question he was coming to dread.

'So what's all this about anyway?'

'There have been some suspicious deaths involving people who were connected with the events at the Trafalgar Theatre.'

'Suspicious? You mean murder?'

'Possibly.'

'And you reckon it might be revenge for what happened that day?'

'Possibly.'

He braced himself for her anger, but it didn't come. Instead, she pressed a hand to her chest. 'Well, that's just awful. Whoever those people were, whatever they did, they've still got families who are left behind to grieve. People who didn't do anything wrong.' She laid her hand on his arm. 'You find who's doing it, Mr Easterbrook.'

Leaving the house, he turned for home, replaying the conversation about Mr Turnbull's illness. A spell in an asylum. That might explain the delay before the murders started. As would a turn in prison. He retraced his steps back to a cab stand. Time to pay John a visit.

Albert looked down at the two lists John had given him, not entirely convinced John hadn't broken several laws. One sheet of paper listed everyone who had lived in the environs of the Trafalgar Theatre and been admitted to an insane asylum in the months immediately following the disaster. Those who would have been children at the time, as well as their parents or adult relatives. It was a short list, with only three names, although that didn't necessarily mean other people hadn't needed help. Just that they or their parents hadn't been able to afford it, so they'd been expected to muddle through. The other was a list of those living in the same vicinity who had been imprisoned within three years of the disaster. A quick glance showed him there was no overlap. The list of asylum inmates was the shorter, so that's where he decided to start.

Clive Turnbull he dismissed immediately. The man had moved to America within a month of his release and never returned. John had placed a letter 'd' in brackets next to the second name followed by the year 1872, indicating that the man had died that year.

Albert looked down at the next name on the list. James Tomlinson. He would have been ten when the disaster happened, and was admitted to Finsbury Asylum three months after it took place. It could just be coincidence but Albert needed to follow it up. Besides, it gave him something to do that didn't involve talking to grief-stricken parents.

Finsbury Asylum was an imposing building, a central rotunda flanked by two jutting wings, and then long corridors extending either side. In front of the building was a large circular bed planted with shrubs and grasses. Impressive, but Albert knew how misleading appearances could be. The asylum had only been open since 1860 but it had become notorious for all the wrong reasons. A year after opening, the ceiling collapsed in one ward and rafters shifted away from the walls in other parts of the building. The chapel, the seventy-five-acre farm, the brewery and the aviary couldn't hide the fact there were serious problems.

And that was just with the fabric of the building. On their release, several inmates had gone to the press with details of their treatment. Founded under the benevolent, progressive gaze of Dr Anderson, the administration had passed over to a Dr Phillips in 1864; by all accounts Phillips favoured a more punitive regime. He'd lasted a few years, then moved into politics, which Albert suspected was a blessed release for anyone who'd been under his care. His successor, Dr Butler, had invited little coverage in the press, which Albert guessed was a good thing.

He was greeted at the door by a benign-looking woman in her forties, dressed in a simple navy dress and white apron. She introduced herself as Mrs Hughes and led Albert through a network of corridors. He caught glimpses of orderlies in the distance, beefy men who looked as if they wouldn't be out of place working for the likes of Jem Blount.

Mrs Hughes followed his gaze and gave him a bland, practised smile. 'Some of our patients can be very violent, Mr Easterbrook. When possessed by the kind of rage we witness here, even the most diminutive of men – or women for that matter – may require restraint.'

Finally they reached the office of Dr Butler. Mrs Hughes announced Albert, and Butler rose from behind his desk, coming forward with his hand outstretched. The man looked like a picture drawn by a child. His mouth was a little too small, his eyes a little too large, his ears asymmetrical. He had the faded look of red-headed men when they age and had an air about him of someone who rarely smiled, but his manner was welcoming enough.

'Mr Easterbrook,' Butler said, inviting Albert to take a seat and resuming his position behind the desk. 'How may I be of assistance?'

'As I stated in my correspondence, I have some questions regarding James Tomlinson, a former inmate of this institution.'

Butler nodded, stroking a buff folder on the desk in front of him. 'I've reminded myself of his case. What is it you wish to know?'

'How old was James when he was admitted?' Albert asked. He already knew the answer, but it was always useful to start an interview with simple questions that put the other person at ease.

'Ten,' Butler said. 'He was first admitted into the care of Dr Anderson. Then, after a few months, Dr Phillips took over the running of this establishment.'

'And James's symptoms?'

'Quite typical for children of that age. Bed-wetting. Nightmares. Disproportionate anger. Nothing exceptional, I regret to say.'

'What had triggered those symptoms? Assuming the lad hadn't suffered from them before.'

'He was present at the Trafalgar Theatre disaster. You may have heard of it.'

Albert nodded, trying to hide his interest. So James Tomlinson had been ten years old and present in the theatre that day. Whatever he'd witnessed, it had led to his parents having him admitted.

'He was not alone in the theatre that day,' Butler continued. 'His twin sister was also there, and she did not survive the tragedy.'

'Is it usual to admit a child to a lunatic asylum for wetting the bed?' Albert asked. 'Isn't that something we'd expect a child to grow out of?'

Butler sighed and slowly nodded his head. 'We work at the behest of the patient's family. His parents sought help initially from their church. Their vicar had connections with parish relief, and he suggested that a spell of treatment here could be paid for by the parish. I would, as you say, suggest to the parents that the child would grow out of the condition. But the founder of this asylum, Dr Anderson, was a more soft-hearted individual. And also somewhat more driven by pecuniary needs.'

'And how long did he stay here? Six months? A year?'

'James Tomlinson was a patient here for seven years. He was released at the age of seventeen, in August 1871.'

Seven years. If he wasn't insane when he first arrived, he might well have been by the time he left.

'It took seven years to cure a spell of bed-wetting and some difficulty sleeping?' Albert asked, struggling to control his anger.

Butler looked down at his hands and smoothed the surface of the folder a second time. Then he seemed to reach a decision and raised his head. 'My predecessor, Dr Phillips, was somewhat unorthodox in his treatment of patients. There are instances – far too many instances, in my opinion – where patients were detained when they could very easily have been released.'

'To what end?'

'Experimentation.'

A chill descended on the room. In the distance Albert could hear shouts and the shriek of a whistle. 'Football,' Butler said. 'The patients have a game every afternoon.' The banality of the activity only served to highlight the horrors Butler had made reference to but, thankfully, had not expanded on.

Butler opened his desk drawer and removed a pack of cigarettes. Albert accepted the offer of one, and the two men smoked for a few moments, both wrapped up in their thoughts, before Butler spoke. 'Why are you interested in James Tomlinson? Your letter wasn't specific.'

Something about Butler told Albert he could be honest with him. 'I think he may be connected to a series of suspicious deaths. And I think it may have something to do with what happened at the Trafalgar Theatre.'

Butler nodded, as if he'd been expecting that exact answer. 'These deaths,' he said, 'how did they happen?'

'Differing types of suffocation.'

Butler nodded again, took a long drag on his cigarette and threw the butt into the fire. 'When James was first admitted, he was encouraged to talk about his experiences, what had brought him to us. Anderson was very progressive in that respect; precious few institutions at that time did much beyond feeding and clothing their patients and keeping them quiet with laudanum and the like.'

'Has much changed?' Albert asked.

'Not enough. We're making some inroads but, no, not enough has changed. That's why Anderson was so remarkable. He genuinely cared for his patients, you can see it in his notes.' He opened the buff folder and turned it so Albert could see the pages covered in a neat cursive. 'Here,' Butler said, drawing Albert's attention to a particular paragraph. 'James told Anderson of an "emptiness" beside him. A space the exact size of his sister, he said. And here' – he gestured to a separate page – 'he talks of his night terrors.'

Albert scanned the page. 'JDT frequently wakes in the night, fighting for air. He speaks of a darkness filling his head and his chest; an inability to breathe. Mother the only one able to comfort

JDT. Father still angry about death and failure to apportion blame.'

'Did his parents visit him?' Albert asked.

'They were discouraged from doing so. There was a school of thought – it still exists – that contact with family can hinder a patient's progress. Mr and Mrs Tomlinson were told to stay away.'

'But the lad was only ten.'

Butler nodded. 'Anderson believed there was every possibility James would be released after a few months' treatment. But then Anderson retired, and Phillips took his place.'

'What did Phillips do to the lad?'

'His favoured treatment for James was what he termed a "water cure". The patient was placed in a large bath of cold water and submerged for increasing periods of time. Phillips even wrote a scientific paper on the purgative benefits of such treatment.'

'If someone holds you underwater—' Albert said.

'—you will feel as if you're suffocating, yes.'

Albert sat quietly, absorbing all he had learned. Butler was very comfortable with silence, Albert was learning. But then, that was part of his job.

'Do you have an address for where James went when he was discharged?' Albert asked.

'He was discharged into the care of his father. 33 Sheridan Street.'

'And do you have a description of James?'

Butler turned the pages in the folder, finally finding what he needed. 'Fair hair. Underweight, but that's not unusual in a patient of James's background. No distinctive marks.' He pushed the folder across the desk. 'We take a photograph of each of our patients when they arrive. Obviously, Tomlinson will have aged since this was taken, but it might prove useful.'

Albert reached forward and pulled the folder towards him. The photograph was pinned to the inside cover. It was difficult to believe the child was ten; he looked no more than five or six. Someone, James's mother probably, looked as if they'd made an effort with his hair, which had been slicked down and neatly combed. His clothes were worn and it was difficult to tell how clean they were from the photograph.

But it was the child's eyes that struck Albert. The eyes of someone much older than his years, staring at the camera lens, but with a vacancy behind them. He didn't look mad, Albert thought.

Just afraid.

TWENTY

Minnie hadn't been sleeping well since Freddy Graham's funeral. Every night Lennie Thomas figured in her nightmares. His hand grasping his neck, struggling to breathe. The other arm stretched out for help that no one was able to give him. Albert had told her strychnine often took effect within fifteen minutes. So it was likely that whoever had given Lennie the poison had been there in the pub. Perhaps standing next to Minnie, pushing past her to get to the bar.

Frances looked as if she wasn't sleeping any better than Minnie. She made them both coffee and they were sitting quietly, allowing the day to start, when there was a knock at the door. It was Tom.

'Oh, God, I'm sorry,' Minnie said. 'You asked me – what? A week ago to meet you and I ain't even got back to you with a time.'

'Don't worry. I heard what happened at the funeral. You've had other things on your mind.'

'But still,' Minnie said, 'you asked to see me and I should have remembered.' She saw his eyes looking past her to where Frances was sitting and introduced them.

'You were there too?' Tom asked.

'I was,' Frances said, the fatigue evident in her voice.

'What about I take you girls out for a cuppa and a bun? My treat.'

Frances shook her head and gestured to the piles of fabric on her table. 'Too much work to do. Maybe another time.'

'I, on the other hand,' Minnie said, 'am never too busy for a bun.'

Tom had suggested a tea room just round the corner, but it was proving to be a disappointment. The tea wasn't strong enough and the buns tasted as if they'd been made by someone who'd never heard of sugar and butter. Minnie pushed the plate away, the bun half eaten. 'So why the meeting?'

'It's about Tansie's monkey.'

'Please don't tell me he's dead. I couldn't take it at the moment.'

'No, not dead. We know who's taken him and we know where he is.' Tom explained about Jem Blount, the Westminster Pit and Tansie's ill-fated plans to turn Monkey into a money-making rodent killer. 'Tansie's asked around, and he reckons they've got Monkey locked in a back room at the Pit.'

'So?'

'So we need someone who can pick a lock.'

Minnie sighed. 'I don't suppose there's anyone else you can ask?'

Tom shook his head. 'Not anyone we can trust to do it right. But we can't let Albert know about this. There's no way he'd let you set foot inside a place like that.'

'I ain't too keen on the idea myself, to tell the truth.'

She pulled the half-eaten bun towards her and picked at it distractedly. 'What's the set-up at the Pit?'

'Fella's coming to see Tansie tonight at the Palace, five o'clock. He's a dog handler at the Pit and knows the layout. He lost a lot of money to Blount a few months ago and is keen to get his own back.'

'I'll see you at five then.'

Surprisingly for one of Tansie's acquaintances, Newrick Briggs appeared promptly at the agreed time. Looking at him, Minnie figured if you asked people to draw a picture of a typical shady character, he'd look exactly like Briggs. Thin, weaselly, with a large scar over one eye, one decent tooth left in his head and a restless habit of hopping from one foot to the other while he talked, as if he were eager to be somewhere else. He sucked on an unlit cigarette. Tansie offered him a light, but he shook his head. 'Lasts longer this way,' he rasped.

Minnie and Tansie shared a glance.

'So,' Tom said, 'tell us about the Pit.'

'There's the fighting area at the front,' Newrick said. 'Usual arrangement. Directly behind the arena there's a door, but there'll be a fella guarding it. Maybe two.'

'Why the bouncers?' Minnie asked.

'Behind that door is where they keep the animals while they're waiting to fight. You don't want no one slipping in there and drugging someone's dog. Or wiping something on his neck. That's why they've got the lickers.'

'Lickers?' Tansie said.

'Fellas who lick the dogs' necks to check no one's cheating,' Briggs said.

'Nope. You've still lost me,' Tansie said.

'You get a lot of dodgy types in the dog-fighting world,' Briggs said, clearly not seeing the irony of his words. 'They'll put ammonia or pepper on a dog's neck, so it tastes nasty to the other dog and it puts him off, see? So it ain't a fair fight. The Westminster's a slightly more upmarket kind of gaff. If it's gonna be dog on dog, they hire fellas to lick the dogs' necks before they go in the pit.'

'What do they do in gaffs that ain't so – upmarket?' Minnie asked.

'Well, you've gotta lick your opponent's dog yourself, aintcha?' Briggs said, as if the answer were obvious.

This was proving to be quite an education. Minnie was intrigued to learn more, but Tansie's face told her they had a job to do.

'So one, maybe two heavies at the door who'll need distracting,' Tansie said. 'Is there any other way into that backstage area where they keep the dogs?'

'You can come round the back, but you'll need a reason to be there.'

'Dropping off a dog?' Tom said.

Briggs nodded slowly. 'That'd get you in. I could get Boris on the line-up tonight. You could drop him off, then go looking for your monkey friend.'

Tansie leaned across the desk and fixed Newrick with a hard stare. 'Why you doing this?' he asked. 'From what I've heard of Blount, he don't take kindly to anyone crossing him. You sure this ain't a trap?'

Newrick sniffed and wiped his nose on his sleeve. 'Blount bubbled me two months ago. Told me it was a million to a bit o' dirt his dog'd win. Took every last farthing I had. Figure he owes me.'

Minnie nodded. 'If we come in the back way, what happens after we get through the door?'

'There's a corridor running straight in front of you. If they ain't moved him, your monkey's in the third room on the left. It'll be locked.'

Minnie nodded. 'Any more big chaps we'll need to watch out for?'

'Not as such. But it's busy back there, there's people coming and going all the time. You'll have to be quick to pick the lock and get inside the room. And then you've gotta get the monkey out without anyone noticing. You doing all this on your own?' He cast an appraising look at Minnie. 'No offence or nothing but I don't fancy your chances, love.'

'She'll have me with her, waiting outside,' Tom said.

'Good with your fists, are you? 'Cos if they get wise to what you're up to, you're gonna need to be. These are not nice men. Punch first and think later. And if one of Blount's fellas hits you, you'll stay hit.'

Tom was a wiry chap. He'd always said he was handy in a fight, but Minnie had never seen the evidence of it. Albert would be the perfect companion, the perfect person to keep her safe. But Albert would never let her put herself in harm's way like this. Time enough to tell him about it when it was all over, and they had Monkey safely back in the Palace. Minnie wasn't going to say anything to Tansie, but she was starting to have her doubts about the whole enterprise. She'd made some quiet enquiries about how easy it would be to get hold of another monkey who looked just like the original one. Not difficult, but Tansie would spot the difference immediately. Even if she trained the new monkey to piss in people's shoes.

After Briggs had left, Minnie slipped into Wardrobe and found what she was looking for. A tired-looking pair of brown trousers, a shirt that had once been white, and a waistcoat. She was meant to look on her uppers and this outfit would do the trick. She took the clothes back to a dressing room, and slipped into them. And just like that, she was back all those months ago, larking around with Cora as the other woman taught her how to be a man. No need to button the shirt collar this time, but the trousers felt just as strange. She sat in front of the mirrors, tried to push the memories of Cora out of her mind. But the woman was everywhere. The conversations they'd shared. Cora complaining about Minnie eating oysters in the dressing rooms. Cora sharing her fondness for Tansie, and asking Minnie's advice about making a move on him.

And, unbidden, the vision of Rose appeared. It never got any easier. The scent of someone's perfume, a woman turning a corner in front of her who shared the tilt of Rose's head, a laugh carried on the breeze. She was right back there, that awful day when she'd heard the news.

But things were different. She had moved on. She'd learned she could survive. That you didn't die of grief. Some days you wished you could. But you didn't. You put one foot in front of the other, and you just kept going.

She blew her nose and stared at her face in the mirror, remembering Cora's instructions. Rice powder to conceal her freckles. Kohl to darken her eyebrows. No moustache or beard. They never looked right. Forcing herself through the pain, slowly she transformed herself into a fresh-faced young lad. Then she stood, and practised walking. Legs further apart. No swinging of the hips. Longer strides.

And finally, the hands. 'It's all in the hands, Min,' Cora had said, showing her how a lad suppressed a yawn with a closed fist, how he'd show you his hands palms up. Then Cora had gone out for lunch with Tansie, and two hours later she was dead.

Minnie forced back the tears. Most people would laugh at what she was about to undertake, tell Tansie to find himself another pet. But she and Tansie had both lost so much. If she could help him, she would. Minnie took one last glance in the mirror.

She had a monkey to save.

TWENTY-ONE

Tom was waiting for her outside the stage door. Since the events of the previous year, he'd been reluctant to come inside the Palace. Too many memories, and most of them bad.

He held a dog lead, at the end of which was some sort of terrier who looked as if he enjoyed a fight. Tom took in her changed appearance and greeted her with a broad grin.

'This is Boris,' he said.

Minnie gave the dog a sceptical look, and kept her distance.

'It's all right. He's a bit of a sweetheart, really. Although Briggs says you wouldn't want to be another dog, or any small animal. You can pet him. He likes it round his ears, and just here.' Tom rubbed his knuckles across the dog's forehead. Boris did look as if he was enjoying it.

'No, you're all right,' Minnie said.

She felt her spirits lifting. She hadn't realised how much she'd missed Tom. It was good to be working together again.

Instinctively, she went to take his arm, then remembered she was meant to be a fella and pulled back, thrusting her hands firmly into her pockets. They set out, weaving their way through the streets until they finally approached the Westminster Pit.

The place looked inconspicuous from the front, a tobacconist's with its shutters down. Most people were passing by, heads down against the cold easterly wind, intent on getting home or wherever else they were heading. But every few minutes, someone would peel off from the crowd, approach the door of the shop and slip inside.

'You ever been to one?' Minnie asked. 'A dogfight?'

Tom shuddered, and she guessed it wasn't just from the cold. 'Albert and I were here the other week, and it was pretty bad. My brother took me once. Thought I'd enjoy it, given that I like animals. It still gives me nightmares.'

She nudged him with her elbow. 'C'mon. Time we got to work.'

Tom handed her Boris's lead. 'You should take him. He's strong, mind, so brace yourself.'

She took the lead and they turned down an alley beside the tobacconist's. Boris got a scent of something and lunged, almost wrenching Minnie's shoulder out of its socket. She lurched forward, nearly dropping the lead and just managing to maintain control of the dog.

At the rear of the Pit were a few men milling around. Minnie and Tom had agreed he would wait nearby, lurking in the darkness of the surrounding buildings.

'You sure you're gonna be all right?' Tom said, concern flitting across his face. 'It don't feel right, you going in there, and me just hanging around out here.'

'Well, unless you've learned how to pick a lock overnight, we ain't got no choice.'

'And you've got the whistle?'

She patted the whistle hanging from a length of string around her neck. She was to blow it if she got into trouble and Tom would come running. And if anyone asked, it was just a whistle to get the dog to do as she wanted.

'Right,' Minnie said, feigning a courage she did not feel. 'Ginger up, Tom. I'll see you back out here in a few minutes. Hopefully.'

She walked purposefully towards the rear of the Pit. A fella who looked to be about twice the width of the doorway blocked her path.

'Who're you?' he growled.

She remembered to drop her voice, speak slowly. 'I'm dropping off Boris here,' she said, gesturing towards the terrier who, thankfully, was remaining calm and making her look as if she was in control. 'Newrick can't make it. He sent me in his place.'

The man glared at her, then crouched down to be on a level with Boris. 'Wotcha, matey,' he said to the dog, who immediately started frantically wagging his tail, thumping it against her leg so hard she was sure she could feel a bruise forming.

'In you go,' the bouncer said. 'Second door on the right. You can leave him in there until it's his turn.'

She nodded, and slipped past him. Just as Briggs had said, she was faced with a long corridor, doors on either side. She could hear the shouts and yells of the crowd out front and then an almighty roar. A few moments later, the door at the end of the corridor opened, the one leading into the arena, and a squinty-faced bloke came through, leading some sort of terrier. The dog's white fur was spattered with blood, its face and jaws a mask of red. He had a large cut above one eye, and was limping, whimpering as he walked. Another fella came out holding a dog in his arms, the body soft and unmoving. With a shock, Minnie realised the whimpering dog must be the victor. She felt a rush of protective sympathy for Boris, and wondered if there was a way she could smuggle him back out without him having to fight. But that wasn't what she was here to do. So, averting her eyes as the two men passed her, for fear she'd see even worse injuries, she opened the second door on the right. The smell of dog was overwhelming, and underneath it the sharp tang of piss. Mentally apologising to Boris for leaving him there, she tied his lead to a hook on the wall and ducked back out of the room.

Diagonally opposite was the room where Briggs had said they

were keeping Monkey. Minnie slid her pick out of her pocket and prayed to the god of lock pickers that the Pit hadn't installed anything very complicated. Luckily, the corridor was empty as she pressed herself up against the weathered wooden door and slid the pick in. A few sharp movements and the door came open with a satisfying clunk. She slipped inside and pulled the door closed behind her. And then realised there was something she hadn't prepared for. The room was in total darkness.

Blindly, she took a few steps to her right, feeling along the wall as she went. 'Monkey?' she hissed into the darkness. 'Monkey?'

Nothing. It might have helped if Tansie had given the creature a more distinctive name. Minnie reached into her pocket and pulled out an old doll that Monkey was very fond of. Tansie insisted the animal only liked to curl up with the doll, but Minnie had caught the creature on more than one occasion in a far more intimate relationship with the toy. She waved the doll in front of her, into the darkness. Not for the first time, she wondered why on earth she'd agreed to this. Here she was, standing in the pitch darkness, waving a doll covered in monkey stench and God knows what else, running the risk of someone walking in at any moment and beating her to a pulp.

Then she felt something tug at her trouser leg and she stifled a scream. There was someone else in here with her. Her hand flew up to the whistle round her neck and she lurched towards the door, the lights from the corridor outside highlighting the door frame. But whoever had hold of her wasn't letting go. His grip was tight. She was on the verge of blowing the whistle, not even sure if Tom would hear her outside, when she felt something leap from her leg to her hip and, finally, to her shoulder. With a mixture of horror and relief, she realised that Monkey had found her.

He grabbed the old doll, and then wrapped his arms around her, leaning into her neck and inhaling deeply. He recognised her smell, she was sure of it. As he moved, Minnie heard the clink of a chain, felt the weight of it resting on her leg. She tugged at the end of the chain attached to his neck and met resistance. Thankfully, Monkey was clinging firmly on to her neck, freeing up both her hands. Minnie inched forward carefully in the dark, uncertain of what else might be in the room. From outside in the corridor, she heard raised voices, what sounded like a celebration. She froze, no longer sure of her bearings. How far was she from the walls? How easy would it be to hide if someone opened the door? The shouts subsided, and now she could hear two men talking in the corridor. It sounded as if they were directly outside the room she was in.

The voices died away, and slowly Minnie started inching forward, one hand reaching over the other along the length of the chain. Eventually her hands hit a wall. She ran her hands down the wall and found a metal ring. The chain was looped through it and secured with a padlock. She reached into her pocket, found her lock picks and tried the first one. No luck. The second worked, and the padlock sprang open. She'd deal with the metal collar round Monkey's neck later, once they were safe and well away from the Pit.

Now she had to get him out of there without anyone noticing. Gingerly, she opened the door an inch or two and peered down the corridor. No one on the way to the exit, but there could be someone the other way and she wouldn't know until she stepped out. Carefully, so as not to scare him, she repositioned Monkey so she could pull her jacket over his whole body. Then she opened the door fully and stepped out into the corridor.

No one. From out the front, she could hear the snarling of the dogs and the baying of the crowd, and she was thankful she couldn't see what was happening. She turned towards the rear exit, remembering to walk slowly, purposefully. She had a right to be here.

She pushed open the door and came face to face with the bouncer.

'You done?' the bouncer said.

She nodded, offering up a silent prayer that Monkey would not choose this moment to make a move. 'Just popping out for a smoke,' she said. 'He ain't fighting for another half-hour.'

'Might be sooner,' the bouncer said, gesturing back towards the arena. 'Satan's out there. I reckon he'll make short shrift of that little runt they've put him in with. Don't go far.'

'I won't,' Minnie said, and walked nonchalantly a few feet away from the bouncer. She peered into the gloom. Where was Tom? He was meant to be waiting where she'd left him, but there was no sign of him. She reached again for the whistle but knew it would only draw attention to herself. And although the bouncer was about as wide as he was tall, that didn't mean he couldn't run fast.

And that was the moment Monkey decided to scramble out from underneath her jacket and onto her head.

'Oi,' the bouncer bellowed. 'What you got there?'

Minnie turned, saw the realisation slowly dawning on his face as she wrestled to grab hold of the monkey. The bouncer took a step towards her, and then, from out of nowhere, Tom emerged from the shadows, lunged at the man and grabbed hold of his leg. The bouncer shook him off as if he was no more than a fly, never even taking his eyes off Minnie. For a moment, everything seemed to freeze, then Tom hurled something at the man, something Minnie couldn't see properly in the darkness. Whatever it was, it was heavy and it hit the fella on the back of the head. He turned towards Tom, his huge hands instinctively formed into fists. Minnie saw the fear in Tom's eyes and then he shouted, 'Run, Min! Run! Now!'

Without thinking, clutching the monkey to her chest, she turned and ran.

She ducked down side turnings and alleys, not knowing where she was going or what lay round the next corner. Half a mile or so from the Pit, she slipped into a doorway, her heart thundering in her chest. Monkey was making a strange whimpering sound, and clinging on to her jacket for dear life. At least he wasn't trying to get away. Tom should be here any minute. She popped her head out of the doorway and realised with a slow, sickening dread that Tom wasn't behind her.

She left the safety of the doorway and carefully retraced her steps back to the Pit, keeping to the shadows and darkness all the way. No sign of Tom. She crept down the alleyway leading to the rear entrance and peeped round the corner of the building.

There was no one there. No bouncer. No lights. No men slipping in and out. The place looked dead, as if it hadn't been open in years.

And there was no sign of Tom.

TWENTY-TWO

Minnie had suffered another sleepless night, this time worrying about Tom. If he didn't show his face today, she'd have to confess to Albert what they'd been up to, and ask for his help. She wasn't looking forward to that conversation.

The letter was propped up on the kitchen table. She didn't need to open it to know it was another missive from Teddy's solicitors. A request for Miss Minnie Ward to visit Lord Linton in Broadmoor, although it would be worded as a command rather than a request. He wasn't giving up.

'Problems?' Frances said, as Minnie laid the letter to one side.

'You could say that.'

'Anything I can help with?'

Minnie shook her head. 'I reckon I'm the only person who can sort this one out.'

Frances gave a half-smile, already distracted. She gazed out of the window as she drank her tea and finished off a slice of bread and butter.

'Problems?' Minnie said, echoing Frances's words deliberately.

'It's Jack. Since all that stuff came out about the Trafalgar Theatre he says he wants to look after me. Make up for what happened.'

'Why's that a problem? I thought you liked him.'

'I do, but he's being a bit much at the moment. He watches me when I'm walking, gazes at my limp, and this soppy look comes over his face. Like I'm a three-legged puppy. Could you have a word? Tell him I'm all right?'

'Of course. I'll speak to him, I promise.'

'Thanks. And you're sure there ain't nothing I can do to help with your problem? You can just talk about it, even if I can't help.'

Minnie fell silent. She was so used to dealing with things on her own, it was never easy for her to open up to other people. But Frances was different. And sometimes a problem shared was most definitely a problem halved. So, cutting out the gorier details, she gave Frances a brief history of her involvement with Teddy Linton, the visit to Broadmoor, and his threat thinly veiled as a request.

'Why don't you just tell him to sling his hook?' Frances said. 'Would he really pull the plug on the Palace? He sounds to me like a chap who likes to feel he's in control. If he takes his money out of the Palace, where's the fun for him?'

'I've been thinking that. But I ain't sure I wanna take the risk.'

'And this Ida woman? Rose's ma? You spoken to her about it?'

Minnie shook her head. 'I was hoping I could avoid it. That it would all just go away. But now he's asking for another visit, and I'm guessing he ain't given up on the idea of Ida showing her forgiveness.'

'Then I'd have a chat with Ida. Maybe the two of you can come up with a plan.'

Minnie sighed. It wasn't going to be that easy, she knew. But she hadn't spoken to Ida for a week or two, and it was always good to see her. The woman was the closest thing Minnie had to a mother, had been for years. She finished off her tea and cleared away the breakfast things.

'You out and about today?' she asked Frances.

'In an hour or so. Gotta drop these off at the Athenaeum.' Frances gestured to a pile of costumes.

'You couldn't do me a favour, could you? Just ask if anyone's seen anything of Tom Neville?'

'That nice-looking fella who was here yesterday? What's happened?'

'He's on the missing list and I could do with finding him before Albert notices,' Minnie said, grabbing her coat and bonnet. '"Nice-looking", eh? We'll have a little chat about that later.'

Minnie popped into the Palace on her way to Ida's. As she passed Kippy's workshop, she spotted Jack sawing a piece of timber. No time like the present.

'Can I have a quick word?'

'Anything for you, Minnie,' Jack said, his face splitting into a broad grin.

God, he wasn't making this any easier. She looked round the room and back out in the corridor. If she asked Jack to go somewhere more private, he'd think he was about to get the sack. And there was no one else within earshot. 'It's about Frances,' she said.

He frowned. 'There's nothing wrong, is there?'

She shook her head. 'No, nothing wrong. It's just – I know you feel there's some kind of special connection between you.'

He blushed so violently his ears looked as if they were about to go up in flames. 'She told you?'

There'd been no need for Frances to tell her. It was obvious to everyone in the Palace, but she didn't need to embarrass the lad by telling him that.

'She did. And she's a lovely girl; I can see why you like her so much.'

He visibly relaxed, the blush subsiding. 'But?'

Minnie inhaled deeply. 'It's just – since all this came out about the Trafalgar, she feels you're being a bit overprotective.'

He nodded. 'I know. She told me. It's just – with everything that's been going on – I feel like I need to take care of her. She was there that day. If you and Albert reckon me and Bernard might be targets, why not Frances?'

Minnie shook her head. 'Whoever it is who's doing this, he's going after people he feels were responsible for what happened. Frances was an innocent victim. He won't be after her.'

He nodded his head again. 'Well, thanks for letting me know, Min,' he said, turning back to his work. 'I'll back off.'

She went to put her hand on his shoulder but thought better of it and headed to her office.

The night before, when she'd got back to the Palace, she and Tansie had removed the screws and eased the metal collar from Monkey's neck. The creature's skin beneath was raw-looking and sore in places. Minnie had soaked a cloth in some salt water and gone to dab it gently on Monkey's inflamed skin. The creature screamed and bared his teeth at her.

'Leave it, Min,' Tansie had said. 'I'll try again later. When he's calmed down a bit.'

Now Tansie was in Minnie's office, feeding Monkey tiny pieces of what looked and smelled like a very nice steak and kidney pudding.

'I don't reckon they fed him the whole time they had him, Min,' he said. 'He's starving.'

'They probably thought hunger would make him a better killer,' a familiar voice said and Minnie turned to see Dorothy holding a jar of something.

'Dickinson's Salve,' Dorothy said, holding up the jar. 'My father—'

'The rabbit-stuffer?' Minnie said, recalling what Albert had told her about the display in Dorothy's office.

'He preferred to be called a natural scientist. But yes, rabbit-stuffer among other things. We had our own small zoo when I was growing up. Father took in damaged animals, nursed them back to health. He swore by this stuff.'

She handed the jar to Tansie, who tentatively started rubbing the salve on Monkey's neck while distracting him with larger portions of pudding.

'Were you looking for me?' Minnie said to Dorothy. 'Assuming you didn't just pop by to tend Monkey's wounds.'

'No. I came to talk about insurance premiums,' Dorothy said, withdrawing a bundle of papers from her bag. 'I saw the state that poor creature was in and remembered the salve my father used. Popped round to my mother's and discovered a jar of it in the cupboard. Not sure if it will still work, but it's worth a try.'

'He ain't screaming,' Tansie said, stroking Monkey between his eyes. 'So that's something at least.'

Minnie popped the papers in her desk drawer. 'Any news from Tom?' she asked Tansie.

'Nothing. I sent Bobby out again this morning, but no one's seen hide nor hair of him.'

A door slammed down the corridor and moments later Bobby appeared, panting hard.

'No sign of him,' Bobby said, gasping for air. The lad always did everything at twice the normal speed, as if he was worried he wouldn't get paid if he didn't go fast enough.

'You went to his rooms?'

Bobby nodded. 'And Albert's. The housekeeper there said she ain't seen him all day. Wanted to know what the problem was, so I made up some old blarney and scarpered.'

Knowing Bobby, the old blarney hadn't been entirely convincing, certainly not for someone as eagle-eyed as Mrs Byrne. Which meant Albert would be in here before long, wanting to know what was going on.

'And you looked in the Red Lion? The Dog and Duck?' Tansie said, the anxiety evident in his voice.

'Everywhere. Any pub near his rooms or Albert's house. He weren't there.'

'Any other ideas, Min?' Tansie asked.

She shook her head. 'We'll have to go back to the Pit.'

'Tansie sent me there first thing,' Bobby said. 'It's all shut up. Quiet as the grave. I knocked on the door, front and back, but no answer, and it just had a feel about it like there was no one inside.'

'Christ almighty,' Tansie said, 'I told you to have a sniff around, not bang on the bleedin' door.'

Bobby winced at Tansie's anger, but Minnie knew it wasn't directed at the lad. Tansie was worried, really worried.

'So, the question is,' Minnie said, 'do I go round now and tell Albert what happened, or do I wait for him to figure out something's up?'

'Lay low, Min,' Tansie said, rubbing crumbs off his hands and all over her office floor. 'Tom might turn up, and then Albert don't need to know nothing about it, does he?'

It sounded like a plan, but somehow Minnie knew Tom wasn't going to be showing his face any time soon.

A tall, angular man in a dark suit appeared in the doorway of the office, clipboard in one hand, pen in the other.

'Mr Tansford?' he said, peering at Tansie.

Tansie grunted an acknowledgement. Official-looking chaps always got his back up.

'My name is Mr Potter. I work for the firm of Wendall and Robinson. Property valuers. I've been sent by Lord Linton to determine the value of this music hall.'

'You what?' Tansie said, his voice low and deliberate.

Minnie and Bobby exchanged a look. Both of them knew that tone of voice. Tansie was about to explode and Potter had no idea. For an instant, she considered warning the man, but he was already ploughing on, now speaking with a deliberation to match Tansie's, as if he were talking to a child.

187

'Lord Linton is the majority owner of this establishment. He is considering selling his share, and has asked my firm to evaluate the property to that end. So, my good man, if you'll be so kind as to show me around?'

A hush settled on the room that felt as if it extended throughout the entire building. Minnie imagined everyone frozen in the midst of their jobs, poised for the eruption.

'I ain't your good man,' Tansie said with disturbing calm. 'And if you know what's good for you, you'll remove yourself from "this establishment" quick smart.'

Potter looked confused. 'I'm afraid that's not possible. I have a job to complete.'

'It's gonna be very difficult to complete it with my boot inserted up your arse.'

'I beg your pardon?' Potter said, horrified.

'So you should. Now, get out of my music hall before I have you thrown out. And let Lord Winky-Blinky Linton know there'll be no selling of the Palace. Not on my watch.'

Tansie deliberately turned away, dismissing Potter. Potter peered questioningly at Minnie. She nodded and gestured with her hand for Potter to be on his way. And, thankfully, he complied. For now, at least. But, knowing Teddy, this wouldn't be the last they'd hear of him.

Ida Watkins was occupied, as usual, with making artificial flowers when Minnie arrived at her house. They hugged, then Minnie slipped into her favourite chair and grabbed a handful of wire stalks and a length of ribbon. She didn't have Ida's skill with making the actual flowers, but she could produce a flower stalk in her sleep. The two women fell immediately into a gentle rhythm, their fingers moving without thought. As she worked, Minnie looked round the room, its contents so familiar to her she barely noticed them any more. Everything was worn with use, furniture scuffed, blankets unravelled and reknitted countless times, cups chipped but not badly enough to be thrown away. She was so at home here, it felt wrong to introduce the subject of Teddy, but there was no longer any avoiding it. She told Ida about the visit to Broadmoor and Teddy's request that both she and Ida provide some sort of testimony stating they had forgiven him.

'Are you saying you've already been to see him?' Ida said.

'I have.'

'Why on earth would you do that? And why are you telling me about it now?' Ida said, her mouth tight, her eyes averted. 'You know I'm never gonna forgive him.'

'I ain't asking you to. I ain't gonna forgive him either.'

'So? What's all this about then?' Ida rose from her seat with the gentle groan that accompanied most of her movements these days; her back was playing up all the time, not helped by the hours she spent bent over her work. She crossed to the stove to put the kettle on. She was still avoiding Minnie's eye, and Minnie knew the woman was angry with her and trying to keep a lid on it.

Minnie said nothing and continued winding the ribbon onto the wires. Why had she told Ida? She didn't want to go to Broadmoor again, and it would be over her dead body that Ida would sign any statement of forgiveness. So why tell Ida? The mechanical motion of winding the ribbon enabled her to think and, as her fingers reached for another length of material, she knew the reason why.

'You're the only one who really understands,' she said. 'Tansie was upset about Rose, but a lot of that was to do with guilt; he felt he should have protected her somehow. Billy's gone. Albert never knew her, although he fought hard enough to find out who killed her. You're the only one who knows who she really was. What a hole she's left in our lives.'

Ida poured the hot water into the pot, stirred the tea leaves.

She said nothing, but her manner shifted. She was less angry, paying attention to Minnie's words and leaving her space to speak. Most of what Minnie knew about being a good listener she'd learned from Ida, the rest from Albert.

'I need you to keep me strong,' Minnie said. 'I'm terrified Teddy's gonna withdraw his money so there's this temptation to do what he asks. For Tanse, and Kippy, and Bernard and Frances, and everyone else who works at the Palace. If I don't think about you, about what you lost, I might be able to convince myself to give him what he wants.'

'What about you?' Ida said, pouring the tea and handing Minnie a cup. 'You talk about Tansie and Frances and all the others. What about you? What do you lose if the Palace goes under?'

'Everything. Everything I've worked so hard to achieve, the life I've made for myself. I'll lose it all.'

Ida leaned both arms on the table and gave Minnie a long stare. 'No, you won't. You'll lose your job, but you'll get another one. You'll miss seeing Tansie and the others every day, but they won't disappear from your life, not unless you want them to. Things will change if the Palace goes under, Min, but you won't lose yourself. The woman you've become since that bastard Beresford – she's here to stay, with or without the Palace.'

Minnie sipped her tea, then reached across the table for Ida's hand. Ida and Rose had been the ones to patch her up after the botched abortion that had nearly killed her. Now Rose was gone, and Ida was the only one who knew just how much damage had been done to Minnie that day. Albert knew about the consequences, the fact she couldn't have children, but he hadn't been there when it happened. He hadn't mopped up the blood, held her while she cried and told her it would all be all right.

The two women said nothing for a few minutes. Then, as if by some unspoken agreement, they quietly resumed their work and began to talk of other less important things.

TWENTY-THREE

'And what precisely am I expected to do with that?'

Mrs Byrne threw a pillowcase down on Albert's desk. There was a large, oily-looking stain across most of one side. Albert sniffed it. Goose grease.

With the realisation that Bernard might be the next victim, Albert had offered to put him up and hopefully keep him out of harm's way. The problem was, if the killer didn't murder him, Mrs Byrne probably would. Albert favoured a quiet home life, particularly when he was working on a case as complicated as this one.

'I'll have a word,' he said. 'Perhaps suggest he applies a little less. Although it's a good sign that he's using it again. Shows his spirits are picking up a little.'

'I don't care about his *spirits*, Albert. I care about how much longer I'm going to have to spend doing the laundry. And he's been in my kitchen. Moved things around. I can't find anything now. He says it's a better system. I liked the system I had before, thank you very much. And while you're at it, can you persuade him to abandon the Shakespeare? I don't understand what he's saying half of the time.'

'That may be a little trickier, but I'll try. Any sign of Tom this morning?' he asked, trying to get Mrs Byrne off the vexatious subject of Bernard Reynolds. 'We've got a great deal of work to get through.'

'Nothing,' she sniffed. 'I've just come from Fletcher's and he's not there. There was a lad here earlier looking for him.'

'What sort of lad?'

'Scruffy-looking thing. Lick of dark hair that kept falling into his eyes.'

'Bobby? From the Palace?'

'He didn't give a name. Said he needed Tom to make up a side in football, which was clearly nonsense with Tom's dicky ankle.'

Someone from the Palace was looking for Tom, and wanted to keep it a secret. Tansie? Minnie? Something suspicious was going on, and whatever it was, it probably didn't spell good news. Secrets and the Palace made very poor bedfellows in Albert's experience.

'In Tom's absence, maybe our Shakespearean friend could lend a hand with the case?' Mrs Byrne suggested. 'It would get him out from under my feet, at the very least.'

'I think Bernard's better off sticking to the theatre, don't you?' Albert said. 'If Tom turns up, you have my permission to insert a flea in his ear. I'm going out.'

Albert took the omnibus to James Tomlinson's family home, getting off a few stops before Sheridan Street. He needed fresh air and the rhythm of walking to organise his thoughts. This interview was not going to be an easy one.

33 Sheridan Street was in a row of shabby terraced houses. One or two tenants had made an effort by keeping the front step clean and washing the windows, but the majority of the houses spoke of a quiet despair. Number 33 was no different. The man who opened the door looked as if he rarely left the house, blinking frantically at the sunlight and backing away into the darkness behind him. Albert introduced himself, explained why he was there, and Mr Tomlinson invited him in.

The room Albert entered was dark, with the curtains drawn

and the only light coming from a single candle that looked in danger of flickering out at any minute. Through an open door, Albert could see a kitchen beyond, and stairs presumably leading up to bedrooms. But Mr Tomlinson appeared to be living in this single room. Blankets and pillows were piled in one corner, to create a makeshift bed come nightfall. A dirty plate and cup sat on a table next to a Bible, open to the book of Daniel.

Mr Tomlinson offered Albert a seat. Truthfully, he didn't want to sit down. But, from his days on the force, he'd got used to hiding his alarm at people's living conditions. He perched carefully on the edge of an armchair.

'So what's he done?' Tomlinson said, after Albert had explained his reason for visiting. His breathing was laboured and he looked as if he was in the final stages of consumption.

'Why do you assume James has done something?' Albert asked.

'Well, look at yourself. Fellas like you don't come calling with good news. So he's either dead or in the nick.'

'Neither. I was just hoping to speak to James about the Trafalgar Theatre.'

Tomlinson's hand reached instinctively for his Bible, as if it might provide him with some sort of protection. His breathing grew heavier, and he erupted into a violent coughing fit, quelled only by several gulps from a bottle of beer.

'I'm sorry to cause you distress,' Albert said. 'I understand you lost a child that day. I wouldn't ask you if it wasn't important.'

'There's nothing I can tell you. My lovely girl died that day, James survived. Some days I wish it had been the other way round. Or that the good Lord had seen fit to take both of them. James, he just weren't the same after. His mother, God rest her soul, she tried her hardest. But we couldn't help him. When Father Mulligan offered to help, it was a godsend, to tell the truth.'

'He was at Finsbury Asylum for a long time. Did you visit him often?'

'We were told not to. Told it wasn't helping his recovery. We just wanted him to get well, so we did as they asked.' He spat into the fireplace, a lump of green phlegm barely raising a hiss from the meagre flames.

'And did you see James when he was released?'

'Only the once. He came here. Said he wanted some stuff from his old room. I couldn't imagine what he'd be after, but he came back downstairs with an old tin tobacco box. Said that was all he needed, and he left.'

'And you've never seen him since?'

He shook his head. 'Not once. His younger sister only lives two streets away. She's got six kids. James has nieces and nephews he's never even met.'

'Have you tried contacting him?'

'How would I do that? I've got no address for him. His sister said we should try to find him when I was first diagnosed. Suggested we hire a chap like you – a private detective. As if we could afford that.' He gave a bitter laugh, which erupted into another coughing fit, this one so strong Albert thought he was going to need medical help. Eventually, the coughing ceased. Tomlinson pulled the handkerchief away from his mouth, the specks of blood clearly visible.

'I don't know where my son is, Mr Easterbrook. And I ain't got the means to find him. If you manage to track him down, tell him his father's dying and would like to see him.'

As he turned his key in the front door, Mrs Byrne appeared in the hallway. 'That lad was here again, looking for Tom,' she said.

'And Tom hasn't shown his face?'

She shook her head. She was worried, he could tell. And he was starting to feel the same. A knock at the door interrupted his thoughts, and he opened it to see Minnie standing on the doorstep. Her face told him she hadn't come with good news.

'Please tell me this isn't about Tom,' Albert said.

'Sorry to disappoint,' she said grimly. 'Something's happened, Albert, and I need your help.'

He led her into the morning room, where she recounted the previous night's events. 'And yes,' she concluded, holding up both hands in a gesture of defeat, 'you're right. We shouldn't have gone there. It was dangerous. I was foolish. I was wrong. But we did it. And now Tom is missing and I've got a horrible feeling about it all.'

Albert knew this was not the time to lose his temper with Minnie. From what John had told him about Jem Blount, Tom was in serious danger, and every minute they spent discussing it, or hurling recriminations at each other, was a minute they weren't looking for Tom. But when was Minnie going to learn that she should tell him what she was planning, instead of hurtling headlong into danger and disaster? She always assumed he would put a stop to her plans and, given some of her hare-brained ideas, maybe he would. Or maybe he'd be able to help.

'Let's find him first,' he said, his voice low and overly calm. 'We can talk later about the idiocy of your undertaking.'

She nodded. If she wasn't taking offence at the suggestion she'd been an idiot, she really must be worried. 'I thought we could try the hospitals first,' she said. 'And maybe John?'

'I'll send a note to him,' Albert said, hastily scribbling something and handing it to Mrs Byrne.

'If you've led that boy into trouble,' Mrs Byrne said, 'you'll have me to answer to, Minnie Ward.'

Minnie said nothing, simply lowering her head and refusing to meet Mrs Byrne's gaze.

They trudged to St Bartholomew's, neither of them attempting to make conversation. Albert felt it was wisest to say nothing.

At Barts, they approached the admissions desk. A weary-looking man greeted them. They offered Tom's name and a brief description, and then, with a heavy sigh, the man consulted a list of names. No Tom.

'Any young men at all admitted late last night?' Albert asked.

'Plenty,' the man said. 'But none matching your description.'

Frustrated, they made their way to Guy's, where they met the same unhelpful reception. No Tom. No one who looked like him. From there, to St Thomas', Westminster and finally St George's. Nothing.

They found a coffee house and ordered tea and cake, which neither of them ate.

'We'll see if John's heard anything,' Albert said, quietly finishing the last of his tea. The unspoken words hovered in the air between them. If Tom wasn't in a hospital ward, and John had no word of him, the next stop was the morgue.

TWENTY-FOUR

Albert's feet were killing him. He'd been unable to sleep since hearing of Tom's disappearance and had risen in the early hours. He'd now been tramping the streets around Lambeth for the last three or four hours and he was very much wishing Blount lived and operated out of a different part of London. Lambeth had to be one of the most godforsaken parts of the city, and that was saying something. Buildings filthy with soot and grime – warehouses, blacking factories, soap works – reared up on all sides, making the streets and pavements feel as if the sun never found them. The sweet, slightly rancid smell from the Red Lion Brewery made him vow never to touch beer again; but at least it masked the stench from a nearby tanning yard. Albert could still remember the first time he'd learned that leather workers used dog excrement, or 'pure', to soften the hides; the word had never been so misused.

Occasionally, he passed a police officer, and they exchanged a few words. John had notified all the local police stations to keep an eye out for anyone matching Tom's description.

'I wouldn't hold your breath, though,' John had said. 'If Blount's got hold of him, this ain't likely to have a happy ending.'

Albert knew he was right. When he'd learned of Blount's involvement in Monkey's kidnap, he'd investigated the man's background and it didn't make for pleasant listening. More than one man who'd crossed Blount had wound up dead. 'We can't pin anything serious on him, though,' John had said with a sigh. 'He's got so many fellas working for him, it's always one of them who's found holding the knife, while Blount has an alibi that places him miles from the scene.'

Slowly, painfully, Albert's steps turned towards the Palace. He knew Minnie wouldn't be there – after much persuasion, she'd finally agreed to go home and get some sleep – but the place felt like home now, and at least he wouldn't have to look at the fear in Mrs B's eyes as another hour passed with no sign of Tom.

Albert found Tansie in Minnie's office, dispatching two young lads with a few shillings and a promise of more if they came back with news. Tansie had enlisted a small army of boys whose knowledge of the backstreets would put any cab driver to shame. So far, no sightings. Albert's sense of unease was growing, and he saw it reflected in everyone who knew Tom.

'Nothing?' Albert asked, although he already knew the answer.

Tansie shook his head. 'I've widened the net. Sent some of the lads further south of the river and over to the west as well. There's no sign of Tom anywhere close to Blount's haunts.'

'So he could be anywhere,' Albert said, slumping into a chair and letting exhaustion sweep through his body.

They heard the stage door slam and, for a brief moment, Albert allowed a surge of optimism. But it was John. And his face didn't suggest good news.

'What is it?' Albert asked, his body stiffening as he prepared himself for the worst.

'Newrick Briggs,' John said. 'The fella who lent his dog so that Minnie could get inside the Pit. He's been found dead. Drowned.'

'And it weren't no accident, I'm assuming,' Tansie said.

John shook his head. 'Not unless he managed to beat himself up and break all his ribs before throwing himself in the river with bricks in his pockets. No accident.'

Tansie swore under his breath, then reached into the desk drawer and took out a bottle of brandy and three glasses. John shook his head, but Albert accepted the drink and downed it in one sharp motion.

'This is all my fault,' Tansie said, staring vacantly into the distance. 'If I'd just kept my mouth shut, Blount would never have taken Monkey. Now look where we are. Newrick dead. Tom missing – probably dead, let's be honest.'

'Don't say that. Don't you dare say that, Tanse.'

All three of them turned. Minnie stood in the doorway. She looked awful, her face grey with fatigue. 'Couldn't sleep,' she said, although she looked as if she'd drop into a deep slumber the minute her head touched the pillow.

'He's right though, Minnie,' Albert said. 'We need to prepare ourselves for bad news. Why would Blount kill Newrick, and keep Tom alive?'

'Because it's Tom,' Minnie said, her hands clenched tightly into tiny fists. 'And because we can't lose anyone else.'

It didn't work like that. But Minnie knew that, as well as anyone did. So the words went unsaid.

John coughed. 'There's something else,' he said.

All three of them looked at him expectantly.

'Another body came into the morgue an hour ago. A colleague of mine saw it when they brought it in. He can't be sure, but he said it matches the description of Tom.'

When Albert had left the police force he'd hoped he'd never have to visit a morgue again. It was one part of his job he'd really hated. And now he was back, probably about to identify someone he knew and cared about. Loved, if he was honest with himself. Tom's enthusiasm and optimism were infectious; life was better when he was around.

Albert had insisted on being the one to see the body. Minnie had put up a fight, had said she should at least accompany him, but he'd told her no and something in the way he spoke must have convinced her because she'd backed down. To Albert's mind, Minnie had had more than her fair share of dead bodies and, besides, Tom worked for him. It was his job to say a last farewell. He'd refused John's offer to accompany him as well; it made more sense for John to be out on the streets, tracking down Blount, rather than holding Albert's hand while he identified Tom's body.

As he navigated his way downstairs into the bowels of the building it was the smell that struck him first, a smell he thought he'd forgotten but which returned to him like a childhood memory. Disinfectant, soap, a clinical smell that couldn't mask something disturbing lying underneath it. The sweetness of decay, Albert thought.

He pulled his coat and scarf tighter round his body as his breath misted in the air. They kept these places so cold. After taking a few dead-end corridors he finally reached a door labelled as the morgue. The room had a high ceiling, with tiles reaching up to the top of the windows. He didn't see the point of the windows; they were in the basement of the hospital and there was nothing to see out of them. Maybe it was to give the illusion of something normal, in a place where nothing normal ever took place. Along one wall was a long sink, more like a cattle trough. And in the middle of the room, drawing all eyes to it, a marble table, large enough to hold a man.

They'd placed a sheet over him, covering him completely. Albert knew the routine. He'd be asked to come closer, then the sheet would be drawn back and he would be asked if he could identify the body. When he'd been a police officer, he'd been the one to draw back the sheet. He'd never expected to be on the other side of the arrangement and, as he took his first faltering steps towards the table, he felt his legs go from beneath him. He paused, inhaled deeply the sharp tang of disinfectant. Told himself it would be over soon. It would all be over.

The attendant drew back the sheet. Albert heard a sharp ringing in his ears, as if someone had struck a tuning fork and, for a moment, his eyes misted. Then he forced himself to look more closely. Fair hair, long eyelashes, a sprinkle of freckles across the bridge of the nose. He could understand why the police officer had thought it might be Tom. But it wasn't Tom.

Not this time, anyway.

TWENTY-FIVE

Albert had delivered the news to Minnie that the body was not Tom's, but the momentary relief had soon been replaced by renewed anxiety. Blount must have Tom kept prisoner somewhere, and Minnie dreaded to think what was happening to the lad. Either that, or he was already dead and they just hadn't found the body yet. Although neither she nor Albert wanted to stop searching, it was clear they both needed to eat, so they'd returned to Albert's house.

Albert had barely spoken to her since the news of Tom's disappearance. She wanted to get the needle with him, but she knew in her heart he was right to be angry. Now, having eaten, and not yet established where the search would take them next, Albert was staring out of his drawing-room window. Ignoring her.

'I know you're angry, but you're gonna have to talk to me sometime, Albert. Shout at me, I don't mind.'

'There's no point, is there? Shouting at you? You do just what you please, no matter how many people tell you to do otherwise.' There was a quiet steeliness in his voice that Minnie found more upsetting than if he'd lost his temper. Next he'd be telling her he was disappointed in her. That was what her ma used to tell her whenever Minnie had misbehaved as a child. It had killed her every time.

'Minnie, Jeremiah Blount hurts people for *fun*. Not because he has to, or as a way of protecting himself and his business interests. He hurts people because he enjoys it.'

'All right, I get the message. What I did was dangerous and stupid and foolhardy. Although, might I point out it was Tom who asked me to help, not the other way round. But, having said that, I was stupid to think Tom and I could pull it off when, if the last year's taught me anything, it's that if a thing can go wrong it probably will. And I was stupid not to tell you about it. I know you'd have tried to stop me, but I'm thinking now you would've been right. So start shouting.'

'Why? To make you feel better? So you can shout back and call me unreasonable and flounce out of here and refuse to forgive me until I've spent a week's wages on cake from Brown's?' He turned back to the window and his voice was low, with a hint of resignation in it that she didn't like. 'Not this time, Minnie. You know what you did was wrong. You don't need me to tell you.'

She hesitated. 'You're right, I don't need you to tell me. I just thought it might make you feel better.'

He said nothing, his back firmly turned towards her. Minutes passed, punctuated by the ticking of the clock and the cries of street sellers in the distance, and children playing closer to home.

'I take it there's no word from the hospitals?' Minnie said, breaking the silence when she could bear it no longer.

Albert shook his head. 'Tansie's got lads going to each of them every hour, but there's nothing.'

'And John doesn't have anything?'

'Nothing. It's been two days, Minnie. They've either got him held captive somewhere, or he's—'

She held up a hand to stop him. 'Don't say it, Albert.'

'Saying it doesn't make it happen.'

She gave him a withering look. 'I know that. Obviously I know that. It's just – I dunno.'

203

She stood up and reached for her coat. 'I should go. I'm in a foul mood, and I'm just taking it out on you.'

As she reached the door, a cry of distress rose from the kitchen below them. Mrs Byrne was shouting Albert's name. Something was terribly wrong.

They sped down the stairs. Mrs Byrne was by the back door, crouched over a dark shape on the floor. As she drew nearer, Minnie realised it was a person, a man. Mrs Byrne was kneeling by him, murmuring his name as she stroked his hair. She looked up, her eyes filled with tears. 'It's bad, Albert,' she said.

He knelt down, Minnie beside him. If it weren't for the fact she recognised the lad's clothes, she wouldn't have been able to tell it was Tom. His swollen face was a mass of bruising and dried blood, and his eyes looked terrible, one of them totally closed, the other not far behind. Albert went to lift him, and Tom screamed in agony. He raised a hand to stop Albert moving him any further, and Minnie saw there was something wrong with the hand, but she couldn't figure out what. Mrs Byrne was still holding Tom's head, stroking his hair, repeating his name as if that would somehow make it all right.

'Get a doctor, Minnie,' Albert said, reaching into his pocket for his wallet. 'Pay whatever you need to, but get someone here immediately.'

Leaning back against the pillows in Albert's second bedroom the next morning, Tom looked even worse than when they'd first found him. Something about the whiteness of the linen threw his skin into stark contrast. His face was swollen beyond anything Minnie would have thought possible, a tapestry of reds and purples and yellows. His left eye was swollen completely shut, his right eye just a slit. The doctor had put stitches in a cut above the right eye and repaired Tom's flapping left ear. What looked like a boot mark was visible on his cheek, he had broken at least two ribs, maybe more, and there were dog bites on his arms and legs.

But it was his right hand that made Minnie cry every time she looked at it.

'They said they was gonna break every one of my fingers,' Tom had told them the night before, as they'd waited for the doctor to arrive. 'They started with this hand.' He held up his right hand, wincing at the pain even this small movement caused. Three of the fingers were at sickening angles. 'One of Blount's thugs wanted to cut them off, a finger at a time. Said he could send them in the post to Tansie, teach him not to meddle. Blount drew the line at that, said they should just break them, it'd be more painful. They did these three, but I managed to get away before they got any further.'

The fingers were broken in several places. The doctor, a benevolent-looking elderly gentleman, was uncertain the fractures would mend. 'There's not a great deal more I can do other than splinting the fingers,' he'd said. 'If he rests the hand and we have a little luck on our side, he might be all right.'

The doctor then gave Tom a dose of laudanum, and left more with careful instructions on how to administer it. Tom had been drifting in and out of consciousness ever since. In his more lucid moments, he'd been able to answer some questions.

'They took me somewhere,' he whispered, wincing as he did so. Even talking caused him pain. 'Couldn't tell you where. Thought I was gonna die. Early this morning, they'd left just one fella guarding me. He had a skinful the night before. Fell asleep and I got away.'

'Did you recognise where you were? Any landmarks?'

'Bermondsey? Maybe. Didn't notice.' He was struggling to stay awake, and Minnie knew the laudanum was taking hold again. 'Ran. Recognised streets. Got here.' His eyelids drooped and then closed.

Between them, Minnie and Mrs Byrne were keeping a round-the-clock vigil, administering the laudanum, trying to coax Tom into eating a little something in his moments of consciousness. Meanwhile, Albert and John were knocking on every door in Bermondsey, patrolling the streets, trying to find some clue as to where Blount had held him. Tansie had offered to help, but the word on the streets was that Blount was looking for him next, so they'd all agreed it was best if Tansie laid low.

Albert had gone round to Jem Blount's house in Oakley Street with John in tow, but the blinds were all down and the curtains closed. No one answered the door. They had a look round the back, but there were no signs of life.

It was now four o'clock in the morning. Tom was sleeping heavily, occasionally crying out. When he became too agitated, Minnie would lay a hand on his arm, whisper his name, and it seemed to soothe him.

She heard the front door open, and Albert mounting the stairs. He entered the room, and Minnie wasn't sure who looked worse out of the two men. Albert gave her a questioning look, and she nodded her head. 'He's fine,' she said. 'He even managed a bit of ham hock earlier on.'

'And Bernard?'

'He got a bit theatrical about having to sleep on the sofa, but he'll live.'

Albert slumped into a chair by the fireplace and within moments he'd fallen asleep.

Minnie watched as the firelight danced across his face and thought about another time, months ago, when Albert had been brought home from Teddy Linton's house and Mrs Byrne had convinced herself he was dead. Minnie had sat by his bedside, watching the steady rise and fall of Albert's breathing, willing him to stay alive, to come back to her. Something inside her had shifted that night, with the realisation of what he meant to her.

With a small cry, Albert suddenly awoke.

'Were you dreaming?' Minnie said, smiling gently.

'Don't remember.' He glanced across at the bed. Minnie understood the feeling, the need to be endlessly attentive towards Tom. Despite what the doctor had said, they were afraid if they turned their backs for a moment he would slip away.

'He ain't going anywhere,' Minnie said, reading Albert's thoughts. 'He's on the mend now.'

Albert frowned, gazing blankly at Tom. 'I can't find any trace of Jem Blount and his men,' he said eventually, his voice flat and dull, with every ounce of his fatigue evident in the way he spoke. 'John and I have been traipsing the streets for hours, and he's got his men knocking on doors, poking around in back alleys, pulling in favours. And all I can think about is you. How it could have been you. And how I can't protect you.'

'You threw yourself in front of a bullet for me, Albert. Remember? If that ain't protecting me, I don't know what is.'

'But I can't keep you safe. No matter what I do.'

'It ain't your job, Albert.'

'But I want it to be my job,' he said, the words bursting out of him with surprising force. 'I want to take care of you. But you've made it very clear there's no future for us.'

Minnie knew how this conversation would go. They'd had it often enough. Albert would tell her how much he felt for her. She'd tell him she felt the same, but she'd fought too hard for her independence to let it go. And, besides, she couldn't give him children. And he'd make such a lovely dad. They'd circle round a few more times and then move on to something else. So she thought of telling him that they worked together and they were friends and wasn't that enough of a future? And she imagined him saying it wasn't enough of a future for him.

But something told her it was different this time. Later, she wondered if it was the fatigue or it being the early hours of the morning, or the worry about Tom and the relief of finding him again that made her speak as she did. Whatever the reason, the words were out of her mouth before she'd allowed herself to think about what she was saying.

'You should move on, Albert. Find yourself a nice young woman.'

He said nothing, his arms resting on his knees, staring down at the floor. And she knew, because she knew him so well, that he was agreeing with what she had said. So she stumbled on, wanting to hurt herself for the pain she'd caused him, for the foolishness that had led Tom into such danger.

'What about Dorothy Lawrence?' she said, a mask of bravado hiding her very real fear. What if he agreed?

'What about her?' he asked.

'She's very beautiful. And clever. Funny.'

Albert gave a gentle smile, almost to himself. 'She's a lovely woman, you're right. The presence of her husband might be an obstacle.'

Minnie shook her head. 'She ain't married. She was playing with her ring the other day, sliding it off and on her finger. There's no ring mark.'

'Maybe the ring's too big to leave a mark?'

'In which case, you'd have it made smaller or you'd wear it on a chain around your neck. No woman's gonna risk losing her wedding ring. I'm telling you, she ain't married. Loads of women do it. Call themselves missus and buy a cheap ring so fellas'll leave them alone. So don't let that be an obstacle.'

'Thanks for the advice,' he said, weariness evident in every word he spoke. 'What about you? Any potential suitors?' He gestured towards the sleeping Tom. 'Or Tansie, perhaps?'

'Do me a favour,' she exclaimed. 'Besides, I ain't looking.'

'But if you were?'

She let her gaze rest on him. 'I ain't looking, Albert. I wish I could give you what you want. You know why I can't. But I want you to know if I was looking for any of that – it would be you.'

Tom stirred, his eyelids flickering. 'Lovey-dovey,' he murmured. 'Just get on with it, the pair of you.' And he slid back into sleep.

At Tom's words, Albert had moved closer and sat on the bed. Now, as the lad's breathing grew heavier again, Minnie moved to his side, slid her hand round his shoulder. 'It's all right,' she murmured. 'He'll be all right.' Albert leaned into her, his cheek pressed against her waist.

'I'm gonna make 'em pay,' Minnie whispered.

Albert took her hand in his. '*We're* going to make them pay.'

TWENTY-SIX

A week later, the swelling and bruising had started to subside and Tom was out of bed, navigating his way around Albert's house with reasonable ease. He'd managed to get himself downstairs unassisted and was now tucking into a lamb chop provided by Mrs Byrne. His biggest problem was when he needed to cough. He'd hold a pillow against his chest, but still it was obvious how much it hurt, a sharp wince of agony contorting his features every time. 'It's my ribs, Min,' he said. 'They're bleedin' agony.'

'Can't the doctor do nothing?'

He shook his head. 'He said they've just got to heal themselves. Told me to take it easy. Which is all very well, but we've got a case to solve.'

And revenge to be exacted, Minnie thought, but said nothing. She didn't want Tom going anywhere near Jem Blount and his heavies ever again. She still hadn't figured out exactly what she was going to do to Blount. But it was going to be painful.

'Albert won't let me leave the house, Min. Mrs B is fattening me up like I'm gonna be on the menu come Christmas Day. Please tell me there's something I can do to help.'

'Talk it through with me? Sometimes that helps.'

So they travelled over the same ground. Five people connected with the Trafalgar Theatre disaster had died; four of them were definitely murder, one most likely the same. The suspect list ran to hundreds, maybe thousands of people.

'We need a break, Tom. A clue. Something to narrow down the numbers.'

'Well, I've got nothing else to do with my time. I'll have a ponder. You should go, Min. Show your face at the Palace. You ain't been there for a while. How on earth are they coping without you?'

'Good question.'

She'd sent a message a few days ago that she could be found at Albert's during the day, but there'd been no requests for her help, no appearance from Bobby. 'You don't reckon Tansie and Bernard have finally managed to burn the place down? Or flood it?'

'I reckon we'd have heard,' Tom said, suppressing a groan as he rose from the chair.

And then it dawned on her that they were coping because over the past few weeks, without her really noticing what was happening, Tansie had taken back the reins.

The Palace was quiet when she arrived there at midday, with no obvious signs of impending catastrophe. Frances was waiting in her office.

'Any news on Tom?' she asked. Minnie noticed a flush creep up the other woman's cheeks. She'd been right. Maybe there was another reason Frances's interest in Jack had waned.

'He's on the mend. He's out of bed and off the laudanum. Eating heartily, so Mrs Byrne's happy. She's spending every minute planning menus of his favourite food.'

'And his hand?'

'Painful. Still splinted, but the doctor was optimistic. We'll just have to wait and see. He's alive, that's the main thing.'

'And any news on Blount and his cronies?'

'No clue where they're hiding, but the word is that Blount's out to get Tansie next.'

Bernard came sauntering into the office. He was back at work full-time and had immersed himself in planning an act incorporating the water tank Tansie had so recklessly installed. He and Jack were currently devising a way to achieve a waterfall effect on stage, with predictable results. He was holding a pair of wet shoes in his hand, a puddle rapidly forming beneath them.

'I don't wanna know, Bernard,' Minnie said. 'Not unless it is one hundred per cent successful. Other than that, leave me out of the whole thing.'

Bernard looked mildly offended. 'One has to expect a few teething problems, Minnie. And it's rather intriguing trying to find a suitable solution. As the Bard would say, "Sweet are the uses of adversity."'

'Bernard, I am delighted you have found something to get excited about. Just remember I can't afford the insurance for flooding.'

The offended look reappeared. 'Thank you for the vote of confidence, dearest one. I was just coming to tell you that I'm going to change my clothes and then we're taking a short break for refreshments and to purchase a few additional items.'

'Such as?' Minnie said, mentally totting up costs.

'Just a length of hose, some rubber sheeting and a pillowcase.'

Minnie looked at Frances.

'Best not to ask,' Frances said.

Bernard left, a steady dripping sound accompanying him as he went back down the corridor.

'I need to get to Rosenberg's before they sell out of poplin. I'll just drop these off in Wardrobe,' Frances said, gesturing towards the costumes she'd brought with her. 'Catch you later.'

With Frances's absence, the theatre fell silent. Along with the moment just before curtain up, Minnie loved this time of day. The Palace was so quiet you could almost hear it breathing. Occasionally, there would be distant hammering from Kippy or Jack, but today there wasn't even that. She leaned back in her chair and closed her eyes.

Someone gave a gentle cough. She opened her eyes to find Albert leaning against the doorframe.

'How long you been there?' she asked.

'Long enough to know that you snore.'

'I do not,' Minnie said, incensed at the suggestion.

'Oh, you do. A delightful ladylike snore. Like angels whispering, or baby turtle doves cooing to each other in the greenwood. But it was definitely snoring.'

'Why're you here?' she said, disproportionately annoyed by him. Sneaking up on her. Watching her while she slept.

'Mrs Byrne told me to remove myself from the house. I believe I'm interfering with her intensive feeding regime for Tom. Strange that I've lived this long without realising lamb chops and sausages could mend a broken finger. Tom survived Blount, but Mrs B might yet finish him off.'

'There's a lot you don't know, Albert, but we won't start on that now.'

'And I thought you might appreciate an update on the Trafalgar murders.'

'Oh, that's what we're calling them, is it?'

'It seemed to make sense. Anyway, much as I really don't wish to do it, I'm slowly making my way down the list of dead children and speaking to their families. With Tom out of action, I was wondering if you could speak to a few.'

'Of course,' she said, all irritation instantly dispelled by the thought of getting her teeth back into the investigation. She took a list of names and addresses from him and quickly scanned it. 'The numbers next to their names? Their ages?'

Albert nodded.

There was no number higher than twelve on the list he'd given her. The full horror of the tragedy struck her anew. So many children.

'I'll get on it,' she said, glancing at her pocket watch.

'You wouldn't like to join me for a bite to eat first? I can't exactly remember when I last ate.'

'You know me, Albert. I can always find time for food.' She turned to reach behind her for her bag. It was wedged in above the safe and, as she pulled it clear, she dislodged a stage weight which had somehow found its way into her office. It fell to the floor with an almighty clang. In the empty theatre, the noise seemed to echo and reverberate through the whole building.

'Lucky that didn't land on my foot,' Minnie said, 'or it wouldn't just be Tom who was out of action.'

Albert crossed the room to help her lift the weight. She heard a door bang somewhere downstairs. Hadn't Bernard and Jack nipped out for food? And then what sounded like a cry for help. Christ, what mess had they got themselves into now?

'Best you come with me,' Minnie said. 'Knowing that pair, anything could have happened.'

As she descended the stairs ahead of Albert, Minnie assumed rehearsals had been going as disastrously as usual and braced herself for the chaos that awaited her. And then she realised something was terribly, terribly wrong.

There were three people in the tank. Two standing, one of them encircled by a mass of material. A third person was floating face down in the water. It was Bernard, and he wasn't moving. Sounds seemed to drop away, and all Minnie could hear was her own ragged breathing and the beating of her heart. She could see mouths moving, arms gesturing towards her for help, but she couldn't hear them.

Frances and Jack – she realised they were the two people

214

standing in the tank – were trying to haul Bernard out, but Frances was worse than useless, the sodden material of her dress billowing around her and weighing her down, making it almost impossible for her to move through the water.

Bernard still hadn't moved.

Albert pushed past her so roughly she almost fell over. She didn't seem able to put one foot in front of the other. Bernard was dead, that much was clear. But how could he be dead? He'd been in her office only half an hour before. There was still a wet patch where he'd dripped onto the carpet.

Albert leapt into the water tank and waded across to where Bernard lay floating. He grabbed the man under both arms and dragged him over to the side of the tank, Jack by his side.

Albert turned to her, shouted something, but she was still locked in a bubble of her own breathing, her own heartbeat. And then it was as if she'd been underwater herself and had finally lifted her head. She could hear again.

'Minnie,' Albert shouted. 'Get over here now.'

Somehow her legs started to move, almost without any effort on her part. Dimly, she was aware of Frances, struggling to get out of the water. Frances was alive; any help she needed could wait.

And then it was as if time suddenly sped up, like someone turning a zoetrope too quickly. She ran to the side of the tank. Albert and Jack were struggling to get Bernard over the edge and out of the water.

Between the three of them, they managed to haul Bernard out, but he fell to the floor with a terrible thud. Minnie ran round the other side of the tank and tried to get Frances out, but the weight of her waterlogged dress was making it impossible. Jack appeared at her side, grabbed Frances by the waist and managed to throw her over his shoulder and pull her to safety.

Albert placed both hands on the side of the tank and levered himself out. He knelt down beside Bernard, rolling the man onto his back and thumping him hard on the chest. Nothing. He did the same again, with the same result.

Bernard's lips were blue, his skin already pallid.

'Try putting him on his front,' Minnie said, some story she'd read about in a newspaper surfacing in her memory.

Albert rolled Bernard over and thumped him hard again. You'll break his ribs, Minnie thought, and then pulled herself up. He won't care about broken ribs. He's already dead.

She knelt down opposite Albert, one of them each side of Bernard's body. Together they alternately thumped and massaged Bernard, desperately trying to force him back to life. Time seemed to stand still. She had no idea how long they'd been working on him when suddenly, miraculously, he coughed. Water spurted out of his mouth and he coughed again. Albert placed his fingers on Bernard's neck and then nodded. 'He's got a pulse,' he said. Bernard gasped and spluttered, then tried to sit up.

'Stay still,' Albert said. 'Just stay there for a while.'

Bernard nodded his head almost imperceptibly. After a few minutes, he raised himself up to a sitting position and leaned back against the side of the tank. He didn't look as if he had an ounce of energy left in him. Across the room, Frances and Jack stood staring at Bernard, as if afraid to look away, afraid to move.

Minnie bolted up the stairs and returned a few minutes later with blankets for all of them, and the bottle of brandy she kept in her office. They passed it round, but Bernard refused.

'What happened?' Albert said eventually. 'Did you fall in?'

Bernard shook his head, glancing nervously round the room.

'What then?' Minnie said. 'How did it happen?'

'Pushed,' Bernard gasped. 'I was on the stepladder, figuring out how much hose we'd need to buy. Someone came up behind me. Pushed me off the ladder and held me under.'

'Did you see who it was?' Albert asked.

'I had my back to them when they pushed me, but I remember them being in the water with me, holding my head under.'

'Who was it?' Minnie asked.

Slowly, Bernard lifted a hand and pointed one trembling finger at Frances.

TWENTY-SEVEN

Bernard was alive, thanks to Albert, but he'd been admitted to hospital overnight. Just to keep an eye on him, the doctor said. Tansie had dispatched a very large and menacing friend of his to stand guard over Bernard: whatever had happened in the area below stage, it hadn't been an accident.

The rest of them had made it upstairs to Minnie's office, and she'd found a change of clothes for everyone in Wardrobe. Under different circumstances, it would have made her laugh, the sight they made in an assortment of ill-fitting items. But not today.

'So what happened?' Albert said.

Both Frances and Jack seemed reluctant to speak, but Frances eventually broke the silence. 'I've been overworked lately, taken on far too much. I had an order due at the Adelphi today and I needed at least another week to get it done.' She paused, glancing at Minnie.

'What?' Minnie said. 'You ain't gonna tell me it *was* you who tried to drown him, are you?'

Frances shook her head vigorously. ''Course not. But you ain't gonna like what I've got to tell you. Like I said, I had an order due and not enough time. I remembered there were some costumes on racks downstairs that would fit the bill. I made them for the Palace a couple of years ago, and they ain't been used in ages. I figured everyone would've forgotten about them. What with everything that's been going on, I thought I could take them, pass them on to the Adelphi and no one would know. Sorry, Min.'

Minnie waved a hand dismissively. A few pinched costumes were the least of her worries.

'When I got down there,' Frances said, 'I saw Bernard in the water. He was floating face down. I knew something weren't right, so I just got in, didn't think about it. Of course, the minute I touched the water, my skirts ballooned out with the wet. They weighed a ton. I could barely move, let alone rescue Bernard. I shouted for help, and that's when Jack appeared.'

'I thought you'd finished for the day?' Minnie said, turning to Jack.

'I had. Bernard was waiting for me while I put some tools back in Kippy's office. You know what a stickler Kippy is, and I figured he'd have my guts for garters if I left anything lying around. So I was in Kippy's office and I heard a door banging somewhere and then a minute or so later Frances called out. I found her in the tank with Bernard. I yelled for help and luckily you were still here.'

'This banging door,' Albert said. 'The stage door?'

Jack paused for a moment, as if replaying the moment, then shook his head. 'Not the stage door. One of the front doors maybe.'

'Did either of you see anyone else? Anyone at all?' Albert asked. They both shook their heads.

'Well, there must have been someone,' Minnie said. 'Bernard don't remember much about it, but he said he was definitely held underwater.'

'By me, apparently,' Frances said. 'Which is just ridiculous. Why on earth would I want to kill Bernard? And, if I did, I could think of an easier way of doing it than trying to drown him.'

'Did we ever have any joy finding the mystery woman who turned up at the Fortune, wanting to speak to Peter, Bernard's brother?' Minnie said. 'Maybe she's made a reappearance.'

Albert shook his head. 'Whoever she was, she's vanished into thin air.'

'What about footprints?' Frances said. 'Around the tank? I read a story the other day and that's how they found the killer.'

'I didn't think to check,' Albert said.

'You were fairly busy doing other things,' Minnie said. 'Like saving Bernard's life. Besides, there was so much water on the floor by that point, you'd have been hard pushed to pick out a set of footprints.'

'I still don't know how you managed to save him,' Jack said. 'I mean, he'd drowned, hadn't he? How'd you bring him back to life?'

'I suspect it was something to do with how cold the water was,' Albert said. 'There was some story in the newspapers recently. Explorers attempting to discover the North Passage. One of them went over the side of the boat. When they pulled him out, he was dead. No heartbeat, nothing. But they managed to bring him back.'

'You should offer Albert a spot here, Min,' Frances said. 'The Mighty Lazarus.'

'Except it was Jesus who did the raising from the dead, not Lazarus,' Minnie said. 'And I reckon we might get in trouble with an act called the Mighty Jesus.'

She looked at Frances and Jack, then back at Albert. 'I think we should let these two go home, don't you?'

Albert nodded, although he didn't look too happy. Minnie saw Frances and Jack out of the building, then returned to her office.

'What's up?' she said. 'You've got a face like a wet Sunday.'

'I'm wondering if we've just let our killer walk out the door.'

'Who? Frances? Don't be daft.'

'Bernard implicated her, Minnie. I asked him who'd done it, and he pointed straight at Frances.'

'And ten minutes later, when we asked him again, he said all he could remember was Frances being in the water with him.

He couldn't say for sure if she was the one who tried to drown him.'

'And he couldn't say for sure she wasn't. Remember, you were the first one who suggested it could be a woman doing all this. Why not Frances?'

'For a start-off, why would she call out for help? Why didn't she just kill Bernard and head off home?'

'You'd just dropped that stage weight. I suspect she thought she was alone in the theatre. Then she hears that almighty racket, realises someone's still there and gets concerned she might get caught. So she thinks she's probably finished Bernard off, but cries out for help anyway, just to cover her tracks.'

'Or it's like she said. She found him like that, and she jumped in to rescue him.'

'Frances was there at the Trafalgar Theatre that day,' Albert said. 'It left her lame, and she still has nightmares about it. That might be enough to make someone seek revenge. And she was very quick to change the subject when you mentioned the mystery woman at the Fortune Theatre, did you notice? All of a sudden, she's asking questions about wet footprints.'

Minnie shook her head. 'I'm telling you, it ain't her. You're just gonna have to trust my gut on this one.'

'Well, I'm still keeping a very close eye on her. I think you should move out of her rooms today.'

'And what reason am I gonna give? If you're so convinced she's the killer, ain't she gonna find it a bit suspicious that I'm suddenly moving out? Besides, whoever the murderer is, they've only gone for people who were there on that day, or somehow involved with events afterwards. I was ten years old at the time, so I think we can say fairly confidently I didn't have anything to do with it. If I stay living with Frances, I can keep an eye on her, have a little nosey when she's out.'

Albert sighed. 'You might have a point. But at the very least you should arm yourself. I've got a ladies' pistol at home. You do know how to use one?' he added, noting the look of bewilderment on her face.

'Why would I know how to shoot a gun?' Minnie said.

'No, of course not. I just somehow imagined it was part of your repertoire. Along with picking locks, passing yourself off as a man and rescuing monkeys from dens of iniquity.'

She smiled. 'An impressive set of skills, you have to agree.'

'I'll show you how to use it, and then keep the pistol on you at all times.'

'As long as there's no danger of it going off sharpish. C'mon. No time like the present.'

Back at Albert's house, he rooted in his desk until he found what he was looking for. A small, rather delicate gun that sat snugly in Minnie's hand. For something so little, the weight of it was surprising.

Albert grabbed a small box and led Minnie out into the back garden.

'Ain't the neighbours gonna have something to say about us firing bullets?'

'It's not the first time it's happened,' Albert said. 'I can normally placate them afterwards with a nice bottle of claret. Now,' he said, opening the box and removing two bullets, 'here's how we load.'

He clicked open the barrel of the gun, slid the two bullets into the chamber, closed the barrel and then placed his thumb over the hammer. It slid back into place with two sharp clicks. Albert aimed the gun towards the end of the garden and took a shot. He re-cocked the hammer and shot again.

'Now you,' he said.

Suddenly, and surprisingly, she felt nervous handling the bullets. He must have registered her concern. 'They can't do any harm until they're in the gun,' he said.

'I know. Of course, I know.' She held the two bullets in her hand and then tried unsuccessfully to open the barrel of the gun.

'Here,' Albert said, placing his hands over hers and showing her the action. His hands were warm, despite the chill in the air. She noticed the hairs peeping out from his shirt cuffs, and reminded herself she was supposed to be focusing on learning how to shoot a gun.

'And now,' he said, placing his hand over hers and moving her thumb, 'you pull back the hammer. You need to pull it all the way back until you hear the clicks or the gun won't fire. You've heard of the phrase "going off half-cocked"?'

'I do work at the Palace, Albert. It's a phrase I hear almost every day.'

'Well, if you try to fire a gun half-cocked, it won't work properly. Now, the gun's ready to fire. Always remember to keep it aimed away from people. Now, fire it.'

She raised her right hand, her arm bent.

'No,' Albert said, 'arms out straight. And aim at what you want to shoot.' He placed his hands on her waist and turned her towards the rear of the garden. Once she was in position, his hands stayed where they were. She couldn't say she minded.

'Arms straight out, hold the gun with both hands.'

Minnie did as instructed. The gun had a surprising kick for something so small, and she felt a tremor pass through her shoulder.

They spent the next half-hour reloading and firing the gun, with Albert setting up targets at the rear of the garden.

'Well,' he said, when it had started to grow dark and the air had turned even chillier, 'I wouldn't fancy your chances in the Wild West, but I think it'll be enough to keep you safe. Let's hope you never have to use it.'

223

When Minnie got home, Frances was sitting by the window, her face turned towards the road. She was obviously waiting for Minnie.

'Bernard pointed at me, but I swear to you, Minnie, it weren't me.'

'I know.'

'Does Albert know that too? He was giving me some very funny looks earlier.'

Minnie sighed. 'He doesn't know you like I do. And he used to be a copper. He thinks everyone's guilty until proven innocent. I'm sure at one point last year he had me in the frame as Rose's killer.'

Frances turned away again, staring blankly out of the window.

'You sure you don't remember seeing anyone?' Minnie said. 'It would help us no end.'

Minnie let the silence build between them. There was something Frances wanted to tell her, she was certain of it. Sometimes saying nothing yielded the best results.

But not this time. After a few minutes, Frances rose from her seat and fetched some embroidery she'd been working on. 'Best I get on with this. It's due tomorrow and I reckon there's still a few hours' work on it.' She paused for a moment, her fingers tracing the delicate work. 'Do you forgive me? For what I was gonna do with them costumes?'

'You should've told me, Frances. If it's stuff we ain't used in ages, I'd have given them to you.'

Frances slowly nodded her head. 'When you see Bernard, tell him it weren't me. Tell him I tried to save him, would you? I don't know him very well, but I hate the idea he might think ill of me.'

Minnie crossed the room and pulled Frances into a tight hug. The other woman laughed with surprise. 'It ain't wise to hug a woman who's holding a needle, you know.'

Or a gun, Minnie thought.

TWENTY-EIGHT

Albert took the parcel of lamb chops from the butcher and left the shop. It was Mrs Byrne's job to collect the shopping, but she clearly didn't feel comfortable leaving Tom's side. Besides, Albert needed a break from the slightly claustrophobic atmosphere in his house, Tom wincing with every step and Bernard trawling his memory for Shakespearean quotes about pain and suffering. Of which there were far too many.

He'd just turned onto St James's Street when he spotted a figure on the other side of the road.

Jem Blount.

The man hadn't seen him. Albert wasn't even certain if Blount knew who he was. He didn't appear to have his lackeys with him, just a young woman in a gaudy dress – not much more than a child – who was holding on to his arm, her face tilted up towards his, bright with expectation but also a flicker of fear. She said something Albert couldn't catch over the clip of horses' hooves as carriages rumbled past. With no warning, exactly as he had done at the Westminster Pit with a different woman, Blount slapped her hard across the face, the sharp crack ringing out across the busy street. A few people turned at the noise, but then seemed to take in the girl's tawdry clothes and turned back again, paying no mind. She had fallen to the ground, her hand pressed against her cheek, but she scrambled to stand up, as if fearful that staying still for too long would invite further punishment.

Barely giving himself time to check for oncoming horses, Albert sprinted across the road. Blount saw him approaching and was on the verge of saying something when Albert punched him hard in the face. The blow was aimed at Blount's nose, but he saw it coming and turned his head at the last minute. Still, Albert felt the reassuring crunch of bone beneath his fist and knew he'd caused some damage to the other man's cheek.

Blount glanced behind him reflexively, and then realised he was alone. The girl, who had righted herself by now, looked from one man to the other and stepped backwards into a newsagent's doorway. Passers-by gave them a wide berth, as if knowing to keep their distance.

Blood thumped in Albert's ears and his focus narrowed to Blount, watching him to see what the man was about to do next. He saw Blount's hands form into fists. Good. The man was tall and broad, but his arms and fists didn't look the strongest: certainly not as strong as Albert's. Blount relied too much on his henchmen to do his fighting for him, but they were nowhere to be seen.

Blount took two steps backwards, and for a moment Albert thought he was going to walk away. He reached down, brushing some dust off his trousers and, just a moment too quickly for Albert to realise what was happening, he had pulled up his trouser cuff and removed a knife strapped to his leg. He leered at Albert, the knife glinting in his hand. Albert shifted his attention to the knife. Knowing what he did of Blount, he guessed the man wouldn't be content with merely wounding him.

Albert's fear must have been evident on his face because Blount laughed, then swopped the knife from hand to hand a few times, as if relishing this moment. He made a few faint lunges at Albert, easy enough to sidestep, but Albert knew he was being toyed with.

226

Soon enough Blount would tire of this game, and one swift move could see the blade inserted between Albert's ribs.

Dimly, Albert was aware of passers-by, other shoppers. Some walked by without seeming to notice Blount's knife. Others registered it and hurried on, heads down. Why was no one calling for help?

He tried to kick the blade out of Blount's hand, but Blount simply shifted out of his reach. If he turned and ran, he had no guarantee Blount wouldn't outpace him. And he'd rather have the knife in front of him, where he could see it, than behind him, ready at any moment to plunge into his back. His options were limited. Astonishingly, he realised he still had the wrapped meat in his hand. He threw the parcel hard at Blount's head. The man moved to avoid it and, just at the moment when he was slightly off balance, Albert rushed at him, slamming a ringing blow to the side of his head. Blount doubled over, but he held the knife firm. Albert grabbed the arm holding the knife and shook it, trying to loosen Blount's grip, but to no effect. Blount elbowed him in the ribs, and Albert stumbled backwards. He was winded, but he ignored the pain and forced himself to straighten up; he couldn't leave himself exposed to Blount's attack.

He heard voices that seemed to be coming from some distance away, but he couldn't fathom what was being said. A shout? A whistle? He couldn't be sure.

The two men faced each other, each of them crouched forward, legs apart. Whatever Albert was going to do, it had to be swift and overwhelming. Blount was stronger than he looked, and Albert knew he'd be lucky to escape with his life.

With his eyes locked on Blount's he was only dimly aware of a blur of movement out of the corner of his eye. The young woman emerged from the newsagent's and rushed towards Blount, calling his name. She grabbed his arm and looked as if she was trying to pull him away from the fight. Never taking his eyes off Albert,

Blount swore at her and swept his arm in a wide arc to fling her off. But something about his movement unbalanced him. He took a step backwards to reposition himself, but he was right at the edge of the kerb and he fell into the road.

He didn't stand a chance. The cab driver tried his best to rein in his horse, but he was too close to save Blount. The horse reared up, his eyes wide with fear, his ears pinned back close to his head. And then an awful sound, a scream of pain and horror that could have come from either Blount or the horse, Albert couldn't be sure. Perhaps it came from both. Then the grinding of the cab wheels and the sharp splinter of wood. What was left of Blount was barely recognisable, his skull caved in on one side.

Instinctively, Albert sprang forward to help, but somebody held him back. A police officer, his face vaguely familiar to Albert. 'No, sir. Stay back. You can't do nothing now. And the nag's still spooked. There's no knowing what he'll do.'

Albert nodded. There was nothing to be done. He looked behind him and then up and down the length of the street. The girl had vanished into the shadows as if she'd never been there.

Albert had just finished giving his statement when John arrived back at the station. He took one glance at Albert, then led him into an interview room and sent a young constable to make some sweet tea. While Albert sipped the drink, John read through his statement.

'A fight, you say?'

Albert nodded. The effort of moving his head was almost more than he could bear.

'You sure about that? My PC says he saw Blount in an argument with some tail and you were just standing nearby. Didn't say nothing about a fight.'

'I think I know when I've been in a fight, John.'

'And I think you've had a terrible shock, Albert. Seeing a fella run over by a hansom cab would tip anyone up. Make them remember things that perhaps weren't what happened after all.'

Albert stared at him, saying nothing.

'Accidents like these, they happen every day,' John said. 'We just write it off and get on with catching the villains. If there was a fight going on beforehand, there'd be a lot more paperwork, a lot more explaining to do. My men are very busy at the moment. And Blount's men – if they ain't already scattered to the four winds – they might want to have words with someone seen fighting their boss just before he died. Now,' John said, screwing Albert's statement into a ball and lobbing it into a wastepaper bin, 'you finish that tea and we'll write your statement together. I think you'll find it's a lot simpler than you're remembering.'

'The man is dead, John.'

'That he is, but not by your hand. Like you said, he tripped and fell into the road. And this is Jeremiah Blount we're talking about. To my way of thinking, you deserve a bleedin' medal. Now, let's get this written and get you home.'

TWENTY-NINE

Minnie was tidying her room when she heard the door slam. She found Frances in the living room, distressed, out of breath, standing by the window looking out at the busy street below.

'What's wrong?' Minnie said.

Frances jumped at Minnie's voice, as if she'd thought she was alone. 'What did you say to Jack?' she said, a hint of accusation creeping into her voice.

'What about?'

'When you spoke to him. Told him to stop treating me like a china doll. What exactly did you say?'

'Pretty much that. We chatted about you. I said you were able to take care of yourself.'

'And how did he take it?'

'He seemed fine.' Minnie paused, replaying the scene in her head. 'Maybe a little too fine. As if what I said was of no consequence. Why? What's happened?'

Frances slumped into an armchair. 'I've just seen him at the Palace. He's accused me of all sorts. He reckons you and I have been having what he called "cosy little chats". That I've been telling you stuff about him. Stuff he didn't want no one else to know.'

'Like what?'

Frances shrugged. 'I dunno. He weren't too clear on the details.

He was just acting really strange. Angry, in a way I've never seen him before. He scared me, Min.' She rubbed her wrists.

'Did he hurt you?'

'He didn't mean to. He just grabbed hold of me when he was trying to get his point across.' She held out her wrists. The bruises were already starting to form.

'Well, that's Jack's days at the Palace numbered,' Minnie said.

Frances lifted her head, a look of panic crossing her face. 'Don't do nothing, Min. He'll know I told you and—'

'And what? If he comes near you again, I'll call the police on him.'

'Don't do that, Min. He's no trouble, really. And he's had a lot to deal with—' She broke off.

'Like what?'

Frances gave her a hard look. 'Swear you won't tell no one? I promised him I'd never tell, but if you know, I reckon you'll think about him a bit more kindly.'

'I ain't making any promises, Frances. Not without knowing what you're gonna say.'

Frances sighed, but it was obvious she'd already decided to tell Minnie. 'We were both at the Trafalgar that day. Both lived through something awful, but it was worse for Jack.'

'How so?'

'He lost someone that day. His twin sister.'

Minnie thought for a moment, reliving the conversation at the Palace after Lennie Thomas's poisoning, when Jack had revealed he'd been at the Trafalgar. 'He's never mentioned a sister to me. Never mind a twin.'

'He wouldn't. He don't want no one knowing about it. I don't reckon he's ever got over it. The problem is, he reckons I look like her. His dead sister. Reckons she'd have been the spit of me if she'd lived. That's why he thinks we're somehow bound together, but why he ain't interested in me as a sweetheart. We both lived through the same thing, both somehow ended up working for the Palace and got to know each other. And I look just like her, he says.'

Minnie dropped into the other armchair. 'That's a bit bleedin' creepy if you ask me. Sounds like you've had a lucky escape.'

Frances shivered. Minnie leapt up and wrapped a blanket round her shoulders.

'You should have told me earlier,' Minnie said. 'I've thought for ages you knew more than you were letting on.'

'It weren't my story to tell. Trouble is, he's getting – well, strange. Intense. If you get him sacked, he's gonna know it's got something to do with me.'

'I can get Kippy to make up some excuse. Jack's only ever been a casual worker. Kippy can just say the money's dried up – which ain't too far from the truth – and there's no more work. I can't have him staying on at the Palace, Frances. Not if he makes you feel like this.'

Frances squeezed her hand by way of thanks.

'C'mon,' Minnie said, crossing over to the stove and checking there was water in the kettle. 'Let's have a cuppa. Unless you'd prefer something stronger?'

'There's a bit of gin left. I wouldn't say no.'

After the first few sips Frances visibly relaxed. 'That Tom fella who works for Albert,' she said. 'What's he like?'

'Interested, are you?'

Frances smiled. 'Always interested, Min, if it's the right fella.'

'Tom's a lovely lad. Had a terrible time of it last year, though. I ain't sure he's totally over it.'

'Might he need consoling?' Frances said, giving Minnie an arch look.

'You,' Minnie said, waving her gin glass at Frances, 'are incorrigible. Besides, Tom's a lot younger than Jack, and you've always said Jack feels like he's too young for you. Aside from the fact he's half cracked.'

'You know what I mean. It ain't Jack's age, as such, it's more how he seems. I told you, didn't I, when I first got to know him, he always looked like he needed a good scrub. Particularly his hands. Black, they were.'

'Why so dirty?' Minnie asked. 'The stuff he does for Kippy, it's mucky work sometimes, but nothing a good wash wouldn't sort.'

'Oh, it ain't what he does at the Palace. It's one of his other jobs.'

Minnie wasn't surprised to hear Jack took on other work. A lot of people she knew had to work more than one job if they wanted to keep the wolf from the door.

'What's that, then?' she asked.

'He's a sweep,' Frances said, leaning forward and topping up Minnie's glass.

'What?' Minnie said, sobering up instantly.

Frances gave her a bemused look. 'A sweep. You know, fella with a load of rods and brushes, sorts out your flue.' She started to giggle. 'Rude.'

'How long's Jack been doing that?'

Frances shrugged. 'I dunno. It's only an occasional thing. Why're you so interested?'

'No reason,' Minnie said, feigning indifference while her head was racing to make the connections. 'It's just he's never mentioned it.'

'Well, it ain't exactly a riveting topic of conversation, is it? Where you going?' Frances said, as Minnie leapt up and reached for her coat and bonnet.

'Need to see a man about a chair.'

THIRTY

From Frances's rooms it was a short walk to the Fortune Theatre. Luck was on her side, and Ned the caretaker was just finishing his lunch.

'You here about the chairs?' he said. ''Cos you can't have 'em back. The punters love 'em. They reckon pink and gold together is a dead classy combination.'

Minnie shook her head. 'You're fine. I just wanted to ask you something. When you came to collect the chairs that day you told me your name and then you said something like "although you know that, don't you?" I've a head for faces, Ned. I'd remember if I'd met you before.'

'It weren't you I was talking to. It was Danny, the young lad you had helping you out.'

'How'd you know him?'

Ned shrugged, seemingly confused by her interest. 'He worked here for a while. Helped me out with a few bits and pieces. He's a handy lad.'

'Why'd he leave?'

'We were having that refurbishment done. The place was gonna be shut for a week or so. No work, so he moved on. Why'd you ask?'

Minnie shook her head. 'No reason.'

She blew the expense and caught a cab to Albert's. Now she was sitting in his morning room, recounting her conversations with Frances and Ned. As she revealed each successive detail, Albert grew more and more animated.

'So,' she concluded, 'he was at the Trafalgar Theatre that day and he lost a twin sister. He's worked as a sweep. He was there at the wake when Lennie Thomas died, and he worked at the Fortune with Peter Reynolds. The only thing that don't really fit is Bernard's drowning. He came running when Frances called for help.'

'I've wondered about that,' Albert said. 'Maybe he drowned Bernard, thought the job was done and was changing out of his wet clothes, when he hears the stage weight falling in your office and realises he's not alone. Frances calls out, and he realises he needs to go and make it look like he's helping.'

'Wouldn't she have noticed his clothes were already wet before he got in the tank to help her?'

'It's not the kind of thing you'd be looking for, is it? And in the heat of the moment, she was hardly going to worry about inspecting Jack's clothes.'

Albert crossed to the fireplace and removed an empty clay pipe from the mantelpiece, rubbing it gently between his forefinger and thumb while he spoke. 'James Tomlinson, the lad who was put in the asylum after the Trafalgar Theatre disaster. He lost a twin sister that day.'

'James Tomlinson. Jack Cassidy. What was the name of that sweep again?'

'Danny Webster. In his rooms there were all sorts of letters made out to other names, but for the life of me I can't remember any of them.'

'Maybe we need to pay Danny Webster another visit.'

'And Jack. If nothing else, we can get him to explain his connection to all these crimes. I don't suppose you know where he lives?'

'As a matter of fact, I do. But we'll have to head back to the Palace.'

Minnie hurried into her office. On the desk was a box holding several pieces of card. Each of them had the contact details of anyone who worked at the Palace. Inwardly, she blessed Tansie for this bit of organisation that he'd impressed on her she needed to maintain when she took over the management of the Palace. 'You never know when you're gonna need someone last minute,' he'd told her, fanning the cards in front of her face. 'And this way, you don't have to keep all those addresses in your head.'

She rifled through the cards, telling herself she should have kept them in Tansie's strict alphabetical order. Finally, she found Jack's. 'Mare Street,' she said. '27 Mare Street.'

'That's it,' Albert said. 'That's where Danny Webster lives. I didn't get much of a look at him that day. He had a hat pulled down over his face, collar turned up, muffler pulled up over his mouth to keep out the cold. So I couldn't swear to it, but I reckon Danny Webster and Jack Cassidy might be the same person.'

236

THIRTY-ONE

Danny Webster's landlady had a face like a bulldog sucking a lemon. 'You here again?' she said to Albert, but he didn't reply. She seemed to take particular offence at Minnie's presence, sniffing her disapproval as her eyes ran up and down Minnie's frame.

'I don't allow my gentlemen to have no lady callers,' she said, stressing the word 'lady' as her lip curled.

'Then we won't have a problem, 'cos I ain't a lady caller. I'm a detective,' Minnie said, sweeping past the landlady and opening the door to what they now knew was Jack's room.

It was much as Albert had described it: large damp patches visible on every wall, and floorboards that felt as if they might collapse beneath your feet. And yet scrupulously organised. Everything carefully folded and tidied away.

'Bit odd, ain't it?' Minnie said. 'Young fella keeping his room so neat?'

She lifted the edge of the rug. 'Book I was reading the other week, there was a secret trapdoor under the carpet.'

No such luck, but just as she went to reposition the rug, Albert stopped her and pointed to scratches on the floor by the wardrobe.

'Someone's moved that,' he said. 'It's a heavy item from the looks of it, even if you took all the clothes out, so they've had to drag it, which would explain the scratches. When John and I were here before, we didn't lift the rug. Didn't see the scratches. Nice work, Minnie.'

'I knew all that reading would pay off one day.'

Albert opened the wardrobe door. Jack's clothes were hanging on hooks, some items neatly folded and stacked on a high shelf. It was a big wardrobe, which made it all the more obvious that Jack had so little to put in it. And why had someone moved the wardrobe and then moved it back again to the same position?

He pushed hard against one side of the wardrobe and it shifted. He looked behind it.

'There's a door. Lend me a hand, Minnie. This is even heavier than I thought.'

Between the two of them, they moved the wardrobe enough to gain access to the door behind. Albert sniffed the air.

'What is it?' Minnie said. 'What are you smelling?'

'Nothing, thankfully.' He turned the handle and opened the door.

Behind was a small room, a cupboard really, about two feet wide and stretching back maybe as far again. It smelt musty and unused, and there was nothing in there. Not a shirt or a pair of socks. Nothing but a single tobacco tin on the floor.

Minnie placed a hand on Albert's arm, her breath catching in her throat as she leaned down and retrieved the tin. Inside was a bundle of papers: old newspaper cuttings worn thin at the folds, official-looking documents, scraps of card with writing on, addresses, sketches of houses and people, what looked like floor plans of houses.

'It's all about the Trafalgar Theatre,' she murmured. 'All the newspaper coverage from the time it happened. Details of the inquest. Witness statements. Everything. This must be what he got from his dad's house, when he went there after he got out of the asylum.'

'And look.' Albert pointed to the scraps of card with addresses.

'Upper Grosvenor Street, that's Eddings's home. Ridley Road, that's Fowler.'

'What are the drawings?' Minnie asked.

'Some of them are from the newspapers at the time of the tragedy. I recognise them from my visit to the *Illustrated London News* archives. See?' He pointed at the image closest to him: hordes of children, their faces contorted by pain and rage, hurtling towards their death.

'What about the others? The houses?'

'That looks like Judge Eddings's from the outside. And that floor plan' – he pointed to another scrap of paper – 'that's the layout of the house.'

'And these notes look like something to do with Fowler's wife. Like he'd been watching the house, noting when she left for work.' She turned to him, her eyes flooded with tears. 'Oh, Albert, I was so hoping it weren't him. I just wanted it to be someone I didn't know. Didn't care about.'

He slipped an arm round her shoulders and pulled her to him. They stood quietly for a moment, Minnie's eyes darting across the documents, piecing together the story they told.

A single sheet of paper contained a list of names. The five men Jack had killed. Then Bernard. And two more names. Martin Taylor and Stephen Collins.

'Ones he hasn't got to yet,' Minnie said. 'Any idea who they are?'

'Stephen Collins I'm fairly sure was the journalist for the *ILN*. Martin Taylor rings a bell, but I can't remember who he is.'

The creak of a floorboard made them both turn. Jack stood in the middle of the room. For a moment, Minnie felt the need to apologise for having invaded his privacy, uncovered his secrets. But then she remembered what those secrets were. And she saw the gun in Jack's hand.

'Minnie,' Jack said, and he sounded so weary, so defeated, she wanted to hug him. Tell him it would be all right.

'It's me, Jack,' she said. 'You wanna put down that gun?'

He shook his head. 'Can't do that, Min. I ain't finished yet. Once I'm finished – well, we'll cross that bridge when we get to it, eh?'

He tossed her a length of rope. 'Tie Albert's hands behind his back. And no funny business, Min. I weren't born yesterday.'

Except that was exactly what he sounded like, his voice wavering like the ten-year-old boy Albert had learned about on his visit to the asylum, who had wet his bed and had nightmares only his mother could soothe. She tried again to speak, to reason with him, but he cut her off before she could say anything. 'Do it, Min. Or I'll kill Albert. And don't think I won't, 'cos I've done it before.'

She nodded. Albert sat on a chair, his hands behind his back, and she tied them securely. Jack waved the gun at her. 'Stand over there by the window,' he said, and he checked the knot, tugging hard at it two or three times.

'Now you,' he said, gesturing towards the bed. 'Lay down. Hands behind your back.'

She did as she was told and Jack tied her hands firmly. He crossed to the cupboard, closed the door and pushed the wardrobe back in place. 'Those are my secrets,' he said. 'No one else's.'

'Where are you going now, Jack?' Minnie said gently, trying to keep the panic and fear out of her voice.

'Never you mind,' and he was gone, the door slamming behind him.

They heard his footsteps recede into the distance, then Albert said, 'Minnie, if you can get yourself over here, and you back up against me, I think I can untie you.'

'No need. Turn your hands so they're back to back and then pull them apart quickly.'

He did as she said, and the rope came loose.

'Where on earth did you learn that little trick?' he asked, crossing to the bed and untying her.

'Three months as assistant to the Great Suprendo. Lock picking, trick knots. He wanted to teach me sword swallowing, but I couldn't stomach it.'

She rubbed her wrists where the rope had been. 'We need to get to the Palace, quick smart. He's gone to finish Bernard off, I reckon.'

The Palace was quiet when they got there. Minnie nipped into her office and slipped the pistol inside her pocket.

Kippy had seen no sign of Jack or Bernard. Minnie was starting to despair of finding them when Frances emerged from Wardrobe.

'You've just missed them, Min.'

'Did they say where they were going?'

'Jack said the Regal's installed a water tank without half the bother we've had here. Said he could show Bernard. What is it? You look like the world's about to end.'

Minnie and Albert shared a look. 'Tell me,' Frances said. 'It's about Jack, ain't it? Something's wrong.'

'It's him, Frances. He's the one who's been killing people from the Trafalgar Theatre.'

Frances fell silent. If she was shocked, she was keeping it well hidden. Slowly, she lifted her head, her face the image of firm resolve. 'Then I think I know where they might be.'

THIRTY-TWO

The theatre had lain untouched since the disaster, and time had taken its toll. The doors at the front had swollen from years of rain, but a hard shove from Albert got them open. The roof had collapsed in several places, allowing broad shafts of light to pierce the gloom. Flights of pigeons took off up into the roof timbers and re-settled themselves with an air of calm acceptance. They would be here long after everyone else had left.

'Watch your step,' Albert said to Minnie and Frances, gesturing towards the bird mess littering the floor and decorating every other surface in the theatre. Mingled with the bird mess were rat droppings, the rats' presence confirmed by a frantic scuttling behind the walls. Minnie pulled her skirts tighter round her legs. 'Bloody rats,' she murmured.

Thieves had broken in at some point in the last fourteen years. Most of the seats had been removed, the tables, the light fittings. But the place still retained some aura of what it had once been. Fancifully, Minnie thought if she were to stay very quiet she might hear children laughing. Or maybe screaming.

Frances gazed upwards at the holes in the roof. 'Floorboards'll be dodgy,' she said. 'God knows how long the rain's been getting in.'

She was right. The place smelt musty and damp and it was certainly not safe to be in there. One of those rotting ceiling joists could fall on them at any minute.

'Has Jack been coming here?' Minnie asked.

Frances nodded. 'He told me he sometimes sneaks in, although why on earth you'd want to is beyond me.'

Carefully, they picked their way through the detritus that covered the floor. Leaves, twigs, bones from unidentified animals that were all the rats had left of them. At one point, Minnie slipped on something unmentionable and Albert caught her before she fell. Hand in hand, they navigated their way through the empty auditorium, towards the staircases leading up to the galleries. They stood silently in front of the east staircase, the door now fully open, but the hole in the floor for the bolt still visible. Minnie became aware of Frances whispering beside her. She turned, and realised the other woman was saying a quiet prayer.

'Can't do any harm, can it?' Frances said.

In this cavernous space all three of them had naturally started to whisper, as if they were afraid to disturb the souls who had died there.

'I don't think we should go upstairs,' Albert said. 'It's dangerous enough down here.'

'Backstage?' Minnie suggested. 'If I was hiding out in a theatre, that's where I'd go. It's quieter. Usually warmer.'

The three of them carefully picked their way backstage. It felt strange to be in this part of the theatre, normally so full of life, now derelict and deserted, layers of dust and grime on every surface. It was as if the place had been evacuated with no warning, everything left behind. The dressing rooms with lockers, their doors hanging open. Old make-up sponges and half-used sticks of greasepaint cluttering the desks. Minnie expected to see the remains of a final meal, but there was nothing like that. The rats and the pigeons must have eaten it all long ago.

They carried on down the corridor, not speaking, as if afraid to break the spell the derelict theatre had cast over all three of them. Albert peered into what looked as if it might once have been

Wardrobe. 'He's been here,' he said. On the floor was a pile of blankets, an oil lamp, some unopened tins of food, a knife and spoon. Albert picked up the blankets and sniffed them. 'These are clean,' he said.

'So he's been sleeping here how long?' Frances asked.

'About three weeks, I suspect,' Albert said. 'It's been that long since I chased him and I know he hasn't been back to his room.'

A noise from the auditorium pierced the quiet.

'He's here,' Frances whispered, turning back the way they'd come. Albert laid a hand on her arm. 'He's got a gun, Frances. You and Minnie stay back here.'

Calmly, Frances removed his hand. 'He won't hurt me.'

'He did before,' Minnie reminded her.

'That was an accident,' Frances said. 'It won't happen again.' She seemed unnaturally calm, as if she'd been waiting for this moment. 'I can talk to him, Min.'

'Well, you're not going out there without me,' Albert said.

All three of them headed for the auditorium. At first they could make nothing out in the gloom. Then they heard what sounded like the scrape of a chair and they turned towards the stage, where the noise had come from. Standing in a pool of sunlight, like an actor about to deliver the final monologue, was Jack, the gun in his right hand. Beside him, Bernard, his hands tied behind his back, his mouth gagged. He was teetering on a stool, struggling to stay upright. He couldn't fully lower his heels because taut around his neck was a noose. At some point, he'd lose the battle to stay upright and he'd hang himself. He made a noise that sounded like Minnie's name, his eyes wide with alarm.

Frances moved calmly round Minnie and Albert, so Jack could see her. The sight of her clearly shocked him. 'Why are *you* here?' Jack asked. 'You ain't supposed to be here.'

'You all right, Jack?' Frances asked, ignoring his words.

'I'm fine, Frances,' he said, and hearing him speak reminded

Minnie of the person she'd known all this time. A young lad, struggling to make his way in the world. A potential suitor for Frances. Trustworthy and reliable.

Frances took a couple of steps towards him. 'Please don't hurt him, Jack.'

'It won't hurt. Not for long, anyway.'

'Or maybe you could just let him go?'

He shook his head slowly. 'If I do that, you'll catch me. And I won't be able to finish the job.'

'It's Bernard, Jack. He's your friend. He didn't cause that accident, you know that.'

'It was him and his brother who threw the presents out into the crowd. That's what started it all.'

'How many more lives do you have to take?' Albert said, his voice casual as if he and Jack were having a conversation about the weather. 'To finish the job? To rest easy? We found your list, but I can't remember now how many names there were.'

'Two more after Bernard. Stephen Collins, another journalist for the newspaper. The things he wrote – as if it was nobody's fault but the children's. As if they should have had better control of themselves. Or their parents or teachers should have been there to take care of them.'

'And who else?' Albert said. 'You said two more.'

'Martin Taylor. He was front of house at the Trafalgar that day. And Bernard, of course.'

'Of course,' Albert said casually. 'You didn't have time to finish him, did you? So Stephen Collins, Martin Taylor and Bernard. And then you'll be done?' He was talking to the lad as if they were planning this together, as if at any moment he might offer to help.

Jack nodded. 'That's it, I reckon. I've gone over and over those newspaper reports and the accounts of the inquest. If there's others who were to blame, I can't find 'em.'

'And then what?' Albert asked. 'What's your plan, then?' Subtly, so slowly Minnie was sure Jack hadn't noticed, Albert was inching closer to Jack with each question. But he was still too far from the stage to do anything. Bernard was looking exhausted. She couldn't tell how much longer he'd be able to stay on tiptoe, but it couldn't be long.

Jack looked confused at Albert's words. 'What d'you mean?'

'Well, when you've applied justice, done the thing that needs to be done, what next?'

Jack looked down, as if the answer might lie at his feet, and then addressed his answer to Frances. 'I dunno. Carry on working at the Palace, I suppose. And maybe you and me, Frances? I know you're fond of me, but I couldn't do nothing about it 'cos I had this' – he waved the gun – 'to do first. But once that's all done, maybe you and me?'

'Maybe,' Frances said. She didn't sound too convincing, but Jack seemed to have swallowed it.

'Frances looks like your sister, I hear,' Minnie said.

'Yeah. Cassie. People never believed we was twins, 'cos we didn't look nothing like each other. But Frances is the spit of Cassie. That's what started it all, really. Meeting Frances.'

'How d'you mean?' Minnie asked. Out of the corner of her eye, she could see Albert edging tentatively forward. If she could just keep Jack talking, Albert might get close enough to rush him. They didn't have long. Bernard was making inarticulate noises that sounded increasingly panicky.

'I'd been away for a while,' Jack said. 'I think perhaps you know about that, my time at Finsbury. They said they was gonna cure me, but they just made it worse. When I got out, I swore I was gonna try to put it behind me. Decided to go by Jack instead of James, and changed my surname to Cassidy. It sounds like Cassie, so it was like I had her beside me all the time. Whole new start. I was gonna earn some money, find a nice girl, settle down. I worked a few places, tried my hand at all sorts, then I got a job at the Palace and, my second day there, in walked Frances. I swear, for a moment I thought I might be losing my mind, she looked so like Cassie. I didn't sleep that night, just reliving it. And I realised I'd done the wrong thing, pushing it away. I had a duty to Cassie and all those other children, to make sure that people paid for what happened that day.'

'You were angry,' Minnie said. 'I understand that.'

'I ain't sure I was ever angry, Min. They beat that out of me in the asylum. It's just people needed to pay for what they did. And nobody else seemed to be doing anything about it.'

'So you started with Fowler. How'd you do it?' Minnie asked. 'I mean, it can't be easy to hang a grown man.'

Jack waved the gun and Frances cried out, flinching and then immediately suppressing the cry. He turned to her, his face marked by distress. 'I ain't gonna hurt you, Frances. I said so, didn't I?' He turned back to Minnie. 'What'd you ask me again?'

'Fowler,' Minnie coaxed him. 'What happened?'

'I spent weeks watching him, learning his routine. His wife left the house every morning at six to go to work, and then he went out a couple of hours later, bundle of papers under his arm, pencil over his ear so he could make any corrections to his work as he thought of them. Getting inside the house was easy enough. His wife was a bit later leaving that day, so I waited until she was gone, made sure she wasn't nipping back for anything she'd forgotten and then I knocked on the door, said I was there to do the chimneys. He let me in without a thought. He barely noticed I was there, I think; he was so caught up in whatever he was writing. Crouched over his desk, frantically stabbing at the typewriter keys like his life depended on it. He was a big fella. He'd have beaten me hands down in a fight. I had a gun with me, and some chloroform I'd swiped while I was doing the chimneys at a doctor's house a few weeks earlier. But I didn't need the chloroform. Just waved the gun at Fowler and told him to throw the noose over the beam. Said I'd hurt his wife when she got back if he didn't do as I asked. I wouldn't have, though,' he said. 'I want you to know that. I wouldn't have hurt her.'

'And he put his own head in the noose?' Minnie said.

'I told him it was just to scare him, that I wanted him to know what it felt like to suffocate. I promised him I wouldn't let him die. I lied. It weren't easy, though. I'd planned it all out, but I didn't think about how it would feel to take a life. To watch a man die in front of you when, with one simple movement of a hand, you could save him.'

From the corner of her eye, Minnie could see Albert edging closer to the stage. Not close enough yet, though. She needed to keep Jack talking.

'And the same for Judge Eddings?' she asked.

'Pretty much. I'd been there before, doing the chimneys. Knew the arrangement of the rooms, the movements of the servants. Knew the time of day I was most likely to find the judge at home. I weren't expecting his grandson to be there, but that made it easier in the end. They were playing hide-and-seek. The judge told the boy to find a good hiding place while he counted to a hundred. The boy scampered out of the room and I took out the gun. I told him I'd hurt the child if he didn't do as I said. Which I could never do. Never hurt a child. But he wasn't to know that, was he? I'd heard the child thumping down the hallway to the rear of the house, so I knew we could safely take the stairs. Up we went, up into the servants' quarters. I figured out if I could get him up in the loft, out of the way, I could take my time. It was even easier than I expected 'cos of the trunk. I hit him on the back of the head with the gun and he went down like a lead weight. I felt his pulse, thin and slow. Maybe he was already dying and I didn't need to do the next bit. But I did it anyway. Dragged him to the trunk and tipped him in. He was heavier than I'd thought, for all he weren't a big fella. Bodies weigh more than you think, Min. I piled some books and suitcases on top of the trunk. He'd never have got out, even if he was still alive. And they'd never hear him shouting up there. Fancy houses, see? Thick walls. Thick floors. Not like my room where I swear you can hear a cat breathing three doors down.

'That trunk, what a stroke of luck. And that made me know I was doing the right thing. If what I was doing was wrong, things wouldn't have come easy like that, would they? It's like with Lennie Thomas. What were the chances of him being at the wake for Freddy Graham? But he was, and he let me buy him a pint even though he didn't know me, and it was the easiest thing in the world to slip in a bit of strychnine. I'd bought it a few weeks earlier. Told the pharmacist I had rats. Been carrying it around with me, just in case I got lucky. And I did, didn't I?'

'And Peter Reynolds?' Minnie asked. 'Were you lucky there too?'

'Sort of. I worked with him at the Fortune. It didn't take long to figure out he liked men, and men dressed up as women more particularly. I nicked a costume from Wardrobe. I was nervous walking from my room to the theatre, dressed like that. Fearful someone would spot me for what I was and start on me. But no one even noticed. I knocked at the stage door, praying it would be someone who didn't know me who'd answer. But it was George, the stage manager, and I thought the game was up then. I'd pulled the shawl over my head already, and I turned my face away into the shadows. He never suspected a thing. Peter came to the stage door. I dropped the shawl, turned towards the light so he knew who I was and what I'd come for. He was confused at first, not understanding what I was offering him. Then he realised, and he was like a kid in a sweet shop. Couldn't believe his luck. We found a quiet spot down a side alley. I let him go so far, then I told him we should have somewhere nicer. More cosy.

He looked worried then. Said he couldn't bring me back to his rooms. If his landlady found out she'd have the coppers onto him. There's spaces in the Fortune, I reminded him. Quiet rooms. We could hang back, I said. Wait until everyone's gone and then be together. Special, like. He was scared we'd get locked inside, but I told him I knew where the caretaker left the spare set of keys. We could do our business, then slip out the stage door, shove the key under the door and no one would be any the wiser. And it was just like I'd promised. Well, in most respects. We hung back in the cleaners' cupboard. I showed him a length of rope I'd brought with me and his eyes lit up. So I tied him up and shoved a rag in his mouth. Then I said I needed something to drink 'cos it was fearsome hot in there, right next to the furnace which was still hot from earlier in the evening. I told him to wait and I'd get us both a beer from the stock down in that cellar. I slipped out, found the caretaker's spare keys in the desk drawer in his office. I'd oiled the lock the day before, so the key turned almost without a noise. I don't think he knew anything was happening, until I spoke to him through the locked door. Told him who I was. Why I was really there. Sat on the floor and took my time telling him. He kicked against the door for a bit. As if that would do him any good. In the end, he fell almost silent. Just the sound of him crying. It brought back memories, no matter how hard I tried to push them away. Every time someone new was admitted to Finsbury, they'd spend that first night crying. Calling out for their ma. Eventually, I couldn't stand it any more. I threw the spare set of keys in a ditch a mile or so away.'

'So the note we found by Peter's body, that was nothing to do with you?'

Jack looked confused. 'No note, Minnie. Not from me.'

He broke her gaze and turned towards Bernard, who looked as if he couldn't remain upright for much longer.

'I want you to know, Min, I never killed anyone innocent. They all deserved it. Like I said, if what I was doing was wrong, it would have been a lot harder.'

'But you did, Jack,' Frances said, her voice low and calm, quiet too, so Jack had to strain to hear her. 'You did kill someone innocent. Freddy Graham, the stage manager.'

A flicker of confusion crossed his face, and then he offered his explanation, as if eager to accept responsibility for all he'd done. 'It was the chloroform what done for Graham. I was gonna string him up, but there was no need. The chloroform killed him. Turns out it can do that, if you've got a dicky heart.'

'But Freddy saved me that day,' Frances said.

Jack frowned at her. 'No, he didn't, Frances. You must be misremembering. That's what Dr Phillips always told me. That I was misremembering the events of the day.'

'I ain't misremembering. I was wedged in the turn of the stairs. It was Freddy Graham who saved me. Not just me. He went back in the Trafalgar countless times, brought out loads of children, some of them still alive. He just kept going back in, coming back with another kid in his arms. I remember his face. Blank, it was. Like he felt nothing. Or felt too much. His skin was grey by the end of it. He looked twenty years older. You got it wrong, Jack. If it weren't for Freddy – me and countless other children, we'd have died that day alongside the ones who did. You killed an innocent man.'

A hush fell on the deserted auditorium. It had started to rain outside, the water dripping through the holes in the ceiling and forming puddles on the floor. Jack had turned completely towards Frances now, enthralled by her story. He seemed to have forgotten there was anyone else in the room. Albert moved forward more rapidly, still carefully but making greater strides.

'You're wrong, Frances,' Jack said, his voice low and troubled. 'Freddy Graham was the one who bolted the door at the bottom of the stairs.'

Frances shook her head. 'That ain't true, Jack. It's what they thought at first, tried to pin the blame on him. But you've read the witness statements from the inquest. No one could be certain who it was, but they all said it was a dark-haired fella. Freddy was fair. It weren't him. It weren't his decision to bolt the door. And it weren't his idea to throw presents out into the audience. He was innocent, Jack.'

The life seemed to seep out of Jack and he visibly slumped. The gun hung loosely by his side. To Minnie's left, a blur of movement as Albert rushed towards the stage. But just as he got close to the steps leading up, Jack turned and raised his gun. He had Albert clearly in his sights. Albert stopped dead. A sound echoed through the auditorium, and Minnie realised it was Frances screaming. Jack took a step closer to Albert. And then, just as Minnie was sure he was going to fire, he turned back to Bernard and kicked the stool out from under him, so hard it flew off the stage and landed in the auditorium.

Immediately, Bernard's legs started to kick wildly, desperately searching for something to secure him. He was making an awful noise. Jack had the gun trained on Albert again and, with a sickening dread, Minnie realised what Jack had planned. Either Albert risked his own life or Bernard died in front of them all.

Frances was still screaming, frozen to the spot. There was no point in asking her to do anything.

Minnie reached into her pocket, her fingers closing round the pistol. Remembering everything Albert had told her, she raised the gun and fired it at Jack. The noise echoed round the empty auditorium, and the pigeons took flight again, their wings filling the air with noise and movement. The shock of the gunshot had silenced Frances, at least.

Without thinking, Minnie ran towards the stage. Jack had gone. Albert had Bernard by the legs, desperately trying to support the man's weight and stop him from dying.

'The rope, Minnie,' Albert gasped. 'You need to cut the rope.'

'But – Jack—'

'Leave him. We need to save Bernard. And I can't hold on much longer. A knife. Or something sharp.'

A knife? Where on earth was she going to find a knife?

'Jack's bedroom,' Frances said, from the gloom of the shadowy auditorium.

Minnie rushed backstage, snatched the knife Jack had been using for his food and ran back onto the stage, grabbing the stool Bernard had been standing on. The knife wasn't the sharpest but, balanced on the stool, she finally managed to hack through the rope and free Bernard. Then, without allowing herself time to consider what she was doing, she hurried backstage again, running up and down the corridor and looking in every room.

But Jack was gone.

THIRTY-THREE

As soon as they were outside the confines of the derelict theatre, Bernard started to shake violently. Albert took off his coat and forced Bernard to put it on, but it made no difference.

'It's shock,' Albert said. 'We need to get him somewhere warm and safe, where he can rest. Frances, too.'

Minnie nodded and ran out into the street to hail a cab.

Ten minutes later, they were at Albert's house. Bernard had stopped shaking, but he looked awful. Minnie offered him her arm, but he waved it aside.

'See to her,' he said, pointing at Frances. 'She's in a terrible state, poor love.'

'And you're as fit as a fiddle, I suppose?' Minnie said. 'You nearly died back there, y'know?'

'Not for the first time. Trust me, I'm not planning on making a habit of it.'

The front door flew open and Mrs Byrne hurried down the steps to meet them. Albert started to explain what had happened, but Mrs Byrne swept his words aside impatiently. She appraised both Frances and Bernard, then took Bernard by the arm, ignoring his protestations, and led him into the house. 'Albert, there's some pea and ham soup on the stove I was just warming up for lunch,' she said over her shoulder. 'Fetch me some in two bowls. Minnie, in the cupboard under the stairs you'll find blankets. Bring them here.'

They did as they were told. Mrs Byrne fed Bernard the soup until he was able to take hold of the spoon himself. When he had finished, his eyes immediately started to grow heavy.

'Guest bedroom for you, Bernard. We'll shift Tom to the sofa. And you, my love,' Mrs Byrne said, turning to Frances, 'can have my room. Clean sheets on this morning.'

Her words seemed to unlock something in Frances, and the girl started to sob. Mrs Byrne held her until the crying subsided, then she crouched beside her, taking Frances's hands in hers and forcing her to look at her.

'You're safe now,' Mrs Byrne said slowly. 'No one will hurt you here. I promise you.'

Frances nodded, her eyes locked on the older woman.

'What's her story?' Minnie said, once she and Albert were left alone.

'Who, Frances?'

'No, Mrs B. She always seems to know just what to do in an emergency. Remarkably calm.'

'I'm sure there is a story, but I've never had the courage to ask. You, on the other hand—'

Minnie smiled. 'I ain't in her good books at the moment. I think she reckons I'm leading you astray.'

'She loves you, Minnie,' Albert said quietly.

'Really?'

'Really.'

He said something else, almost to himself, as he turned away. She didn't catch the words.

'Remind me why we're here again?' Minnie said, after Jack's landlady had admitted them to his room for the second time that day. 'Jack ain't likely to be coming back here, is he?'

'There might be something,' Albert said distractedly, opening the chest of drawers and rifling through the papers. 'Something to tell us where else he might go now we know about his hiding place at the Trafalgar Theatre. And, at some point, he may come back. There are personal effects here which I can't see him just walking away from.'

'Here, give me some of them,' Minnie said, gesturing towards the papers in Albert's hand. He halved the bundle and the two of them started looking through it. Minnie looked up. Albert was squinting at a page, holding it further away and then closer again.

'You need spectacles, Albert,' she murmured.

'I've never needed them before.'

'First time for everything.'

They carried on skimming through the papers, and suddenly a wave of nausea swept over Minnie, so abruptly that she had to sit down.

'Are you all right?' Albert said. 'Do you need some fresh air? A glass of water?'

She shook her head. 'Must be something I ate not agreeing with me.' Although all she'd had for breakfast had been a cup of tea and a bread roll. Sweat prickled under her arms and along her hairline. She looked up at Albert. He was looking a bit peaky, too.

'Why's it so hot in here?' she said, glancing at the fireplace. 'Fire ain't lit.'

'I know,' Albert said, wiping his handkerchief across his forehead.

Minnie looked again at the fireplace. 'If it ain't lit, why does it stink of burning coal in here?'

Albert's eyes grew wide with alarm. He moved towards her, then all the colour drained from him, and he swayed ominously. 'Get out, Min,' he said, his breath rasping as if it was taking an immense effort to say the words. 'Get out of this room. Now.' He straightened up and lunged at her, pushing her towards the door.

She reached for the door handle, but she saw double and couldn't place her hand in the right spot. She was having trouble breathing too, and getting out of the room seemed an insurmountable task. Albert reached round her, grabbed hold of the handle, opened the door and pushed her into the hallway. 'Right out,' he gasped. 'Outside.'

Minnie's brain didn't seem to be working properly, but she managed to do as he said, opening the front door and stumbling down the steps. She almost fell, but managed to right herself in time, grabbing hold of the railings. The sour-faced landlady appeared from the rear of the house. 'I don't know what you're doing in there,' she said, 'but you ain't got no one's permission to go burning stuff.'

Albert grabbed the landlady by the arm, ignoring her protestations, and pushed her down the front steps after Minnie.

She felt Albert beside her, his hand on her back, pushing her head down between her knees. After a few minutes, the nausea passed, and she sat upright. She turned and looked at Albert. He was regaining some of his colour.

'I need to go back in there,' he said. 'Open the windows and get everyone else out of the house.'

'There's no one else in there,' the landlady said. 'And what on earth is going on?'

'That smell,' Albert said. 'Someone's been burning charcoal. In a confined space, it releases carbon monoxide. It can kill you before you even realise what's happening.'

'Then you're staying put,' Minnie said, grabbing hold of his arm, horrified at the thought of him placing himself in further danger.

'I have to, Minnie,' he said. 'If I open the windows and doors, the gas will disperse fairly rapidly, and then we can help Jack.'

'You think he's – in there? How can he be? We'd have seen him.'

Before she could say anything further, or had the chance to stop him, Albert ducked back inside the house. She heard the scrape of the windows opening, and in a few moments he was back outside, taking large gulps of fresh air.

'We need to give it a moment,' he said. 'And then we'll go back in.'

'If he's in there,' Minnie said falteringly, 'it ain't an accident, is it?'

Albert shook his head. 'I doubt it. Frances's insistence that Freddy Graham was a hero that day, it didn't fit with Jack's plan, did it? He murdered an innocent man.'

'But why charcoal?'

'It suffocates you. It devours the oxygen in the air, and you suffocate.'

The wardrobe door was locked, but it didn't take too much effort on Albert's part to wrench it open.

The smell of charcoal grew stronger the minute they opened the door, and Albert insisted they retreat again for a while. Once he was confident the gas had dispersed, they went back to the wardrobe. On the floor to one side was a small burner full of the remains of burned charcoal and newspaper. And beside it, curled up in a ball, like a child fallen into slumber, lay Jack. His face was swollen and congested, but it was still him; the only thing that marked his death was the deep-red colour of his skin.

He lay curled, his knees pulled up close to his chest, one hand tucked under his head, as if he had grown tired and simply lain down for a rest. In his other hand, a single piece of paper. Gently, Albert loosened the lad's fingers and removed the paper. It was a list of names. The children who had died that day. Their ages and addresses. And underscored with pencil so many times it had gone right through the paper, one particular name. The only name that had ever mattered to Jack.

Cassie Tomlinson. Ten.

John arrived at the same time as the doctor. The medical man took one look at the burner, and the colour of Jack's skin and confirmed what Albert had suspected. 'Carbon monoxide,' he said. 'I'll have to write it up as suicide.'

'I don't think so,' Albert said. 'Miss Ward here knew the lad. There's no reason to think he'd take his own life, surely?'

Minnie shook her head. 'Happy as a sandboy, he was. Not the brightest spark, mind. We had an act at the Variety Palace a few weeks ago. Magician locked in a cupboard with a fire blazing. When the door was opened the magician was gone and the fire had been transformed into a live parrot. It looks to me like Jack was trying to figure out how it was done, not realising what would happen. See' – she pointed at the burnt embers of paper – 'he was burning something or other. Just didn't know what it would do in such a small space.'

'Family?' the doctor said.

'His father's still alive,' Minnie said. 'And a sister. There's young nieces and nephews too.'

The doctor looked from Minnie to Albert and then back again to Minnie. An unspoken understanding passed between all three of them. The doctor held Minnie's gaze a moment longer and then nodded his head, almost imperceptibly. 'Accidental death,' he said. 'Easily done.'

After Jack's body had been removed, Albert and Minnie filled John in on the incident at the abandoned theatre. 'I don't get it,' John said. 'That fella killed five people. He nearly killed Bernard. Why were you in such a hurry to make his death look accidental?'

'He has a family who've done nothing wrong,' Minnie said. 'If it's suicide, that means burial in unconsecrated ground, and a stigma that might follow Jack's family for the rest of their lives.' She thought back to Rose, and Ida's desperate need to have her daughter buried inside the confines of the churchyard. 'Jack's father's a religious man. It would destroy him, I reckon, if Jack's death was declared a suicide.'

'Well, he's gonna be declared a killer, Minnie,' John said, his mouth forming into a hard line. 'And you're showing a remarkable level of compassion for him.'

'I ain't condoning what he did, John. But I don't think he could help himself. He'd spent his whole life trying to live with what happened. And then he met Frances, and it brought it all back, how no one had paid for what happened that day. He felt someone had to do something.'

'That don't make it right. If we all felt like that, there'd be bloody chaos on the streets.'

'You sure that ain't the case already?' she said.

THIRTY-FOUR

Minnie stood back and surveyed Frances's handiwork. Dorothy looked stunning. The dress flattered in all the right places and the red suited her colouring perfectly. Mind you, Minnie was starting to think Dorothy looked good no matter what she wore. Maybe a bit too good.

'Tell me again why it's got to be me,' Dorothy asked.

'The bouncer likes blondes.'

'But you've got a music hall full of wigs, you could easily disguise yourself, Minnie.'

'He also has a fondness for—' Minnie struggled to find the right words.

'—the more Rubenesque woman?' Albert suggested.

'If I knew what that meant, I might be able to offer an opinion,' Minnie said. 'Let's just say he likes his ladies with a bit of padding.'

'Fella after my own heart,' Tansie said.

Dorothy frowned. 'I've never done anything like this before, Minnie. I'm worried I'll let you down.'

'Dorothy, you are a very beautiful woman,' Minnie said. 'He's a man. Just act like everything he's got to say is fascinating. Giggle a bit. You spend your life doing clever things with numbers. You know more about monkeys than is strictly healthy, and if the bookkeeping ever dries up, you could set yourself up as a taxidermist with no problem. This is gonna be the easiest thing you've ever done.'

Dorothy didn't look convinced.

'Look, why don't I coach you for a bit?' Tansie said. 'Just imagine I'm quite a stupid fella.'

'Shouldn't be too much of a stretch,' Minnie said.

'Shut yer trap, Ward,' Tansie said. 'We'll be out front if you need us.'

When they were out of earshot, Minnie turned to Albert. 'Are you sure this is gonna work, Albert?'

'If everything goes *exactly* as planned, we've probably got a fifty per cent chance of success.'

She stared at him, open-mouthed. 'You didn't say that earlier.'

'I was swept up in your enthusiasm. And now it's a bit late to back out.'

'But—'

'Ssh,' he said, grinning at her with an optimism that seemed oddly misplaced. 'It's all going to be just fine. Blount's out of the picture and the man who's taken over the Pit has no idea who we are. Now, isn't it time you got changed?'

She glanced at her watch. 'It is. But I've got another question first. If we're successful – and I'm just starting to realise how big an "if" that is, thanks for that, by the way – what are we going to do after? We'll have all these—'

'Don't worry,' he said. 'Dorothy and I have a plan.'

There it was again. Dorothy and I. That coupling was tripping far too readily off his tongue these days.

'Fancy sharing that plan with me?'

He grinned again. Christ, she'd never seen him so happy. 'It's a secret, Minnie. You'll find out soon enough.'

Minnie's dress didn't look quite as spectacular as Dorothy's, but she still felt horribly conspicuous in it. Emerald green wasn't a colour she normally opted for and she felt like something off a greengrocer's stall. But then, it wasn't her who needed to catch the bouncer's eye. And next to Dorothy, she felt almost invisible.

They finally reached the alleyway running behind the Westminster Pit. Minnie turned Dorothy towards her, holding both her hands. 'Remember,' Minnie said, 'you're irresistible. And I'm gonna be right beside you. I'll do the talking. You just bat your eyelashes and try to look like he's the most fascinating fella you've ever met.'

Minnie checked her pocket watch. It was time.

The two women walked slowly up the alleyway, feigning a conversation. 'Giggle,' Minnie murmured. Dorothy did as instructed. 'Louder,' Minnie said.

Dorothy let out a maniacal laugh which, quite frankly, made her sound demented. But it got the bouncer's attention. He turned to face them and immediately gave Dorothy an appreciative look.

'Well, hallo, ladies,' he said, puffing out his chest completely unnecessarily as he walked towards them. The man was the size of a house. 'And what brings you here tonight?'

All his comments were directed at Dorothy. Minnie might just as well not have been there. Which was fine. It really was fine.

Dorothy laughed again, dropped her head and then peeped out at the bouncer from underneath her eyelashes. Not bad, Minnie thought.

A broad grin spread across the bouncer's face, revealing his three teeth. Behind him Tansie, Kippy and Albert were slowly creeping towards the rear door of the Pit.

'Ain't ya got nothing to say for yourself?' the bouncer asked Dorothy.

'Oh, she's the quiet type,' Minnie intervened.

'Are you now? Well, you know what they say about the quiet ones.'

Dorothy giggled again. Minnie wondered if perhaps she should have taught her to extend her repertoire a little, but the bouncer seemed transfixed.

'Off anywhere nice, are you, ladies?' he asked.

'We've just been down the Spotted Dog,' Minnie said. 'Thought we might take a little stroll. I'm meeting a gentleman friend of mine in ten minutes.'

'Will you be all on your own then, darling?' the bouncer said to Dorothy, reaching for her hand as he did so.

Dorothy froze. Minnie could tell she was resisting the urge to slap his hand away, but the bouncer misread the signals. 'Shy, are you?' he said, leaning in closer, engulfing them both in the smell of stale beer and tobacco.

'She takes a bit of time to warm up,' Minnie said, growing a little desperate. Where the hell were the boys? What was taking so long?

'I can think of a few ways to warm you up,' the bouncer said, now openly leering at Dorothy. He reached into his back pocket and produced a hip flask. 'Let's start with a little nip of this, shall we?'

Minnie was about to stop Dorothy taking any of the drink, but she was too late. Dorothy grabbed hold of the hip flask and took a long swig, gasping and coughing as she handed it back to the bouncer. He gave her another admiring glance. 'Like a tipple, do you, love? Well, there's plenty more where that came from.'

Minnie was just wondering how long they could keep this up before the bouncer started questioning whether or not Dorothy had the power of speech, when three figures emerged from the rear of the Pit. Each of them held a dog cage in either hand. Tansie had hold of one of the feistier mutts who was jumping up at the cage handle, trying to bite Tansie. The dog was one of those little rat-like creatures known for their barking.

Just as the terrier started to fulfil his reputation, Dorothy grabbed hold of the bouncer's face and pulled him down towards her for a kiss. Minnie was transfixed. This was going well above and beyond. Receding into the distance, the terrier was raising merry hell. But

Dorothy's kiss seemed to have rendered the bouncer deaf. As Tansie, Kippy and Albert disappeared out of sight round the corner, Minnie tugged on Dorothy's dress. Instantly, Dorothy leapt back from the bouncer, wiping her mouth with her hand. The bouncer lunged for her, but she jumped back further.

'That was just a taster,' Dorothy said, narrowing her eyes and staring at the bouncer as if she intended to devour him. 'You stay here, I'll ditch my boring friend and I'll be back in five minutes.'

He nodded in mute astonishment. Dorothy grabbed Minnie's hand and they scooted off down the alleyway in the direction Albert and the others had fled. Once they were round the corner, they broke into a run. As soon as somebody realised the dogs had been taken, they'd be after them in a flash.

Three streets on, Dorothy stopped, pressing her hand to her side.

'You all right?' Minnie said.

'I may need to wash my mouth out with carbolic soap,' Dorothy said, 'but, yes, I'm fine. Just a stitch. How far are we from the Palace? I've completely lost my bearings.'

'Not far,' Minnie said, taking Dorothy's arm.

Back at the Palace, a cart and horses were pulled up behind the stage door. Tom was holding the reins and, behind him, six very angry fighting dogs were making their displeasure known.

'Where now?' Tom said. 'I mean, we can't just let them loose, can we? They're fighting dogs. They could kill someone.'

Albert and Dorothy shared a knowing look.

'I'll go with you, Tom,' Albert said. 'You others, grab a cab. Dorothy knows where we're going.'

Twenty minutes later, the cab pulled up in front of a small house just south of the river. Tom and Albert had arrived not long before them, and Tom was looking as confused as Minnie felt.

'Does this place belong to some mate of yours, Albert?' Tom asked.

'In a manner of speaking,' Albert said, and withdrew a set of keys from his pocket. 'It's yours, Tom.'

Tom looked blankly at the keys. 'I don't get it,' he said.

'The house is modest. Two-up two-down. But I thought that would be sufficient for your needs. The main thing is the land. Five acres. It used to belong to an equestrian gentleman, so there are already stables. And there's plenty of land to build kennels.'

Tom looked at Minnie. 'Do you understand what he's talking about?' he said.

Minnie shook her head, then slowly a memory emerged of a conversation many months ago, when she and Tom had strolled through the Cremorne Gardens and he had told her of his dream to have a place in the country and look after horses. The realisation must have showed on her face, as Albert smiled and nodded at her.

'My mother left me a very generous sum of money in her will,' he said. 'Far more money than I would ever know what to do with. Minnie told me about your dream. I thought maybe you could fulfil it here. And look after the dogs as well, if that's something you think you'd like to do. It'll be quite a job, mind you.' He looked at the nearest cage, which the rat-like terrier was trying to dismantle with his teeth. 'Those dogs will need a lot of training. Don't feel you need to save them if they're beyond it.'

Tom stood, his mouth open in disbelief. He turned towards the house. 'You're saying this is – mine? And five acres?'

Albert nodded and then, before he could say anything more, Tom hurled himself at Albert, wrapping his arms around him.

'I take it that's a yes.'

THIRTY-FIVE

Between them they'd managed to deposit the dogs in the stables without too much bloodshed. Bullet, the fearsome fighter with the terrifying reputation, proved to be fairly docile outside of the ring. The terrier, which Tom had decided to call Nipper, had turned out the most ferocious, with Tansie's trouser leg an early casualty. Minnie wasn't holding out a great deal of hope that Tom would be able to train any of them into domestic pets but, knowing Tom, he'd give it his best shot. And a life with him was a great deal better than what faced them at the Pit.

The following day Minnie was sitting in her office, which she realised she was going to have to hand back to Tansie. Under his resumed management, the Palace had magically improved its takings. If she didn't know him as well as she did, she'd think Tansie was siphoning his own money into the coffers. But, given how notoriously tight-fisted he was, that was impossible. He just seemed to have a knack. For keeping the performers happy, even though he spent his life yelling at them. For knowing what the punters wanted, even when it seemed to make no sense at all. But despite the upturn in takings, there was still the problem of Teddy Linton's part-ownership of the Palace. Another letter had arrived at the Palace that morning, asking Minnie to contact Teddy's solicitor and arrange her next visit to Broadmoor. Teddy wasn't going away. She would have to comply, and the thought left a sour taste in her mouth.

A gentle cough disturbed her thoughts. Albert and Dorothy stood in front of her. They were both – and there was no other word for it – beaming.

Dorothy ceremoniously handed Albert an envelope. She even gave a little squeak of excitement as she handed it to him. Other people's happiness was really irritating sometimes, Minnie thought. Albert placed the envelope on the desk, pushing it towards Minnie.

She tried to smile, but her lips refused to submit.

'Open it,' Albert said.

'What is it?' she asked.

'Open it,' Albert repeated.

Minnie was in no mood for games. She reached for the envelope; as she did so, the thought swept into her mind, unbidden, that Albert and Dorothy were presenting her with an invitation to their wedding. After all, she'd encouraged Albert to find someone else. She couldn't blame him if he'd followed her instructions. She scanned the room, desperately trying to find something else to do. But, of course, there was nothing. They'd solved the crimes, rescued the dogs and the Palace was closed for a couple of days to drain and remove the disastrous water tank. Nothing left to do but put a brave face on it.

She opened the envelope. Inside was a single sheet of paper. Not a wedding invitation, then. Obviously. They always came on card.

She read the words on the paper. The world shifted. For a moment, she thought she was going to faint. The letters blurred in front of her and her mouth went dry. She looked up, helplessly, at their two smiling faces.

'It's yours,' Albert said. 'Or, rather, it will be once you sign all the necessary documents. That piece of paper isn't exactly legally binding. Something Dorothy and I concocted for now.'

'I don't—'

'My inheritance from my mother.'

'But the land—? For Tom—?'

268

'There was quite a lot left over even after that purchase. And I sold some rather ridiculous gifts I'd received from satisfied clients with more money than sense. It's surprising what you can get for a diamond-encrusted snuffbox.'

'But Teddy—' Jesus, why couldn't she complete a sentence?

'That's where Dorothy comes in,' Albert said, turning towards the woman and sharing that smile with her that had been slowly driving Minnie insane for the past few weeks.

'I approached Lord Linton's solicitor,' Dorothy said, 'told him I was acting on behalf of a client who wished to purchase Linton's share of the Palace. Linton was sceptical at first, or his solicitor was, at least. Henry, a friend of mine, posed as the fictional client. Said he wanted to buy the Palace for the land, intended to pull down the building as soon as the purchase was complete.'

'And Teddy believed that?'

'I think the generous sum of money being offered by my "client" may have been the deciding factor.' Dorothy looked at the letter on Minnie's desk from Teddy's solicitor. 'I wonder how long he was going to make you suffer before he told you.'

'I don't think he ever really wanted the Palace,' Albert said. 'He just wanted to torment you. Which he can't any more, because you will be the majority owner. I couldn't persuade Tansie to surrender his share, so I'm afraid it's not all roses.'

Minnie looked down again at the sheet of paper. There it was. Minnie Ward. Seventy per cent owner of the Variety Palace Music Hall.

'Albert, I can't. It's too much. And it's your mother's money.'

He grinned. 'I know. She'd be spinning in her grave if she knew I spent all that respectable money on a music hall and a dogs' home.'

'But you should do something – important with it. Something better.'

He took her hand in his. 'What could be better than this, Minnie?'

What on earth could be more important? Think of the fun we're going to have.'

Tansie shouted from the auditorium.

'They're waiting for us,' Dorothy said.

Minnie looked at her blankly.

'The party?' Dorothy prompted. 'For Christmas? You know, Jesus's birthday?'

Minnie groaned. She could really do with some time to process Albert's news. And, besides, she'd had her reservations about Tansie's idea for a Christmas party the moment he'd first suggested it. Jack had murdered five people and then killed himself. Bernard's brother had died a horrible death. Bernard himself had nearly died. Twice. What did they have to celebrate?

Albert must have read her mind. 'I know,' he said softly. 'But Tansie felt – and I have to say I agree with him – that we should mark the happier moments. We've grieved enough to last us a lifetime. Besides, it's Christmas Day tomorrow.' He held her gaze and she was the first to look away.

'Do you need a few minutes, Minnie?' Dorothy said. 'It's a lot to take in.'

She shook her head. If she was left on her own or, worse, alone with Albert, she couldn't be sure what she'd do.

The three of them made their way into the auditorium. Somebody had lit hundreds of candles and placed them all along the bar. It looked beautiful. Like something out of a fairy tale. Tansie was opening bottles of champagne, Tom was passing round the glasses. She looked across at Bernard. He tilted his head gently to one side and smiled at her. 'I know what you're thinking, dearest one, but don't tell me we shouldn't be celebrating. I know Peter is gone, but he always loved a party. Besides, I understand the Palace has a new owner.'

'*Part* owner,' Tansie shouted from across the other side of the room.

'*Majority* owner,' Minnie corrected him. She took a sip of champagne, felt it rushing through her. Maybe alcohol wasn't a good idea tonight.

Dorothy sidled up to her. 'Are you all right? We did spring it on you, didn't we? Albert wanted to tell you weeks ago, but I'm rather fond of a surprise.'

'I think I'm all right. It hasn't sunk in yet. Particularly as I thought you and Albert were coming to tell me you were getting married.'

Dorothy had just taken a mouthful of champagne, which she promptly spat out in astonishment. 'Me and *Albert*? Where on earth did you get that idea?'

She shrugged. 'All those secret looks. Shutting up every time I walked in the room.'

'Oh, Minnie, you foolish girl. There's only one woman for Albert. Besides, he's a bit tall for me.' And Minnie couldn't be sure, but she could have sworn Dorothy looked over at Tansie, who was repositioning a Christmas hat on Monkey's tiny head.

Further along the bar, Tom was making Frances squeal with horror as he showed her his broken fingers, which hadn't healed terribly well. He was enjoying himself far too much. Mind you, so was Frances. They made a nice couple. And maybe it would be the first Palace romance with a happy ending. For a moment, she projected herself into an ideal future. A successful music hall, running smoothly with all the drama left on the stage. No more deaths.

Albert appeared at her side and topped up her glass. 'Excellent work, Miss Ward,' he said, clinking his glass against hers.

'Bang-up job, Mr Easterbrook.'

'Oh, one more thing.' He fished in his pocket and presented her with a small piece of card. She knew what it was before she even looked at it.

Easterbrook and Ward: Consulting Detectives.

'You're right, it does sound better that way round. But we're equal partners, Minnie. And no chucking this one in a drawer full of make-up and old cake,' he said.

She kept her head down, afraid to look up, afraid to meet his eye.

'All that money, Albert,' she said, stroking the card with one finger before finally raising her head. 'All that money, and you still couldn't stretch to vellum.'

AFTERWORD

This book's original working title was 'The Safety Coffin'. Hardly likely to spring off the shelves, I know. But my plan was to write something about the Victorians' obsession with being buried alive and their ingenious solutions to overcome the problem. Then lockdown came along and I found one way of staying sane was to do lots and lots of random research, not that I needed an excuse. A history of *The Illustrated Police News* by Linda Stratmann led me to the event which inspired *The Innocents*. On 16 June 1883, at the Victoria Hall in Sunderland, a stampede for free toys resulted in the death of 183 children by asphyxia. The caretaker at the Victoria Hall, Frederick Graham, managed to save some 600 children by diverting them to another exit. When I first read of this disaster I was appalled, as anyone would be. I talked to people about it and, aside from those who lived in the vicinity or with a background in theatre history, no one had heard of it. Whilst the disaster did lead to national safety legislation for entertainment venues, no one individual or group of individuals was found guilty of what occurred. I would love to say we have moved on, but I'm not so sure we have.

Whilst I have borrowed Frederick Graham's name, that's as far as any similarity goes. All other characters associated with the Trafalgar Theatre are entirely fictitious.

On an irreverent sidenote, fans of terrible poetry might like to know that William McGonagall (author of 'The Tay Bridge Disaster') commemorated the event in a poem entitled 'The Sunderland Calamity'.

The exhibits in Dorothy's office are based on the wonderful work of the Victorian taxidermist Walter Potter. Feel free to look him up, but be prepared never to sleep easily again.

ACKNOWLEDGEMENTS

The Innocents is the second book in the Variety Palace Mystery series. The first, *The Tumbling Girl*, ventured into the world in 2023. I want to thank the following for the endorsements and support they gave that novel: Tom Benn, SJ Bennett, Elizabeth Chadwick, Julia Crouch, Essie Fox, Femi Kayode, Sheila O'Flanagan, William Ryan, Emma Styles, A. J. West, Mark Wightman, Trevor Wood.

I am blessed with some wonderful beta readers. Jayne Farnworth, Liz Hullin, Natasha Hutcheson, Jane Still and Helen Walsh saw early versions of this book and gave invaluable feedback.

When I'm not writing, I'm crafting. Caroline Birks and Maria Butcher, you're my girls. Don't know what I'd do without you.

I owe a huge debt of gratitude to Joe Harper, Claire Handscombe, Polly Mackintosh and Jane Barringer at Gallic, also to Lucy Ramsey and Meryl Zegarek, my UK and US publicists (I'll never get used to saying that). Isobel Dixon at Blake Friedmann remains the world's best agent, closely followed by Sian Ellis-Martin.

However many of these I write (and I hope there will be many, many more) my biggest thanks will always go to Micky. No one does more than him to keep this rickety old bird on the straight and narrow – in every sense.